B E S T
LESBIAN
EROTICA
2 0 0 4

B E S T
LESBIAN
EROTICA
2 0 0 4

Series Editor

Tristan Taormino

**Selected and
Introduced by**

Michelle Tea

CLEIS PRESS

Published in the United States by Cleis Press Inc.,
P.O. Box 14684, San Francisco, California 94114.
Printed in the United States.
Cover design: Scott Idleman
Cover photograph: Michelle Serchuk
Book design: Karen Quigg
Cleis Press logo art: Juana Alicia
First Edition.
10 9 8 7 6 5 4 3 2 1

"A Tangle of Vines," © 2003 by Cheyenne Blue, was originally published on www.cleansheets.com (May 2003). "Never Say Never," © 2003 by Rachel Kramer Bussel, was originally published in *Best Bondage Erotica,* edited by Alison Tyler (Cleis Press, 2003). "Breathing Water," © 2003 by Bethany Harvey, was originally published on www.cleansheets.com (April 2003). "The Last Pan of the Season," © 2002 by Debra Hyde, was originally published in *The Best of the Best Meat Erotica,* edited by Greg Wharton (Suspect Thoughts Press, 2002). "Devil's Dew," © 2003 by Abbe Ireland, was originally published in *Underneath It All* (Eros Press, 2003). "The Way She Does Me," © 2003 by Miriam R. Sachs Martín, was originally published in *Cliterature,* edited by Madalena M. Christian (Doublewide Press, 2003). "The Chick Magnet," © 2002 by Skian McGuire, was originally published on www.scarletletters.com (September 2002) and is an excerpt from her book *Remote Control and Other Weegee Stories* (Top Dog Press, 2003). "A Bushy Tale," © 2003 by Jean Roberta, was originally published on www.pervgrrl.org (May/June 2003) and www.sliptongue.com (August 2003). "Look but Don't Touch," © 2003 by Sparky, was originally published on www.dykediva.com.

TABLE OF CONTENTS

Foreword

When I came out as a dyke more than a decade ago, I felt truly liberated. As clichéd as that sounds, it's true. When I began getting it on with women, I felt freed from the script of heterosexual sex that defines sex as cock-in-pussy intercourse and labels anything and everything else as appetizer to the main course. The delicious things I started doing with my girlfriend—oral sex, jerking off, finger-fucking, playing with toys—were considered merely "fooling around" when I was straight. But what we did between the sheets did not feel like dabbling in foreplay, it felt like sex—bigger, better, and more intense than I'd ever had it. As quickly as I could purchase my first purple leather strap-on harness (it *was* the early '90s), everything I thought I knew about sex was out the window. Suddenly, all body parts, erotic acts, and desires were fair game. I experienced firsthand what Joan Nestle, Amber Hollibaugh, Pat Califia, and others were raving about: lesbians *were* on the cutting edge of sexuality.

Our foremothers packed, pounded, and paved the way, the next generation grabbed the veritable dildo-cum-baton, and we continue to run with it. I believe, in fact, that queer sex has revolutionized the sex all people have, including those who consider themselves straight. Part of what gives lesbian (and all queer) sexualities such radical potential is that we create our own vision of what sex is and what it can be. We invent it, we name it, we practice it.

And we put it down on paper: one of the ways we document our unique carnal visions is through erotic writing, and that documentation is critical to our cultural history. If we don't share our authentic stories that spring to life from our cunts and our minds, others will do it for us. If it weren't for collections like this, there would be nothing to contradict—or at least complicate—mainstream media images of lesbians. On television, queer girls can be wacky but asexual (hello, "Ellen"), fantastical vampires like Buffy's Sapphic friends, or motherly and argumentative (example: while the guys on "Queer As Folk" are going at it like crazy, the lezzies are adopting children and fighting). In porn, we're blonde, busty look-alikes with long fingernails licking each other for the pleasure of men. This book is less slick and ambivalent, more glamorous and bold about women fucking women.

The contributors to *Best Lesbian Erotica 2004* have transformed heat and passion into words, and had the courage to share their tales with the world. They have captured an incredible variety of sexual moments we have all experienced in one way or another: experimenting with a first sex toy; daring to pick up a stranger; indulging in a secret fantasy; and pushing boundaries, our own or those of others. The characters in this book have short nails, and they know how to use them. The stories reflect our experiences, our fantasies, our fears, and our hopes about all things horizontal. They are ready and waiting to get you off, but they have another mission as well: to influence what we wear and want, how we flirt and fuck. That's why it is important to keep writing, reading, and supporting lesbian erotica: not only does it inspire our desires, but it alters the landscape of sexuality for everyone.

Tristan Taormino
New York City
August 2003

Introduction

When I was around twenty-one years old I began to understand that I could probably look forward to a lifetime of
backbreaking, soul-cracking shit-paying employment. It was a
tradition I inherited from both my workaday family and the
bummed-out town that had nurtured me in the style of
Rappaccini's daughter, raising me in a greenhouse of bleak
expectations until I was virtually allergic to opportunity.

The next revelation clocked the first one in the jaw—
having sex with girls could elevate my inconsequential
existence to the mythology of an outlaw. Because it was
romantic, because in most places it could straight-up get your
ass kicked, because it was dangerous. All filled up with out-
sider thrill, inspired by these tough and vulnerable girls who
kept letting me fuck them—the tunnel between their legs that
seemed to wind darkly toward their hearts; the complicated,
twisty walls that guarded that same raw place—I thought, if I
could write it all down it would be real, it would be that myth,
that dangerous and true story. If I could just get it all down my
life would be way less meaningless, way less pointless than

what it felt like right then—when I was hustling shitbum jobs, pretending I gave a rat's ass about the work, hoping they wouldn't send me home for my clothes being ripped up or simply too strange. Capitalism owned my body until the time clock bit its evening chunk from my card; after that it belonged to girls.

I remember casting a desperate, unemployed glance around Boston, looking for a place I could trick into hiring me. I didn't feel like I had a lot going for me—no school, raised too poor to know how to pass as middle-class, lacking the clothes or the confidence or the ambition. I was inside a cavernous and run-down mall and all that was hiring was the Taco Bell. I knew enough to understand that working at a fast-food joint was a concession to failure, maybe reaching the bottom of the workforce, like you were too stupid to figure out how to get on welfare. The girl behind the counter had smudgy blue rings around her eyes, from eyeliner smeared away in the steamy heat of her job; blue-rimmed eyes, the whites shot with red, hungover red or overworked red, maybe freaked-out-crying-jag red; her red-white-and-blue, totally American, fast-food wage slave eyes. I was in love with her. I thought: we could save each other with our bodies. It was so simple it made me manic and gleeful. We could fuck in the back behind the racks of chrome and frozen bulk foods, we could fuck in the desolate mall bathrooms, in the roomy handicapped stall or precariously close to the slimy stinking toilet in the narrower ones. By the time I handed in my application I had intricate visions of us living together in a tiny, lousy apartment, fucking on a mattress, one square window open to the night and sucking a breeze in to cool us, us churning hot and churning humid over and under and inside each other's bodies. And the next morning at the mall her eyes would have a new streak of crimson marring the whites, the up-all-night-fucking red, and on my break I would write her poetry, I would write out the story of us together and make us the heroes that I knew we really were, write it so the world would know and we would be okay, so we would have lives that actually mattered.

Okay, none of this happened because Taco Bell didn't hire me, but the point is I believe that sex and writing can save people, especially queer people, because it shoots our lives up with hot, crucial meaning and gives us the power to create and recreate that meaning, even after the girl is gone and your heart is broken and your sheets are ruined forever. I loved Debra Hyde's "Last Pan of the Season" because it's a working-class story, plus it's messy and a little gross, my favorite kind of sex. Lisa Archer's "Loved It and Set It Free" is *Are You There God? It's Me, Margaret*-era lesbionics, and its realness makes it both hot and hilarious. The play party Rachel Kramer Bussel takes us into in "Never Say Never" is vivid queer-girl territory, a place where sex dramas get made into myths, just like the dirty peep-show booth in Sparky's "Look but Don't Touch" and the women's coffee shop that spawns some bestial role-playing in Jean Roberta's "A Bushy Tale." Tattoo parlors and boozy nightclub bathrooms—our landscape. All of the stories selected have elements, slight or overwhelming, of queer outlaw culture—Jeni Wright's daddy-play in "In the Beginning There Was a Fantasy," queer sex worker meets gender-fucking trick in Tara-Michelle Ziniuk's "Does She Look Like A Boy?," the extravagant queer freak-show underworld existing in a Las Vegas of Tina Cristina Maria D'Elia's imagination, shared with us in "The Lost Blackjack King in My Eyes." I could write essays on many of the stories in here—how fantastic and mythical America looks from Peggy Munson's knees in "Blowing Across America." I could keep prattling on and on about our righteous outlaw legacy and how girls fucking girls—and girls who've become boys and boys who are most definitely girls—is still radical, still crucial, but there's a whole book in front of you that makes that point super clear, so I think I'll just let you get to it.

Michelle Tea
San Francisco
July 2003

Loved It and Set It Free

Lisa Archer

In 1985, my first dildo drifted out into the Baltimore Harbor on a broken bookshelf. I'd owned this dong for less than a day, but we'd been through a lot together. The night before, I'd eased it inside me, while my high school best friend lay next to me faking sleep. Most people keep their first dildos until they rot. But I was different. I loved mine and set it free.

"The Boss" was a single piece of beige rubber shaped like a billy club or toy sword—with a handle, a cross-guard, and a ten-inch dong in place of a blade. The label on the package said "anatomically correct," but even then I knew ten inches was a little on the long side.

I first laid eyes on The Boss when my friend Kim took me to a porn shop on East Baltimore Street. Kim was a born comic with gawky limbs and a wide, pouty mouth. The summer before our senior year, she carried bottles of Sun-In and hydrogen peroxide wherever she went. When we weren't swimming, she poured them over her head and lay in the sun.

By the time we went back to our all-girls school that fall, Kim's hair hung in clumps like bleached snakes. People said she dyed her hair orange to match school colors—orange and green. So she dyed it green for one of the field hockey games. This was in the mid-'80s, before Grunge Rock.

Around that time, Kim and I were playing "I Never"—one of the few games you can win through sheer inexperience and naïveté. In "I Never," players take turns confessing things they've never done. If the other player has done something you haven't, she owes you a penny. I won two cents easily, because I'd never bleached my hair or dyed it green.

It took me a bit longer to come up with my third confession. Finally I said, "I've never really gotten a good look at another person's genitals."

This was true: Although I'd made out with both boys and girls, we rarely took off our clothes. Instead, we groped each other in dark, semipublic places—fumbling with buttons, bras, belt buckles, and zippers, and glancing over our shoulders every few seconds, expecting our parents to catch us in the act. I'd even lost my virginity in the classic sense on the floor of a toolshed. In short, I'd had plenty of action, but little chance to look at naked bodies or genitalia. I had rarely ever seen boys naked, except when our neighbor little Billy ran across our backyard with his babysitter chasing him. I saw girls' bodies in locker rooms, but felt much too self-conscious to stare.

I expected Kim to question my confession, but she just nodded and tossed me another penny.

"You should come over and watch porn movies the next time my parents go away. That'll give you plenty of chances to check out other people's genitals."

Unlike my parents—the last in town to buy a microwave or any new appliance—Kim's family owned a VCR. When her mom and dad went out of town, Kim rented porn. We planned our porn adventure months in advance and waited for her folks' next vacation.

Kim rented porn videos from a seedy shop on "the Block." The Block—the 400 block of East Baltimore Street—is Baltimore's red-light district, where the locals go to see naked girls dancing and buy porn. Growing up in the sub-suburban sprawl of Baltimore County, I'd never been to the Block, so we drove me past it one night, when Kim borrowed her mom's Honda Civic.

"That's the Block." Kim pointed out the window. "Look now, or you'll miss it."

I pressed my face against the passenger window. Neon lights danced against the starless sky; then darkness swallowed the neon, as we dove back into the night.

"Was that it?"

"Yeah. It's only one block. I'll go around again."

The second time, she drove more slowly, so I could read the neon signs: Golden Nugget Lounge, the Crystal Pussycat, Gresser's Gayety Liquors, Savetta's Psychic Readings, Crazy John's, and the Plaza Saloon. Glamorous names—at least for kids growing up in Baltimore.

We didn't rent videos that night. We just drove by, and Kim pointed out Sylvester's Videos, the store where she rented porn.

"They have booths in the back where you can watch videos, but you don't want to go in there. The walls are sticky and gross. Let's just wait until my parents go away, and we'll rent videos to take home."

Finally Kim's parents scheduled an overnight camping trip. They left on a Friday; my heart and stomach fluttered all day at school. After our last class, Kim and I met in the locker room and changed out of our school uniforms and into jeans.

"Hurry up," said Kim. "I want to get down to the Block while it's still light out, so no one will break into my mom's car." Kim had her mom's car for the weekend. We slung our backpacks over our shoulders and walked out.

As we drove downtown, I pressed my face against the window and marveled at the dirt on the streets. City dirt is different from country dirt. Where I come from, dirt is brown like mud or red like sandstone. In the city, black grit cakes under your fingernails and sticks to the concrete. The wind writes messages on the sidewalk with black dust and dead leaves. I soon realized we were driving in circles, passing the same buildings.

"Are we lost?"

"No, I'm looking for parking."

"Where are we?"

"The Block, silly."

I winced. "It looks different by day."

While night had hidden everything but the neon signs, the sun exposed gray concrete buildings and trash in the street. Turned off, the neon signs were only pale plastic tubing and dusty electrical cords. We passed the same ones I'd seen at night—the Crystal Pussycat, Savetta's Psychic Readings, the Plaza Saloon. At night, they had seemed intimidating, but seeing them by day was like watching a flashy porn star sleep in her underwear and snore.

"Why didn't you take that parking space we just passed?" I asked.

"I want to park in front of the porn shop so I can keep an eye on the car."

After we'd made several more loops, a car pulled out right in front of us, across the street from Sylvester's Videos. Kim pulled up alongside the space.

"That's tiny. You can't fit in there."

"I'm going to try." She cranked her steering wheel all the way to the right and backed into the space much too fast. As her back tires rammed the curb, her elbow struck the horn with a loud honk. A siren squealed in the distance. Across the street, the door to Sylvester's Videos creaked open, and a guy with beady eyes and slicked-back gray hair stepped out of the store and glared at us.

"Shit, Kim. Let's get out of here."

"Get out and direct me," she said calmly.

Trembling, I climbed out of the passenger seat and motioned her into the space. When I glanced over my shoulder, the beady-eyed man had vanished. Kim got out of the car.

"That's the first time I've parallel parked since my Driver's Ed test," she said.

I followed her across the street. The door to Sylvester's Videos was covered with ripped, faded posters and random thumbtacks. The paint was chipped. It hadn't been painted in years.

I looked at Kim.

"Come on, let's go in." She hoisted the door open—revealing a heavy black plastic curtain. Glancing at me, she pulled aside the curtain and slipped inside. I followed her into a dimly-lit square room. Videos lined the walls floor to ceiling.

The beady-eyed man—the same one who had glared at us outside—sat behind the cash register.

"Howdy, girls." He smiled with crooked yellow teeth.

At the sound of his voice, two customers in the front room turned and peered at us. Both were bent over videos, with their collars turned up and hats pulled down over their eyes. Kim and I were the only two women in the store—perhaps the only women who had been there in a long time.

Kim took me on a tour of the narrow, low-ceilinged rooms, pointing to X-rated videos with titles like: *The Penile Colony, Hannah Does Her Sisters, Astropussy Strikes Back, Public Enema Number One, Two,* and *Three.*

"The booths are in the back." Kim pointed to a man slipping behind a black plastic curtain. "You can rent your video, close the curtain, pop your video in the slot and jerk off—Lisa...Lisa!" She poked me.

I had frozen facing a wall of rubber penises and sundry other body parts, including hands and arms. I had never looked at a penis this way before. For the first time in my life, I could look at it without worrying about what the person attached to it thought of me. At the time I was too inexperienced to know that one never quite looks at penises the way one looks at dildos, propped up on shelves, strapped onto harnesses, or packaged in plastic, hanging from hooks on walls—like toys in Toys "R" Us, or meat in a butcher shop. Through my entire childhood, I had been looking at Ken dolls without penises. Suddenly I was looking at the opposite of Ken dolls: penises without bodies attached.

Given my deprivation, this wall of "anatomically correct" models—in black, brown, and beige, complete with rippling rubber veins—was an embarrassment of riches. Some of them, labeled "stints," were hollow and attached to elastic straps. One even had leather straps. What were they for? Then I saw the flying-saucer-shaped "butt plug." Why would anyone need that? Plugs were those things you put in sinks to stop the water from draining. Was a butt plug the opposite of an enema? I was used to things having practical purposes. This was the first time I'd encountered something intended strictly for sexual pleasure, and I just didn't get it.

"Haven't you ever seen a dildo before?" asked Kim.

"N-no," I stammered.

"Check this out." She pointed to a plastic package containing a foot-long rubber forearm with the hand clenched in a fist. I'd never seen anything like it, except those dismembered arms you find in Walgreens at Halloween.

"What do you think you're supposed to do with this?" Kim asked. "Bonk somebody over the head?" I was pretty sure that wasn't what you were supposed to do, but before I could say anything, she yanked the plastic package off the hook and bonked me over the head with the rubber forearm.

"Kim! Stop!"

She clasped her hands over her mouth and burst into giggles, shoulders shaking uncontrollably. Customers in the store turned and stared.

"You're going to get us kicked out of here!" I hissed.

"Shhh! Lower your voice!"

"Look. Here's the description." We huddled over the package and read the label in excited whispers:

12.5 inches long, 3 inches wide, 9 inches around
Size: Huge
Product Category: Anal stimulation
Color: Black
Made of: Rubber
For use in this part of the body: Anus

"It's for the…the…anus?" I asked in disbelief.

"That's the butt," she whispered smugly.

"I know what an anus is, but I don't see how it could fit."

She shrugged. "Don't ask me."

"Do all these things go up your butt?" I gestured to the wall of dildos and butt plugs.

"They don't go up my butt," she giggled. "But you can put dildos up your vagina. Haven't you ever put vegetables up there?"

"No. Have you?"

"Of course."

"You're kidding. What kind?"

"Cucumbers, carrots, and zucchini. When I was about twelve, I used to sneak them out of the vegetable drawer in the refrigerator and put them back when I was done."

"Ew! Yuck!"

Kim hung the rubber arm back on its hook. "We're not getting this," she whispered. "Let's get some dildos. Here's a thin one. It's eight ninety-nine."

Kim handed me a package. I stared at the label: *The Boss: Anatomically Correct Dong.*

"Are you suggesting I buy this?"

"Why not? I'll buy one too."

"How do you know it'll fit?"

"You just have to try your luck. You can't try it on in a dressing room like a pair of jeans."

I laughed nervously.

"Come on," she said. "Let's move on to the videos. That's what we came here for."

I followed her back into the front room, where we rifled through hundreds of video boxes and decided on two orgy movies: *Farm Family Free for All* and *Group Grope 9.*

Growing up in the '70s and '80s, I had become familiar with the made-for-TV Roman orgy—where toga-clad patricians get it on with priestesses of Isis in the Roman baths (made to look like contemporary Jacuzzis). My parents allowed me to watch these programs due to their so-called historical significance. Hence much of my early sex education came from *I, Claudius,* and the head of a penis still reminds me of a Roman centurion's helmet. When you watch orgy scenes in historical dramas, perhaps you are supposed to think, *My god, how decadent,* and believe rampant orgies caused the fall of Rome. Modern libertines should learn from history and beware! But I watched the orgies and wondered, *Why don't people do that anymore?* I thought Roman orgies, like Egyptian mummies, were ancient history. *Farm Family Free for All* and *Group Grope 9* were my first signs that the orgy lived on, at least in contemporary porn.

After nearly an hour of X-rated shopping, Kim and I finally carried our lurid wares to the cashier and spread them out on the counter. The beady-eyed man winked at us.

"You want some K-Y Jelly for those dongs?"

"That's not a bad idea," said Kim. "We'll take some."

Outside, dusk had fallen, and the neon signs flickered on in orange, pink, and green. We crossed the street. Kim's mother's car was still intact. As we drove back to her house, I shivered when a cop car whizzed by. What if they pulled us over and found the porn videos and dildos? I pictured our mug shots on the front page with photos of The Boss underneath.

When we finally made it back to Kim's, we emptied our bags onto the living-room rug and tore open our dildo packages.

"Hey, this isn't very realistic. It doesn't have balls!"

The Boss, as I mentioned earlier, had no balls. Instead, the penis-shaped shaft ended in a handle and cross-guard, like a toy sword. I looked down at the dildo in my hands.

"Darn. I really wanted to see what balls look like."

"You'll see them in the movies," said Kim. *En garde!* She held the dildo by the handle and brandished it like the sword Excalibur, but the rubber weenie just flopped around.

I giggled. "That's one lame weapon."

"Oh well. Let's watch the videos." Kim switched on the TV and took the videos out of their plastic boxes.

"What do you want to watch first, *Farm Family Free for All* or *Group Grope 9?*"

"How about *Farm Family Free for All?*" We unzipped our sleeping bags and curled up side by side, propping our heads up on pillows so we could see the TV. Punching buttons on the remote control, Kim fast-forwarded to the opening scene, where a well-endowed hottie, looking much like Heidi with a blonde mullet and cleavage, skipped through a cornfield in an astonishingly low-cut blue gingham dress. The scene changed to the inside of a barn, where two men in plaid flannel shirts and overalls were milking cows. The younger man stood up and stretched.

"Gee, Paw," he drawled. "Ah wish Sissy would git here with those vittles. Ah need a break."

Outside, the blonde in blue gingham peeked through a crack in the barn door. Seeing the men, she slipped one hand up her gingham skirt and opened the door.

"Did Ah hear y'all say yuh need some refreshments?"

The men turned and gaped as she stepped into the barn, toting a straw basket in the crook of her arm and fondling her breasts.

I shook my head. "God, Kim! Can you believe these accents? Nobody talks like that."

"Watch this." Kim pointed the remote control at the TV. The video flew into fast-forward. Three more people in plaid flannel, calico, and gingham speed-walked into the barn, where they all tore off each other's clothes, sprawled on the hay, and plugged themselves into each other's orifices, fucking and sucking as fast as an assembly line.

"Dammit, Kim! I'm never going to see genitals this way!" I grabbed the remote control and pushed "play." My jaw dropped. Two tanned, tight-bodied girls, locked in a 69, were licking each other. With identical big boobs and blonde mullets, they looked like twins. In fact, they were twins. This was *Farm Family Free for All*. My heart beat faster. I'd never seen two girls having sex, even on screen. Out of the corner of my eye, I peered at Kim. Did she know this was going to be in the video? I knew orgies meant sex scenes with more than one man, more than one woman, or several of both. Somehow it hadn't dawned on me that girls would be getting it on with each other. I gaped at the screen transfixed, crotch tingling under the covers. I crossed my legs and squeezed my thighs together. Finally, I couldn't stand it anymore. I slipped my hands between my thighs. Kim's elbow brushed against mine, so the tiny hairs on our arms stood on end. She was doing the same thing I was, but I didn't dare look at her. I wondered if the people at school would be able to tell we'd watched lesbian porn. Would they see it in our eyes?

In English class earlier that year we had been talking about Virginia Woolf. The class was sitting in a semicircle around the edge of the room, facing our teacher, Mrs. Byrd. My mind was wandering, when someone mentioned the word *lesbians*. Patty raised her hand.

"Have there ever been any lesbians in our school?"

"Yes," said Mrs. Byrd. "We've had some."

"How can you tell?"

"Sometimes two girls are...closer than normal."

"Does the school do anything about it?" asked Patty.

"We try to split them up," said Mrs. Byrd. "Sometimes we tell their parents."

A hush fell over the room, as we all exchanged nervous glances. I looked at Kim, who sat across the room from me doodling. She didn't look up.

If they found out, would they separate us? Tell our parents?

Meanwhile, on *Farm Family Free for All*, the rest of the family joined the girls with mullets. The scene turned into a more traditional orgy with writhing bodies—a monster with multiple arms and legs. I circled my clit with my fingertip, less interested in the family scene, but barely admitting—even to myself—the girl-on-girl porn had turned me on.

Kim grunted next to me. She was snoring.

"Come on—I know you're not really asleep."

No answer.

"Kim?" I put my hand on her shoulder.

She was really asleep. I thought about waking her up, then changed my mind and circled my clit faster, feeling lucky and slightly out of control. My back tensed and my heart quickened, as I tried not to make any noise or move anything except my hand. I had played this game before—many times. The goal was to come without waking the other person. Sometimes, no doubt, the other person woke up and just pretended she was still sleeping. I had faked sleep myself when someone was masturbating beside me.

On screen the camera zoomed in on the girls. A man fucked one of them from behind, while she licked her sister's pussy. Next to me, Kim was breathing slack-jawed—either sound asleep or damn good at pretending. Her legs twitched under the covers. Reaching my arm outside the blankets, I groped around on the icy hardwood floor. My hand landed on the dildo—cold, hard, and ribbed with veins. I dragged it into the sleeping bag and pushed its cold head against the wet lips of my cunt. With a deep breath, I tried to ease the rubber cock inside me. It didn't fit. I pushed, took another breath, and pushed again. Still no go. Suddenly I remembered the K-Y Jelly. I ran my hand over the floor and found the K-Y. It looked like a tube of toothpaste. I squeezed a glob of clear lube into my palm. I couldn't believe how cold it was. I thought of Kim's refrigerated cucumbers. I didn't want anything that cold near my pussy, but if I wanted The Boss inside me, I knew I had to get the lube in there first.

I soaked the head of The Boss in K-Y, then—wincing—squeezed the cold lube directly into my cunt. It spilled onto the sleeping bag, spreading out in a puddle under my butt. Shivering, I glanced at Kim. Her eyelids fluttered. She was dreaming. With several deep breaths, I shoved The Boss inside me. My whole body shook—my cunt was so full, it almost burned. I looked at Kim again. What would it be like to kiss her? I brushed my lips against her cheek. Mustering all my courage, I stretched out the tip of my tongue and licked her hair.

Kim stirred and turned over on her side. I froze. Was she awake? I listened for her breath. I was sure she was awake, but I couldn't stop now. I eased the dildo in and out of my cunt. The woman on the screen came like a swimmer gasping for air. The man squeezed his cock and squirted white jizz on her tits. I came with them, melting into the scene. The cock inside me was his cock. My sounds shot out of her mouth. My wave of pleasure rocked her body on the screen. My cunt contracted and spit out the dildo—wet between my thighs. Warmth spread through my belly, heart, and limbs. I sank into the floor—and yet I was floating.

Someone nudged me.

"Stop it."

"Wake up."

"What? What time is it?"

"Five-thirty."

"What the fuck?" I glanced around the dark, unfamiliar room.

"Wake up." Kim's shadowy form bent over me.

I suddenly remembered where I was—sprawled out on Kim's living-room floor. I must have dozed off after I came.

"Lisa, listen to me. We have to get rid of these now."

"Get rid of what?"

"These." She bumped me on the cheek with something rubber. I winced, as the overhead lights blinked on. What was she talking about? Then it dawned on me. *Jesus, what did I do last night?* I remembered the wall of dildos, The Boss, and licking Kim's hair—shit! Was she awake when I did that? What did she think of me?

"Lisa!" Kim repeated, bonking me on the head. "We've got to get rid of these things before my parents get home. They'll be back early this morning."

"We can't just throw them away. They weren't cheap."

"Do you want to take them home with you?"

"Shit." I peered at the dildos as my eyes adjusted to the light. "I don't think I can."

"What should we do with them then? We can't just throw them in the trash, or bury them in the backyard. The dogs'll get at them."

"Can we burn them?"

"God, no! They'd stink."

"Well then, let's just walk a few blocks down the street and throw them in someone else's trash."

"Good idea. We can take the car and drive a little ways away. We'll take the videos back to the store too." She put the VCR on rewind.

It was still dark outside. The crickets were chirping as we stepped out into the cold, wet air. Kim drove. I dozed in the passenger seat with the dildos in my lap wrapped in newspaper. The car screeched to a stop.

"Where are we?" The sky had turned dark blue. I rolled down my window, tasting the salt air.

"We're at Fells Point. I was thinking we could throw them in the water," said Kim. We climbed out of the car. I followed her to the edge of the pier. Water was lapping at the dock, and the seabirds called out, flapping their wings. One swooped within inches of the water, a white ghost.

Holding the dildos wrapped in newspaper, I peered down into the black water.

"It's a shame to let these sink to the bottom of the harbor."

"I know! Let's float them out to sea on one of those boards over there." Kim darted away and came back seconds later, dragging a dismantled bookcase. She pulled off the top shelf and dislodged several long rusty nails.

"We'll put the dildos on a raft. That way, someone might find them.

We lowered the board into the water. Kim tore off a sheet of newspaper and wrote:

S.O.S.
FREE TO A GOOD HOME.

I leaned over and placed the dildos side by side. Wrapped in newsprint, they looked like twins in swaddling clothes.

I thought of Romulus and Remus—the twins abandoned to the elements, who washed up on shore and founded Rome. Who knew what great fortune or conquest lay in store for our dildos? Would they be suckled by she-wolves? I watched them float away, convinced that some lonely soul, who desperately needed dildos, would find them.

Breathing Water
Bethany Harvey

"Look." May reached out from where she sat on the rain-slick log, feet swinging over the water, to scoop two handfuls of soft clay from the riverbank. "This is you." She showed me one hand, then the other. "And this is me." And she took the two lumps and pressed them together, squeezing until the soft, slick mud oozed between her fingers. "And this is what I want to do." She opened her hands to show me the single lump, double-sized, with ridges marking where her fingers had been.

Her mud-caked hands and something in her voice stirred deep in my belly. We weren't even touching, but it was as if she'd just kissed me, long and hard. I stood in the river, leaning against the log, with the water tugging at my legs. My jeans were wet up to the crotch. The river was shallow here and rain-cool, and the color of the water was weak iced tea. In the deeper places, by the undercut banks, it was garnet-red as though something other than cypress roots were bleeding into it. In this humid Florida spring, the air was half water, my skin coated always with a glaze of sweat. I wore the loosest, lightest clothes I could find and it was still too much.

Watching May I felt even warmer, but it was a welcome warmth, spreading through my core and turning my legs liquid.

I hadn't expected this from her. Starting out as casual lovers, we had become more like friends in the years we'd lived together. We'd never had the kind of sex they write songs about, but lately I had wondered if she was interested in me at all anymore. In fact, I'd asked her to come to the woods with me because I missed her. I had intended to sneak in a kiss or two to let her know that, although most of the time she was just my friend, there were times when I was struck by an aching desire to sink into her; my whole body into her whole body, like those lumps of clay. I never thought she could be hiding such a feeling.

I stared at those muddy hands, and the teasing brown eyes above them, and sloshed through the water toward her. I wrapped my arms around her waist and pulled her into the river with me. She landed feet first, splashing us with a wave of cool red water. Her body yielded against mine. May is soft and rounded in a way that screams sex. Without a bra, her breasts overlap her ribs and sway heavily when she walks. I am tall and unwieldy; my bones long and heavy and dense.

She kissed me, pried my lips open to draw me in. Our tongues twisted and wrestled past each other. I felt the ridges on the roof of her mouth, the sharp edges of her front teeth. Warm breath from our nostrils billowed against our faces, mixing with sweat. The backs of my eyelids were garnet-red, river-red, kissing-May-red. When she pulled away, my glasses were fogged around the edges, so the bank was a green blur. Silt had settled in around my feet in the current and sucked at them when I moved.

We found a sandbar and I pulled her down with me, our legs trailing in the river. We peeled clothes off, our own and each other's, enough to get to skin. Our shirts were bunched under our armpits, her shorts snagged around one ankle and streaming in the current as I bent over her. Sweat and water dampened her belly, and the hair guarding her cunt was coarse and wiry, holding water droplets at the ends, and long enough to catch my fingers in. My own cunt was swollen and drooling between my legs. I sucked her nipples, wore away at them with my tongue. We were melting, blending into the water. Water was in everything; the ground soft and muddy, the air steam-humid and sticky, and the two of us, leaking moisture together.

I scooped my fingers into her the way her fingers had scooped the bank. Inside, she was soft and slick, like wet clay in that state between earth and water. I molded her with my tongue, widening trenches, deepening valleys. She comes more easily when I use a light touch, but I didn't have the restraint. I wanted to bury my face in her cunt for a year, learn to breathe the waters of the womb again. My own cunt egged me on, swollen and aching. Touch it and I would crack open like a too-ripe melon. May's soft thighs shuddered and gripped my head, and I kept on until she let me go. We panted together on the bank, lying still. My cunt pulsed and I waited.

She thrust a knee between my legs, rolled us over and into the water. I went eagerly. Then her hand pressed between my legs, finally. I tried to open my cunt like a mouth and suck her fingers in. I barely noticed her weight on my chest, the silt under my shoulders sliding and giving way.

And suddenly I was choking, gasping, snorting water up my nose and stinging in my throat, and blind panic grabbed my mind and I heaved her off me and sat up. We stared at each other for a moment, me angry and coughing, her looking stung.

"You tryna kill me?" Fear does not turn me on. The ache consuming my pelvis, the swollen-to-bursting hill between my legs, was forgotten, drowned by panic.

She flinched. "Oh god, I'm sorry. I didn't mean... Are you okay?"

Of course I forgave her. I always did. I forgive easily, suddenly; May is the one who holds a grudge. Breathing deep between coughs, I tasted the bitter tannin water and smiled. "Yeah. Just let me get my breath."

May stroked my wet breast with one hand as I tried to stop coughing. By the time I was breathing normally, my desire for her was already coming back, and May's caresses gradually shortened, making smaller and smaller circles around my nipples. I moaned through a tight throat, because she liked to hear me, and she took her hand off my breast and bowed over me to replace it with her mouth. I wanted my whole body to open up and gulp her as she moved over me.

She teased me until she had me writhing and thrusting my cunt into her hand. Her thumb fit perfectly inside me, anchored me to her as her tongue lapping my clit sent me quivering and my head tried to float away and join the leaves shivering in the breeze above. I closed my eyes. The light-and-dark pattern on the backs of my eyelids danced and shuddered, and then my whole body was dancing and shuddering with it.

Then May crawled up beside me, and we lay together in the shallows, the damp yielding sandbar under our heads. A breeze too high for us to feel it stirred the treetops, making splotches of yellow-green light and gray-green shadow dance over the ground and our bodies. My limbs were heavy, sinking into the sand and water, the current pushing vainly at my thighs. I didn't want to move ever again.

But after a while I started to notice the mosquitoes and gnats whining around our bare bodies, and the broken fossil jabbing me in the shoulder, and the way the mud was drying on our bodies in spite of the sweat. May must have noticed these things too because she slid out of my grasp and got up and started getting dressed. I dragged myself up to follow, pulled my own wet clothes on. I found her shorts downstream a few yards, caught on a branch, and fished them out of the current for her.

May reached up to run her fingers through my hair, playing with the sand-matted ends at the back of my neck. The woods lay quiet around us. We turned our backs to the river, trusting it to keep our secrets, and found the path back to civilization.

"Why don't we do this more often?" I said.

"I guess I forgot how much fun it was."

"So now that you remember...?"

May grinned. "Don't tell me this isn't enough to satisfy you for at least a week."

"A week's not so bad," I said, carefully neutral. I wanted to chew her labia.

May skimmed her water-wrinkled fingertips down the edge of my face, down my neck, reaching under my shirt; brought them up again, and licked them. "So we have a date? Next week?"

"Hell, yes."

We ducked through the whippy sweet-gum branches and out into the bright day-lit road. We swaggered home feeling good, and the sun cracked the mud from our skin, leaving little flakes of sex on the hot asphalt.

In the Beginning There Was a Fantasy

Jeni Wright

This is a story about loneliness, the kind of loneliness that starts off as a piece of sharp-edged sea glass and ends up being smooth and worn and safe. I was in the middle stage, where the broken parts are still jagged but don't draw blood anymore. Then you called and instantly I was back at the beginning. Wherever that was.

Maybe the beginning is the night I got drunk at the beach and used the empty bottles to make the sea rocks feel my pain, maybe the beginning is the afternoon you met me for lunch, maybe the beginning is the morning I wanted to wake up next to you. I don't know anymore.

This is a story about loneliness and its value. I know loneliness, it works me like a starved jaw, trails me like the wedding veil I want to wear one day. Morning noon and night I plot myself out of its reach.

You called last week and I felt everything I wasn't supposed to, wished for everything I was supposed to ignore. I'm tired of being out of your reach.

Today I was too slow, my loneliness caught up, and now I have to lie here and pretend you're with me.

There is so much hardness in you I want to feel next to me, on me, in me. Your dick over my clothes as we slide up and down the living room couch, your knee on the inside of my thigh when you kiss me at the front door, your belt-buckle under the heat of my dripping pussy. There's so much hardness in you: the bones of your forearms, elbows, fingers, pelvis, thighs, shins, ribcage, and the rawboned hardness in your dark brown eyes.

It's dark outside. I lie here, doors locked, lights out, window open. I get up to look for matches and a candle. I light the one with the longest wick and go back to my mattress.

Your hand lifts the strap of my thin white tank top, the one with the faded pink triangles, and slips it over my bare shoulder.

You have magic inside you, you draw a line with your thick black boot and dare the beast to cross it. Fuck loneliness, I've got a fantasy. You're in it.

My left nipple is exposed now, my left arm also. I'm getting goose bumps. The rest of me is hidden under a white cover, newly-washed. I removed your boots at the bedroom door but your feet are still big, and black. Your sleeves are rolled up and I want to place my tongue in the crook of your arm.

This is my fantasy and it's as real as the fierce-ass wind running wild though the treetops outside my window.

You place your tongue on my nipple, the left one, the one that's all sharp and pointy because it's cold in our bedroom. Your warm mouth makes me wonder what it would be like to have a baby. Can I have a baby with a butchdaddy? I decide. Yes.

Did I imagine her voice in my ear, whispering I'd be the flyest mom on the block? I imagine the pictures I'd carry in my wallet. The expressions of straight people who'd never believe me.

Your teeth on my nipple make me bite the insides of my cheek. I want more. I always want more.

I know you will give it to me.

Your smile is a sliver of total wickedness when my eyes finally focus. My dizziness does not prevent me from turning over on the bed we set up ourselves. Together. I follow the hand guiding my hip and allow myself to be open to you.

I want you to give it to me, sweetheart. Please. Please. I won't say God or any other word that has no place here. I've learned the hard way to give credit where it is due, and God is not the one who makes me open my mouth wide and beg.

You do. You're in my asshole like you promised me, you came in like the gentle daddy you are, but now I'm hot and you're fucking me so fast I forget to breathe. Now you're going slow, slow, slow enough for me to feel every inch of your thickness, your rock-steadiness, your assurance of your right to view my open asshole. I blush. Somehow you know my embarrassment, even though you're behind me. My face is tilted to the side, pressed to the sheet, staring at the ocean you've painted on our walls. I know you like to see my face, my eyes and mouth especially, see how they change shape as you fuck me. You put your hand to my cheek, gently, trail it down to my neck. You order me to talk, to tell you how I feel inside. I feel safe and very lucky.

"Your...thing feels so good...in me."

How can I be so shy when it comes to saying it out loud?

You pull out quick enough to make me hiss. You flip me so quickly your eyes are a shock when they appear. Looking straight down at me, you hold your tool inches from my chin, say

"This is not a thing. What is this?"

I don't want to answer, my shame is hot and delicious and incapacitating, but you wait for me, eyebrow cocked.

"I know my little girl knows the name for what was inside her."

I do. I do know the name. I know it by heart, I learned it the same night first your dildo then your fist went inside me, made me open up more than I ever had before.

"This is your cock, your dick, your hardness, your gift to me." You smile.

You help me see what I don't want to witness. My loneliness trails me, snaps at me, helps me to see. I need both of you to survive until I can become my fantasy.

You Can Write a Story about It
Jera Star

1.

I wait to meet you on the porch, your silver roller blades shining all the way down the street. I finger the chain around my neck as you approach. We are still awkward at first on these casual rendezvous we've been having. You're used to fucking friends. I'm used to fucking strangers. We are neither friends nor strangers. I'm a pink-haired hippie bi chick. You're a crew-cut wanna-be-cop boy dyke. Sometimes, we fuck.

"Hey, T," I say.

You've come over after watching that movie you love with the character named Troy in it. Where you got your boy name, the one you just told me about today. I haven't yet called you by it.

"Yo, what's up?" you ask. I ignore your question. I'm distracted because you're wearing a red baseball cap backwards—my weakness. You sit down beside me on the porch to take off your blades. "Oh, I saw a shooting star on the way here," you tell me, excitement in your voice. You remind me of a little kid and I find it endearing. A nice change from your usual cocky, obnoxious talk. We sit for a while and talk about the stars. Then I bring you inside. You swagger up the stairs to my apartment. Follow me down the hall to the couch in the spare room.

"How was your day?" I ask.

This time you ignore my question. Instead you say, "You have strong hands." I know you are trying to move things along to what we both really want to be doing. But still, it's one of the few compliments you have ever and will ever (I realize later) offer me. I relish it. And take your bait.

"You want a massage?"

You sit on the floor in front of the couch. I start massaging your shoulders through your clothes. After a minute, you bring out a little container of strawberry massage oil from your pocket. I laugh, getting the point. I take off your shirt. Drip the oil onto your back. You say it feels like lube: cold and hot. I massage again, starting at your neck. Mold your skin. Flex my fingers around your muscles. Shoulders, upper arms. Move my hands in front to your pecs. Careful to avoid your breasts. I stretch your arms up and lay them back down against your sides. Touch my fingers to your lower spine, one of your erogenous zones. Stay there for a while, applying pressure. Playing. You cut right to the chase.

"So, Sue, tell me about your first kiss." You want to get at my fantasies. This is what we do for each other. I like the question.

"It felt so good I thought I could go on kissing him for hours. But then later, behind the portable, after school, he said, 'What do you want to do to me?' I didn't want to do anything to him. I wanted him to do things to me. I wanted him to lick my whole body. All the way from mouth to clit."

"What else?" you ask as I work on your shoulder muscles.

"Hmm, I was too shy to tell him what I wanted. So we just kissed some more," I answer, absorbed in my hands pushing into your back. "Eventually I told him I didn't want to be monogamous and he didn't like that." You laugh, not sure about it yourself.

"Tell me, Sue, what you want me to do to you. Who, what, where you want me to be."

I smile.

You try and grab my tits and I love it. You try and tickle me and I don't like it. We laugh as you try to tickle me and I tell you to stop.

"Don't," I say.

"Don't what?" you say, grabbing my tits again, putting your hands in my pants. "Don't Boy-T? Don't Daddy? Don't Troy? Don't touch my tits? Don't touch my clit? Don't make me come? Huh? Don't what?" I squirm. Hot, fucking hot.

"Daddy," I moan, wanting your hand on my clit. "Daddy, please." I squirm more as you fondle me, feel me, make my clit swell. You take your hand away.

I whine, hurt, sad, "Daddy, please. Come on Daddy. Give me. Give me please. Daddy, please."

You give in and give me some more. Turn me over on my stomach. I moan and cry with the sensations in my cunt. Your hand still fingers my clit. I want more, you pull your fingers away. I whine.

"Oh, poor baby," you say. "What's wrong? Is there something wrong, baby?"

"Please, Daddy." I'm close to crying. You put your fingers back.

"There you go, baby. Come on. You're a good girl." You move your finger faster on my clit. I moan and say "Please, daddy," again and come madly, sweetly, sadly in your arms.

"Do you love me?" you ask.

"Yes, Daddy, I love you."

I shed some tears. We are both quiet.

Finally I say, "And you, T, what do you want me to do, be for you?"

I straddle you. Take off my shirt. Kiss you. Take off my bra while you watch. Take off your jeans and boxer briefs and spread your legs. Move down your body to your belly. You feel vulnerable with it exposed, I know. I linger there, my eyes on you. My tongue licking around your belly button. I start fingering your clit slowly, gently.

"Do you do this to all the boys?" you ask.

"Just my slave-boys," I say. You make small moans. I stop playing with you. Ask, "Were you a good boy today?"

"I hope so," you answer. You always make me laugh.

"You think you deserve this?" I ask.

"Yes, Mistress," you moan as I push one finger inside your cunt.

"Why do you think you deserve this?" I play with your clit some more.

"Because it feels so good." You start humping my finger. I bend down to kiss you and just when you're ready for it, I pull away. You try to bring my lips to yours again. I don't let you.

"Ah, Boy-T wants to kiss me does he?" I say to you, holding your arms above your head.

You close your eyes. "Uh-huh," you say, still humping.

"Now why would I want to let him do that?"

"You know you want it," you say, impatient. You shake your hands out of my grasp. Pull me down against you again. I let my tongue brush your lips. Then I grab your hands and put them above your head one more time. You like it.

"Slave-boys don't kiss without asking," I say. "I want Boy-T to learn how to be a gentleman." You smile and grab my boob real quick. Cocky, as usual.

"Ask nicely," I tell you, speeding up my hand on your clit.

"Oh, fuck."

"I said ask nicely." I push two fingers in your cunt. You clutch my arm.

"Kiss me, damn it," you say as I play with your clit and move my fingers in and out of you.

"What was that?" I ask. I start fucking your wet cunt, pushing my fingers deep. My thumb on your clit. You're groaning with each thrust. Keep trying to grab me, pull me to you. I keep pushing you down. Keep thrusting.

"Please," you moan, your hips rise, try to push my fingers deeper into you with each thrust.

"Please what?"

"Please, please, kiss me, please." You pant between words.

"Ah, that's a good boy," I say. I let go of your arms above your head. You yank me down on top of you, cover my mouth with yours, groan and swear as I fuck you. You come smooth and heavy. Your moans vibrate through me.

2.

It's been a few weeks since our last encounter. Another fight. They keep happening. Our fights remind me of my best friend at ten. How we used to touch tongues in the corner of the schoolyard, get mad and not talk to each other for weeks at a time, then one day start touching tongues again.

You call and ask me to come over. You have something you want to show me. When I hear your obnoxious laughing voice on the phone asking for me, I forget why I was so mad at you.

You come over to show off your new boy clothes. You say you really feel like a guy in them. Shirt and vest. I tell you that you look hot because I know you want to hear it. You tell me, like it's not a big deal, that I'm the only person you've mentioned all this boy stuff to. I'm surprised. Flattered. I offer to take pictures of you exploring your guy self. You refuse. But I persist and get you. Sitting on the couch, legs spread, taking up space; the rapper look, you call it. Your arm bent, scratching your chin; intellectual. Standing, doing a muscle pose; jock. This is all leading up to one thing, only I don't know it.

You want to go out together to the local straight slutty bar. We've talked about it before. I haven't been since I was in high school. Avoided it since I came out. But I love the idea. I put on lipstick for the first time in ages. Tight jeans and a skinny-strap tank top. For me, this is a performance. Reclaiming sixteen with more power than I ever felt I had then. I know for you, this is *it*.

We take the bus downtown in silence. Avoid stares. It is our first public appearance as any kind of couple. Your first public appearance as a guy.

Once in the bar we meld into the place. You quickly become my tough-ass boyfriend for the night. Stand on the sidelines, cocky and casual, and watch me dance. I play up to the bio boys until you can't resist and try to feel me up on the dance floor. I pretend to protest, giddy and turned on. You work on one of the straight girls dancing beside us and I pout and act like I'm pissed off. A jealous girlfriend. Until you turn back around to me, push me up against the speaker and dry hump me, in front of all the bio boys and their straight girl-friends. Your packing cock in your skater pants bulging against the crotch of my pretty-sixteen-year-old-girl jeans. We stay long enough to make a scene. Both of us wet.

"I've decided," you say as we head home to your place, high on the night. "I want you to fuck me with my cock."

I'm shocked. I've brought up the idea of me fucking you before, but you've always refused. Fingers yes. But never the cock.

"The only way it's gonna happen," you say, not looking at me, "is, you've gotta be a guy."

I am never *boy*. My cunt drips.

"Are you sure?" I ask, anxious about my boy performance abilities.

"Yeah, I'm sure." You pause. We approach your apartment. "You can write a story about it," you say finally. " 'I fucked this guy once...' "

I smile casually, acting as if I'm not completely nervous and turned on at the thought of being a guy myself, let alone fucking you. You look at me, knowing.

Once we're inside your apartment, I close the door, kick off my shoes and push you against the living room wall. "Sounds good. But first I want slave-boy to work for his pleasure." You lift up my shirt and start playing with my boobs. "I want you to eat me out. Some good, old-fashioned, cunt licking. And if you're real good," I say slowly, "then maybe...I'll put on your big old cock and fuck you with it." Which makes you smile and move your arms into a surrender position.

"You think you can handle that, slave-boy?" You nod keenly. I push you to the floor. Unbutton my fly. "And you know what I think about good head," I say as I take off my shirt. "It's hard to come by, don't you agree?" You nod again. I unclip my bra. Get rid of my pants and underwear.

"I want it like this," I say, and kneel over you. "With a wall to cling to when I come." I put my arms, my boobs against the cold wall. You slide down onto your back. I bend over your mouth and feel your tongue. My breath catches. "But, as you know, few people can ever really satisfy me." I bend down lower. You grab my cunt with your whole mouth. I groan. "Do you think you can, slave-boy?"

"Oh, yes, Mistress." I shiver.

"Good. Because I want to come. So you've got to keep it up good. Do you think you can, long enough? Suck my pussy with all its fur until I come? Yeah, that's right, just like that. Oh fuck yeah. Do you think you can keep it up slave-boy? Cause I want to come and I want to come good. Long and full and all through me like electricity or something.

Can you do it slave-boy? Come on, keep it up, keep it up. Come on do it keep me coming come on, keep me coming, I'm going to come, no, keep it slow keep it slow, I don't want to come yet. I said, do it slow now, slow now, yeah, that's right. Can you keep it up boy? Can you? Come on, more tongue, I said more tongue boy, yeah that's right, faster now, speed it up a bit, tongue and mouth, faster...just like that. Yeah, that's right. Do it like that.... Can you keep it up? Cause I want to come so you better keep it up, I said yes, more, faster, faster, fucking fast I said goddamn it. Fuck, keep it coming keep it coming keep me coming there I'm there, I'm there I'm fuck I'm coming goddamn you fucking coming fuck fuck fuck fuck. Commming. Unh unh unh unhhhhhhhh. Fuck boy, that's it. Hold me now. Just hold me."

I press my cunt into your belly and let your arms go around me. Just long enough to get myself together. Then I sit up and look at you smiling. All proud of yourself.

"So you think you deserve a fuck for that?" I laugh into your neck for a long time.

In the bedroom, you dress me up in your shirt and vest.

"So who am I?" I ask.

"Steve."

"Who's Steve?"

"Just Steve," you say. I laugh.

"And who are you tonight?" I ask, expecting you to say Troy.

"Tammy."

"Your girl name?"

"Yeah, or you can call me slut, bitch, whore."

I'm blown away. You are never girl. Talk about gender fuck. I get even wetter. Wonder if I'll be able to comply. "Those are harsh words," I say. "You know what a good girl feminist I am."

You smirk. "Just wait, you'll like it. It'll be easier than you think." You get out your big rubber dick and strap it on me.

I like it. You are right. I immediately start to feel cocky. Don't know exactly what you mean by, "Be a guy," but I like the feeling of the cock between my legs, attached to *my* body for a change.

"I want you to dominate me," you say. "I want it hard. Lots of swearing and shit. I'll protest, but you make me take it. Be aggressive. Be an asshole. Call me a cunt. Yeah, cunt, that's a good one."

I'm unsure of how to begin. I push you down on the bed.

"Oh, please stop," you say. Your voice is suddenly higher pitched. I take it as a sign to start being an asshole.

"Shut up, cunt, Steve's going to do whatever the hell he pleases."

You jump up at me, ferocious. I make you stop. Tell you to lie back and shut the fuck up. And you do it. You moan. A moan I've heard many times. A pleasure moan. I still don't feel like a guy, just an asshole wearing a guy's shirt and vest. But it's enough. I start to get into my role. I put my hand on my new dick. It's hard. So am I.

"And what I please is to fuck you, bitch."

You moan again like you like it. "Please don't," you say, pulling me toward you at the same time.

"Ah, come on. I know you're a whore. I know you want my big fucking dick pumping your nasty cunt." I shock myself with what I'm saying. You like it.

"Oh, don't make me, don't fuck me," you say. Then cry, "Oh fuck yeah," when I slap the cock against your thigh. That makes me hot.

"Take your goddamn pants off and turn over, slut," I say. I rub my hand up and down my dick. You stay where you are and watch me. "You heard me. Turn the fuck over, slut! That's right. Now just lie there while I boot up." I put on a condom, drip some lube on your ass. You moan loudly.

"Shut up, bitch." I say and put my cock against your thigh again. You catch your breath.

"Oh no, please."

"Oh yes. Lift your ass, girl. I said lift, bitch." You lift.

"Here I come. Oh yeah, take it like the whore you are." I slowly move my cock into you.

"Oh no, please don't." Your voice is still high. You moan a moan I've never heard before. Then grunt, "Fuck yeah." An affirmation.

"Can you feel that?" I ask. I reach my hand around in front and finger your clit. "Can you? You fucking whore." You grunt loudly.

"I said shut up and take it, bitch." I push in further and start thrusting.

"Yeah," you say, "fuck me hard."

"Oh I will. That's right. Take it. Fucking take it, bitch. Steve's going to fuck you silly. Fuck you till you can't see. Fuck you till you come all over my cock."

"Fuck. Yeah."

"That's right, Tammy, let Steve fuck you like you deserve. Take it, girl. Fucking take it till you come. You're going to gush aren't you? All over me. I said you're going to come, aren't you? I said come, goddamnit. Fucking do it."

"Oh yeaaah, fuck me...."

"I said shut up, cunt, and come for your Daddy." And you do. Loud and labored. You soak the sheets. Your cunt throbs long after I stop thrusting. I lie on top of you, exhausted.

"Hold me," you say. You've never asked me to hold you before. Boy. Girl. T. I hold you.

3.

We don't talk for months. Why? Because you're an asshole. Because I'm a bitch. Because you're insensitive. Because I'm too sensitive. Because we walk two completely different worlds. Today, I don't remember why. Just remember wanting you. Today, I walk through this street. *I miss T* goes over and over in my head. When I get home I call you. Ask you to come over. And of course you do. You always do. No questions asked. This is what we do for each other.

I put on lipstick and meet you on the front porch, even though it's freezing out. I don't tell you about my day, even though it was bad. I don't ask about yours. I am so glad to see you. I can tell you're glad to see me too. But we pretend we're not. We stare at each other in the cold. You and I, we sure know how to pretend.

"Well, aren't you going to ask me in?"

"Yeah, yeah, come up."

You follow me to the top of the stairs, through my apartment door. "Look, T," I say, turning around. Your arm is in the air. You drop a snowball on my head.

"Oh, you bastard," I laugh.

"Aw baby, what's wrong?" Your annoying sarcasm. You laugh too. Brush the snow off my head, my shoulders. "What's wrong?" You stop laughing. "Baby?"

I don't say anything. Bring you into my bedroom. Pull you down beside me on the bed. Lie with you. You caress me. Move your fingers over my clothes, over my body. My eyes are closed. If this is the only thing we can do for each other, so be it.

"So T, tell me about your first kiss."

You don't say anything right away. Then, "I was nine. He was a man." You say it so calmly. Like it's normal. Then I wonder, what the hell is normal?

"And how was it?"

"It was an all right kiss," you say.

I'm quiet. You continue to caress me. Slow, sensual. Unusual for us. We stay like that for a long while. Until you move your hands gently under my shirt. My skin gets goose bumps. My cunt gets wet. My body responds with movement. You take my shirt off. Get more aggressive. Kiss my body where your caresses were. Pull at the button of my jeans.

"I want you," you say.

"I want you too. I want your fist."

"You got it."

You move down my body and undo my jeans, pull them off. Slide your hand over my underwear. Apply pressure on my clit. My hips rise and grind. You take off my underwear. Slide your hand along my wetness. Rub a finger against my clit. I open up to your fingers. You push and play with my clit. In no time my cunt gathers around your whole fist. It is always faster and easier with you than with anyone else. I love it more than anything else we do. But I always have to remind you I don't want thrusts. You like getting pumped and don't understand why I don't. But you do what I ask. Just leave your fist there in me. Still.

"It feels so...comfortable," I say.

"I haven't heard that one before," you say. I smile. We're quiet. You keep it in until I'm ready for you to take it out.

"You're still bleeding." You show me your hand covered with my blood. "Do you have a piece of paper? I'll make a handprint."

I still feel full. Flayed. Prelingual.

"Well, you've got one inside you already, anyway." You lie down beside me. Lay your hand on my breast. We stay like that for a long time.

"Will you run me a bath?" I ask.

I stay in bed while you go. You clean the tub for me. Then run the water hotter than I'd like. Use shampoo to make bubbles. I know you feel chivalrous. Like this is what a guy does for a girl. Takes care of her.

"I wonder if what we are is anything like being straight," I call from the bed.

"We're still dykes," you say, sounding offended. Sometimes

it's true. That's exactly what we are. Sometimes we're not. Sometimes, I guess, it just doesn't matter.

When the bath is ready, you call me. I get in and the water is too hot like you thought it would be. I turn on the cold and swirl it around. You close the toilet lid and sit on it. Watch me. You've got your boy vest on. I like you watching. I turn off the cold water and lie back. Warm. Smothered. A feeling I rarely enjoy. When I ask you to join me in the tub, you refuse. You don't say why, but I know you well enough to understand what makes you feel vulnerable. You leave the room.

I think about how it feels to do this typical boy-girl thing with you. Sometimes I play girl, and sometimes I am girl. I get confused about which one is which. I think about who you are to me. How, sometimes, you are what I need in the most surprising ways. I hear you in the kitchen.

"Hey T," I call from the bath. You stop moving. You're quiet.

"Yeah?" you finally respond.

"Co'mere."

You come back into the bathroom with your swagger. Your casual air. "What?"

"Kneel," I tell you.

"Kneel where?" you ask, pretending to be unsure about wanting to kneel for me.

"Beside the tub," I say, pointing beside me. You just look at me for a second, making like you don't want to. But you do.

"What?" you ask again as you kneel. There's a staccato sound in your voice.

I sit up a bit in the tub and look at you. "Kiss me, Troy."

You hesitate ever so slightly. Then get yourself wet leaning in for the kiss.

Stazione

Sarah Bardeen

It was a late afternoon during school holidays.

I was on vacation from my life. I'd taken myself to the Italian Riviera, less for the culture than for the sun, the cliffs, the good food. For the there-ness of it.

I'd been riding trains for a week. I would spend just a few days in each town, taking day trips to the beaches, staying in cheap rooms let by eager men who met the trains as they came in. I had been to the beach at Riomaggiore, a few towns away, and was waiting for my train to take me back to Vernazza and my room when I saw her.

She was standing with four or five friends. They were all impeccably stylish as Italian fashion demands, and none of them were older than seventeen. She towered over them, her calves and thighs stretching from three-inch platform heels. The platforms slipped a little as she stood, knocking to one side or the other. As she laughed and chatted, one set of painted toes slipped in and out of the strap, scratching her left ankle and then returning to its shoe. She was in a tank dress, no sleeves. The material had big red flowers on it. Close fitting, it ended just below her ass. The other girls looked at her with trepidation or longing—they each longed to be the thing that would capture her attention, and feared to be.

The open platform was crowded in the late afternoon, full of attractive families with attractive children, teenage boys, young lovers, packs of brown, saggy-breasted grandmothers holding woven baskets. The girls—and particularly the tall girl—stood out. They stood in the center of the platform, against no walls. They drew everyone's attention, and they knew it. The late afternoon sun made everything golden. Even them, even the tall girl's skin.

Our train came in a whirl of dust and whistles. It made a steamy exhalation and the doors parted and drew back. The people who'd been waiting on the platform stumbled on. I took my eyes off her and grabbed my bag. The group of girls clambered up the steps ahead of me, climbing to the top deck, along with most of the other passengers. I chose the deck below, for privacy and quiet.

One town passed; another. I dozed against the inflexible headrest, one hand on my backpack, drained by a day of sun, salt water, and Italian waiters. One more town; another. The express steamed by. It was a shadow that woke me.

"You was staring at me. At the *stazione*." The girl stood before me, her eyes throwing darts at me, her knees knocking as she braced herself against the swaying of the train.

"I wasn't staring."

"Oh! You wasn't estaring. What was you doing." Her skirt strained against one thigh, then swung with the train. She had a hand on the seats on either side of her.

I had no answer.

"You are what? A lesbian?"

"I have a boyfriend. In America. A-mer-i-ca. Boy-f-rend." I felt like the crazy mother in this teen movie I once saw, exaggerating my English as if it would make it easier to understand.

"Ah." The train lurched and one knee lunged closer, into the space in front of the seat next to me. "A boy-a-fren." She slipped into the seat beside me, her knees just brushing mine. She leaned over. "What-a is his name?"

"Steven."

"And-a what does he do?" She leaned close enough that I could feel her breast suggested against my shoulder.

"He's a television producer. He works in TV. He lives in Anaheim."

"Ahhh." She settled back in her chair, her flesh withdrawn. The interchange had satisfied her; she leaned her head back and closed her eyes. I felt bereft.

"And you?" I ventured. "You're a student, no?" The *no* was good; it sounded Italian, I thought.

Her eyelids rose halfway and she looked at me without turning her head. "No..." she drawled. "In the summer I am just a girl." She laughed a throaty laugh for someone so young, watching me, then closed her eyes again.

The train had been winding along the coast, just above the beaches. It was approaching the cliffs. We were plunged into darkness as the train entered a tunnel. I felt a hand on my knee. The breasts against my shoulder again. Her voice asked, "Do you miss your boy-a-fren very much?"

I didn't.

My hand found her waist. I couldn't stop myself. I touched all the way up her side to the edge of her breast. I leaned my head nearer to hers and inhaled that sweet, salty adolescent scent. When I touched my lips to her throat her back arched suddenly, as if a spring had been tripped. She grabbed my hand and guided it across the fabric over her breasts.

The train shot out of the darkness and into the blinding Mediterranean light. I hadn't realized she'd thrown her left knee over mine. As she pulled it back I saw a white triangle trapped by two thighs.

She leaned back again. "Boy-a-fren..." she sang softly, looking the other direction.

We stared out the window. A town: a boy looked up at the windows as we passed and did not wave. After a minute, she swung her knees over my lap without looking at me. Her torso shifted toward me but her face looked forward. Without looking at her I put my hands on her knees, I let one hand move to the inside of her thighs. She shifted her pelvis and as she did her dress straps fell from her shoulders. Her hands stayed at her sides, steadying her. Her torso threatened to burst the dress at the seams.

She moved herself so that she was under my left arm. I let that happen. I could just slip my fingers into the top of her dress.

Shhht. The train plunged headlong into another tunnel and the fingers of my other hand sought that triangle inside her skirt. The bikini material was thin. Through it, I could feel her labia and the little knob that was her clit. She leaned and I touched each side of her ass. I let my fingers play over her. She was now taut, her breathing as labored as my own.

The train exploded with light. She disentangled herself from me, stood shakily. Strips of black hair escaped their clasp. Without looking directly at me, she motioned for me to follow her. We tottered to the end of the car, ascended the steps. She fumbled at the bathroom's latch and I stood close behind her, pressing my pelvis against her ass.

When we had latched the door and were engulfed in the smell of urine, she lifted the dress over her head and drew out the strings that held those few scraps of material to her. Her areolas were rust-colored, and seaweed clung to her pubic fuzz. I took off my top and put myself against her. My small white breasts felt clammy against her warm brown ones. She kissed me, and let me kiss her. Her lips were lovely, soft, and knew just enough—but not too much—about how to kiss.

Finally my lips were at her labia, and I stuck out my tongue to taste her. She raised a leg over my shoulder and made a sound. I lapped and groped, and finally snuck a lone finger into her. She took it, and wanted more. Her fingers traced the outlines of my breasts. Her shoe had slipped off and I could feel her foot pushing into my back.

The train gears screamed; we were nearing the first stop of the express. "This is my *stazione*." She barely managed to speak. She moved her leg, and I stood up. She turned and retrieved her dress from the sink. The train had slowed but not stopped as she struggled with the dress. I helped her put it back on.

"Stay."

"No."

We sounded like any lovers, I thought.

The dress was on, her bikini in her hands. It occurred to me that I knew how naked she was under her dress; I knew her nudity.

She unlatched the door. There was no room for anything, no room for a kiss. The train stopped and she stepped out while my hands were still on her hips. I was without a top. People were coming down the stairs from the upper deck. Her eyes gave me a look and the door closed. I turned to the window. She descended the train steps and her friends converged on her, their hands flying. Asking, I supposed, where she had been. She shrugged and they moved away from the train. After a few steps her head jerked back and her eyes searched the train windows for a moment. Then she walked away.

Soap City
Kate E. Conlan

She lies in a colorful city. Her bedroom hovers above the
ground letting orange afternoon light in through the huge
windows. She is fifteen and enamored with her body. She lies
there on her not-too-soft bed and strokes over her skin, underneath the clothes that decorate her. She smoothes fingers over
her ribs, up to the curve at the base of her breast, around to
her sternum and down to the curving belly and its tunnelled
center.

She breathes the late afternoon air and anticipates where
her fingers will go with a sort of naïve pleasure. She wants
to have something to look back at when she's older. So her
fingers reach lower. The city hums its song as she sings
her own.

Afterward, she lets other things into her mind. She forgets
the tiny goose bumps that huddle over skin. She thinks about
dressing again. She imagines tight blue trousers that hang low
on rounded hips. She thinks about over-long-sleeved tops that
touch at her chin.

Then she is out in the street looking for you.

"Anya…"

She waits for you to look before she continues.

"There was a girl in here earlier looking for you."

You bend down and rifle through your bag.

"She was young and very pretty; she had teeth just like a child's."

You pull another chair closer and sprawl over it, lithe limbs folding easily over one another.

"Anya!"

"Yes, yes, Magdalene. A girl, young, pretty, teeth like a child."

"She was looking for you. You promised me that you wouldn't do that anymore."

"Promises are like water Magdalene. Just as easily solid and unmoving, as free and flowing. I cannot remember what I said."

"You did."

"Promise? Was it a bargain so that I could lick you from top to toe?"

"Anya." That comes out in a warning tone, yet you aren't perturbed.

"Or was it a bargain that meant I could be inside you, for a few glorious moments?"

Magdalene turns and walks away. Her heels click on the linoleum floor as your arm muscles flicker while you write. She delivers coffee to the only other person in the house, subtly trying to ignore you and send her fury at the same time. You write her a poem. You haven't decided yet whether it will torture or soothe Magdalene's violent soul. The poem floats under your hand waiting for a decision. Just as you think you may have decided on something, you lift your darkened head to see her, the girl, standing before you in tight blue trousers. A line of hip showing, otherwise covered from neck to toe.

You feel stupid that you let the secret of your favorite place away to such a youngster. However, when she sits down next to you and her tight blue trousers slip to reveal even paler hip, you forget about your privacy and start thinking about something else. She is too young really, and you know you won't let her touch you till she is sixteen, her rule too. She provides a taut sort of pleasure that you will feed later. A taut sort of pleasure that Magdalene might have even thanked the girl for had she known where it came from.

Virginie stands outside a café, for about ten minutes. She spots Anya from across the street. Sees her dark hair flicking over her forehead and curling at the nape of her neck. She sees the worn jeans so soft her fingers have to stray along them. She sees arms that are made for touching, muscles that are there, but just enough. A long neck bends, small breasts point, fingers scribble. Virginie knows that underneath that hair there are eyes thickly lashed, and swooping brows. She knows that there are teeny ears covered in soft down. She knows that there are smooth large lips that could smile easily, but don't. She knows more, but right now she notices her feet have started walking, so she follows them. They walk inside. They end up right next to Anya, in the late afternoon sun that is brightly reflected around the room from Magdalene and her linoleum floor.

The street is hard under your four A.M. tired toes. The girl, Virginie, traipses beside you, not showing anything other than the pretty outline of her body. You have been thinking all night how amusing her name is. Virginie, it rolls pleasingly from your drunken tongue. You don't say this to her though. A miracle. She is far too eager to progress to another level with you. She might take your joke as a hint. All night she has been dragging you into hallways and shy corners. She isn't sixteen for four full days. The waiting it seems is getting to her, now she finds the rule to be arbitrary. At 4:12 A.M. you cannot take her soft body and her smooth kisses any longer. You throw her in a taxi with too much money. She stares at you questioningly from the taxi window, her fingers tapping something out in Morse code, perhaps, on the dirty glass. You progress to Magdalene's house. Your feet know the way, even if you don't.

After knocking for too long, you forget where you are. Then you remember, then you forget again. Magdalene comes to the door. She is used to this. Apparently all the time that you have been knocking Magdalene has been doing something else. Her breasts jut pleasantly from a robe. Her face is slightly flushed, as if she were rushing. And her eyes are dilated.

"You want to come in then?" Her voice isn't mocking. Instead she is realistic, stating what she sees standing slightly slumped on her doorway.

"Yes." You pull your tired self up and take hold of her fragile body. She leans into you almost automatically, but your perceptive powers were used up on her body twenty seconds earlier. You miss this. The kiss starts just inside the door as her foot closes it. It's a soft kiss. One that speaks of lips that know each other well.

Soon, though, you are fucking. You find yourself mesmerized by the way her buttocks ripple as you fuck her from behind. Your fake cock going where you cannot. You can see her breasts swinging slightly out of time. They are like a percussionist that has a problem with delay, slow reflexes. You don't care. The two separate rhythms make good accompaniment for your splendid love. You enjoy how animalistic Magdalene sounds with your cock inside her, your fingers on her clitoris. She makes little grunts, yelps, and murmurs all of which add to the slap your stomach makes against her buttocks. You have a sudden urge to slap her cheeks on the offbeats. You don't. Her head sways. You enjoy watching her spine flex and bend in front of you. You close your eyes and imagine her cunt is really Virginie's mouth: soft, petulant, and perfectly warm. You stop, one finger poised over Magdalene's juddering clitoris, another pressed against the wall within her, measuring the spasms. She pushes against you wildly for a few seconds and then she falls silent. Much to your surprise she comes toward you. She eyes you as she removes the cock that covers your own delicate folds and takes your clitoris into her mouth. You have one moment of fear, you think you've said something and maybe those teeth will bite, but then her sucking and her liquid tongue take over. You are hers in the final seconds before you come. But as the first whisper of orgasm hits you, Virginie's face appears. You try very hard not to say her name. The noise that you make turns Magdalene on so much that she slips several fingers down to her own sex and orgasms again.

Virginie has just celebrated a birthday. It's the morning and she is slightly unhappy to be walking in such bright sunshine, however the thought of eggs Benedict is helping her along the street. She follows the smell of coffee, shutting her eyes and hoping for the best.

This is how she bumps into you. You can't believe your fucking luck. You've spent the last eight years traveling, having sex with fast women in seedy bars, or with slow ones that want to make you theirs. You've ridden scooters and motorcycles, walked till you couldn't walk anymore, and driven till you made yourself sick. Somehow you got back here. You were heading to a favorite haunt when she placed herself so easily into your arms. There are all the words that people say when they bump into each other when it is socially inappropriate. There is much bowing and scraping. Then she steps back and looks at you. Your name comes out as breath from her lips. Her face doesn't smile and then she laughs, like glass breaking, you're not sure if it's a good sound.

"You," she says, her fine eyes trembling in the morning light.

"You would appear to be right." You congratulate yourself on the witty repartee and then think; maybe you should have just shut up. She still takes hold of your arm.

"I'm going for some breakfast, come with me." And that's it, you are dragged along by a whirlwind, a dust devil, something that you have never seen before.

There are days between sightings. She turns out to be one of these rare things that you hunt, like blue jelly beans or the last loaf of fresh bread at seven P.M. Sometimes you will see her as the day approaches high noon, her arms waving from a car. Other times you will only see her at night; she will be wearing clothes that seem to want to be worn by her, and her smile and the cigarette that she holds between lips will welcome you. You dance around each other for almost a year. Sightings and visits mediated by months of nothing. You find this lust frustrating, you are the one that is sought, you are the one that hides like a silverfish between book pages. You hate this befuddlement, but what can you do? You can sleep with Magdalene. She likes the fever that your frustration brings, and she doesn't mind that you want her often and then sometimes not at all. Magdalene is not fussy when it comes to you.

It is high summer; the trees are their greenest green, threatening to wilt without water as most of the flowers have already done. Grass is yellowed, except on the most wasteful gardener's lawn. It is twilight, which means it is about 9:30 P.M. You are wandering down a stretch of city street, smelling the air, thinking that you would like to eat. And as if she was offering herself up as a morsel, who should appear? Your cunt jumps.

Virginie is out in the summer, letting her skin soak up the warmth, letting it glint in her hair. She is hungry, and a little tired. Her feet touching the last strains of sun-warmed pavement, her hair sticking in curls to the back of her neck. She sees you, and her own cunt glistens moistly all of a sudden. She takes this as a sign and walks toward you. Her feet are firm in their path, her legs know where they want to go. As she reaches you, you reach her, and you kiss at almost ten P.M. in summer, on the street where boys in cars whistle as your breasts jostle for position. She slides up your body and suddenly her voluptuous frame is wrapped lightly around you. You wonder what she is made of. You didn't know you were this strong. You imagine that what you can feel on your belly is the heat from her cunt seeping through two people's clothes.

Getting home takes effort. Her house is two hundred meters up the street. But it seems that fingers and lips, eyes and teeth have all become impatient. She rips open the top of your jeans and slides her hand down to your wet crotch. You almost think that you won't be standing when you recover from this touch. Yet you are. People stare. Cars almost stop. So you remove her hand and struggle ten feet till you have to cup a spectacular breast in your long fingers. Then once again you are kissing and her cunt is riding your leg. You force yourself away from her, because you know that soon you will both be naked in the coming darkness, helpless to your own desire.

So you grab her hand and run, fleeing it. You are puffed and laughing when you arrive safely inside her doorway. Then you realize that you want her slowly. Revealing small piece by small piece. You lick and bite her earlobes. Tease your teeth down her neck. You stand behind her, fitting her buttocks into the curve of your body. You circle her nipples through the fabric of her clothing and feel her breath sigh up into your hair as you kiss and nibble upon her neck, her shoulders.

One strap, some kisses, observation of the point most recently uncovered, careful consideration of where to go next, debate, and then the next piece of flesh is uncovered. By the time you have both her naked breasts in your hands the fire from her cunt can be felt even when she is not pressed up against you. It is about midnight before you both stand naked against each other. There is some lazy air about you that makes both of you wonder if you can carry on. But you do. Fingers, mouths, eyes; you could make a list of all the parts that long to touch. Instead you just press your dark, sweaty bodies together.

You feel your heart stopping sometimes. You figure either you are just so far out of your body that you can't feel it, or that what she is doing to you is killing you. You can't decide, though: should you beg her to stop, or beg her to continue? You leave the decision to her, your heart flapping around like some dying fish. You are surprised to find that your mouth is on her; sliding around her wetness you taste her.

Then you lie gasping beside each other. That is all you do, gasp for successive minutes. She would leave, but it is her house. You would leave but for the fact that you can't move let alone create a thought. Your head is inside you. Your head is inside her. Virginie wants to go back to that hunt. She wants to be the wraith that hides from you, and joins up occasionally for this. But she can no more usher you to the door, than you can her.

There has always been a certain randomness to your ways. The next day you are swept from her house easily by the arrival of her brother. He leers at you as much as is possible for quite an attractive man. You take your chances with the outside world. You find yourself, somewhat ashamedly, wondering if anything will have changed. Nothing has. The espresso that you have in fifteen minutes is just as creamy as you remember. And the sky looks just the same. Suffice to say you are wildly disappointed. This is as romantic as you get. You hop a ride on a passing scooter and head out of the city limits still smelling of Virginie's soap and shampoo. You imagine it leaving a trail in the air as you go. You are like Hansel or Gretel leaving a trail to get home by. People on the street eating up the smell like birds.

Unraveling the Stone
Kristen E. Porter

The first time I saw Melissa was down at Jake's Tavern. I showed up late that Friday hoping to run into Billy. I heard he caught his old lady in the sack with his best friend and up and left her, so I figured he might be up for some comforting. I was watching him shoot pool when Melissa walked in. I wasn't alone in my stare; the whole bar took notice of her. I heard Red, the bartender, mutter under his breath, "Goddamned dagger," as the guys at the bar laughed.

I had never seen a woman quite like her before. Her white T-shirt was clean and crisp, sleeves rolled up just above her bicep. Her worn leather pants hugged her frame perfectly and melted into the blackness of thick boots, scuffed around the edges but polished up real nice. She certainly wouldn't be what one would call pretty, but there was something hand-some about her. The buzz was that she just bought old man Harris' farm, so I knew she must have been from out of town. Hell, everyone knew that land's been barren for years.

I couldn't help but stare at her. I finished smoking the last cigarette I had, and grabbed my keys to head out when she began walking toward me. Her stride was strong and purposeful and when her eyes caught mine, it was like she was looking right through me. As she was about to walk past my table, the scent of her cologne made me feel so dizzy the keys dropped right out of my hand onto the floor. She stopped, and bent down to pick them up. She didn't say a word, just placed them in my hand, winked and left. I nervously looked around, relieved to find the guys at the bar oblivious. That's when Billy gave a holler over: "Hope you didn't touch her, might rub off on ya!" Again, the barflies belted out their laughter. Nothing makes a bunch of guys more nerved up than a woman like her. Full of the confidence they lacked. Somehow fucks with their manhood, I think.

As much as I tried, I couldn't get her out of my thoughts. Daydreams, night dreams, she snuck into all of them. Her smell and the feel of her hand as she placed the keys into mine were burned into my memory. About a week after that, I saw her again. I was in town picking up a few bags of feed and struggling to get them to my car when she pulled up next to me in a blue 1963 Ford pickup, with just enough rust peeking through the paint you knew it was lived in. She jumped out the door and rushed over to me.

"Let me help you with that, little lady. Shouldn't your old man be lugging this home for you?" she asked as she lifted the bags into my trunk. She was the first person to ever call me a lady and I liked it.

"Yeah, right," I muttered. "I seem to have skipped the husband part and gone straight into having the kids."

"Oh, sorry for the intrusion. I just assumed that a pretty lady like you would have some fella to help out. I'll mind my business, forgive me," she said, looking down.

"It's all right. Times like these that a husband sure would come in handy, at least to lug this stuff out to the barn for me," I replied, laughing.

"Well, I've got some time right now, why don't I follow you home and help you with this load at least," she said as she winked. That same damn wink that got her stuck in my head to begin with.

"Thanks, that would be great," I said, wondering where this was all going.

She was a great help and a perfect gentleman, if I can call her that. Ever since that Sunday, she's been dropping by for coffee, a cold drink, and on occasion for a whisky after the kids are in bed.

One particular day I heard the knock on the door as I finished washing the breakfast dishes.

"Come in," I called out as I dried my hands on my worn apron. Getting both kids out to school on time was an ordeal, but for now the house was quiet. Jimmy wasn't quite used to the routine of juggling morning chores on a schedule, having just started first grade a few weeks ago. Ben had it down pat, being a few years older, and was never much trouble, besides playing with his eggs instead of eating them.

"Hey there, pretty lady," she said as she swaggered into the kitchen. Today her hair was freshly cut, shaved close in back, with a little bit of bang hanging over her green eyes.

"This is a nice surprise," I said as I began to brush away the stray hairs from her collar.

"I've got another surprise for you," she said. "Do you have time to take a walk with me and the boys?" The boys were her dogs, but they were more like children to her. A golden named Buck and some sort of herder breed named Toby.

I grabbed my sweater as we headed out to the trail behind the house. Melissa gave a whistle as Buck and Toby jumped out of the back of the pickup to lead the way. When we got down to the river, she stopped so the boys could take a drink. She held out a clenched fist and smiled at me.

"What's that?" I asked as my gaze caressed her muscular arm. Her sun-drenched hands were weathered from years of mucking goat pens. You could begin to see the first signs of arthritis in her knuckles from milking during the damp rainy seasons.

"It's a gift," she replied, opening up the palm of my hand and dropping a small newspaper-wrapped item into it. As I opened the paper, a stone fell out. Its cool gray surface glittered with the rising sun.

"Thanks," I replied. I wasn't quite sure what to make of it, but it felt like something special nonetheless.

"It's shaped like a heart," she said as she turned the rock upside down in my hand.

I could feel my face flush with embarrassment. Maybe it was because this was clearly a move on her part, but probably more so because I wanted it. As I looked at the stone heart I thought of mine, hardened by the loss of a lifetime of dreams. It made me think of my grandmother. She was a wise woman, and a beautiful one at that. When I was a little girl she'd scoop me up into her apron and sit us under the crab apple tree in the back-yard. Under that tree she taught me as much about life's truths as she could. One thing she always told me was this: "Suzie, hearts come boxed or bruised. Can't have 'em any other way." Gram nicknamed me Suzie on account of singing that song "Wake Up Little Suzie" at the end of my nap time, even though my real name is Contessa. Mom thought a royal sounding name would give me a better chance of getting the hell out of Missouri some day. People always just call me Tess though.

Melissa and I hiked farther along the path next to the river as I turned the rock over and over again in my hand. The feel of the dewy damp leaves underneath my feet, the weight of the small stone in my hand and the scent of her beside me made my insides twist up. But it was like that from the very first moment I saw her.

She finally asked me out one afternoon while we were sitting on my front porch in the wooden swing. I mentioned that I could not remember ever having seen a shooting star before. She couldn't believe it, with me living out here on these lands all my life. She asked me to get a babysitter for the evening and she'd take me stargazing. Although I wasn't sure if it was a date in the proper sense of the word, I felt excited about it all the same. The fact that she was a woman never much mattered to me and I tried not to think about how it would matter to everyone else.

As that day melted into night my anticipation grew. My thoughts went around and around in my head, as I wondered what to expect. Would she kiss me? Would I like it? I had only kissed a girl once before, as a kid. JoBeth and I were climbing up the empty flagpole that stood in front of our old school. When we finally wore ourselves out she said rather matter-of-factly, "Do you feel that tingling in your privates, Tess?" I did. "Well," she went on to say, "that's what it feels like when you fall in love." This was all news to me, having never felt anything quite like it before. "Does it go away?" I asked. "Yup, it sure will, but you have to kiss first," she said. So we put our lips against each other and moved our heads all around like on TV. I never told JoBeth that the kissing made it worse for me. Figured that meant there was something wrong with me and that it was better to say nothing.

Melissa picked me up that night and for once I was glad there was so much land between the houses up here. Since arriving in town, she was all folks could talk about and I didn't want anyone to be putting bad thoughts into Ben and Jimmy's heads about the whole thing. She opened up the truck door for me and I got in.

"No boys tonight?" I asked as I noticed the dog hair was meticulously cleaned off the front seat.

"Nope, got a sitter for them," she laughed. "Tonight is just for you and me."

She drove out to Riley's field and parked. We climbed into the back of the flatbed and talked as we passed the bottle of Jameson's between us. The liquid burned my throat each time it went down, but made my insides feel warm. It was good to feel desire again after so many years.

The only way I can describe the sky is what I imagine must be the color they call indigo. The deep purple blanket surrounded me in the crispness of the night. I could feel her gaze as it began to burrow through my skin. I felt the heat rising in my face and sweat began to bead between my breasts. The smooth skin of her hand grazed my thigh.

I turned my face toward hers as her eyes met mine. The scent of the honeysuckle swept me up into a moment that I wasn't quite sure I even wanted as my head instinctually moved toward hers. I took her mouth against mine and kissed her hard, feeling the sharpness of her teeth beneath the flesh of her lips. Her hand slowly moved from my thigh over my belly and settled on my throat. The firmness of her grasp across my neck made my mouth water and each swallow more pronounced. Her other hand found its way up under my dress as she moved her legs up over mine. Her weight felt solid against me. My chest heaved to her firm touch as her breathy voice sent shivers through my ear.

"Baby, I want you so bad. Let me take you. I'll be gentle," she whispered.

Gentle? If she only knew the roughness of the hands that have had their way with me over the years. In gas station bathrooms and backseats of cars. The emptiness that went along with "drive-in sex." That's what Gram called it. "Those boys want nothin' from ya but drive-in sex," she'd say. "They drive in and they drive out. When are ya gonna learn, Suzie? Ain't it bad enough you got one baby to care for?"

Melissa's hands felt good, felt right, like nothing had ever before. She began to knead my breasts and responded to my moan by moving the thin cotton that covered them aside with her teeth. My nipples hardened in the open night air. Her tongue moved across my flesh like a skimmer on silky water. With each sigh she bit harder, leaving me breathless. The weight of her small breasts across my chest felt good and I moved my hands down to feel her.

"Don't do that," she pleaded urgently as she grabbed my wrist and abruptly pulled it taut above my head. I gasped from the thrill of her taking control. In a strange way, her forcefulness made me feel safe, protected.

Our lips met and our tongues danced to silent song. Her body released its tightness and softened back into mine. Her hipbones melted into my body like a pat of butter over piping hot pancakes. With her arm above my head still holding my wrist, I could smell the sweet musky scent from her armpit. Her smell. I wanted to take it in so deep it would be impossible to forget. As she kissed me, her thigh ground into me, and my hips responded by rising and falling to her motion. Her hand moved aside the damp material covering my crotch, and behind my shut eyes I could see the veins lining her hands and arms that I had stared at so many times. The confidence, power, and strength in her blood was bulging just beneath the surface, awaiting its release.

Her fingers played with my untrimmed hair, soft, like it was meant to be. Her fingers slid along my swollen labia, full and succulent.

"Girl, you are so wet," she moaned softly. Hearing her voice speak about my pleasure, the pleasure she was providing, just about pushed me over the edge. My anxieties about being with a woman were suddenly overpowered by an exhilaration that somehow felt strange and comfortable at the same time. The pressure in my pussy ached.

"I want to feel you. Let me take you into me, baby, please. Don't make me wait any longer," I begged, hoping for even one finger to calm the throb inside of me.

As she entered me, my insides expanded like the pop of an ice cube as it enters a glass of lemonade on a hot day. My hands were burning to touch her, her skin, her breasts. She kept them away, overpowering each reach I made, which only made me want her more.

Her thumb rubbed ever so slightly on my swollen clit as it began to twitch. I felt myself opening up to her, and for more reasons than one, this was new for me. I relaxed into receiving her. At the same time, my thighs tightened as my hips bucked and my cunt clenched around her fingers. I came in waves as her fingers continued rocking me from the inside.

"Are you crying?" she asked, her lashes fluttering against mine in a butterfly kiss.

"Oh, it's nothing," I answered. Sometimes a release takes you by surprise and shatters the very foundation you thought you were standing on. Our coming together was like being immersed in a great thunderstorm, surging with electricity. Wet with power. And I always did prefer being wrapped in the arms of a storm. Gram said I was a born storm lover, having come into the world during one of the worst flash floods Jackson County had ever seen. She'd say, "Nothing more free than a lightning storm, Suzie, and you got the storm in your veins."

We went on like that for months. Hiding out in fields and woods. Sneaking around like teenagers. Getting to know even the messiest parts of each other. Our sex became more intense, more aggressive with each piece of armor removed. Like peeling an onion, each layer of insecurity that came away made me cry, but Melissa always held me through it. I began to understand that although I wasn't sure if I had always been a lesbian, I was sure that I loved her. As our shooting-star searches became more frequent, my desperation to make love to her as she did me began to consume me. Thoughts of my fingers in secret steamy places and the desire for her in my mouth grew beyond just a want to a need.

One night I sent the kids over to the neighbors for a sleep-over. As usual I was finishing up dishes when she snuck in and put her arms around my waist from behind. Her mouth on the nape of my neck sent shivers down to the pit of my stomach. She grabbed my hips and thrust her pelvis into my ass so that I could feel her packing.

I released her hands from my hips and without words led her to my bedroom. The smell of the passing rain wafted through the open windows, as the movement of the gauze drapes created dancing shadows along the stark walls. As I began to rip at her shirt she spun me around and pushed my hands down on the bed. Nothing had ever come close to this feeling of being taken by her. I heard her unzip her jeans as she placed one hand on the back of my head, grabbing a mound of my thick curls. She kicked my legs open with her boot and pushed my torso toward the bed.

"Baby, I'm gonna fuck you just like you like it. I'm gonna watch my hard cock slide in and out of your wet pussy." She knew I melted when she talked sex talk. I gasped as I took in her hard thrust. She understood that the call to fuck fiercely and without restraint is sometimes as deep as the need to be tender. When I felt she was worked up enough, I reached down and began to rub my hard clit with my middle finger. It didn't take much as she talked me through my orgasm. My body shook violently as my head pressed into the bed, squelching my screams of pleasure. Her full body weight fell upon my back as she caught her breath.

"Oh, baby, I love it that way. Your ass in the air. The way your hair moves when you throw your head back. Seeing me inside your cunt." She sighed.

I used all my force to flip her over on the bed and straddled her hips. Her cock was shining with my juices as I carefully began to remove the harness.

"That's okay baby, I'll go in the bathroom to do that," she said as she reached for my wrist. I was so used to this routine I cut her off at the pass and yanked her arms above her head.

"No, it's not okay. I want to make you feel good. I want to have your taste in my mouth," I begged.

"It doesn't work like that, Tess," she said firmly. Gram used to say that telling me no was the best way to make sure I did exactly what it was I was being told not to do. This was no different.

"C'mon, you are so unfair to me," I pleaded jokingly.

I noticed Melissa's eyes starting to well up. It stopped me short. I released my hold on her wrists feeling stupid for pushing it. I had never seen her cry before; that was usually my department.

"It's okay, baby, you're safe," I said as I took her face in my hands and kissed her tears.

"It's not you," she said, avoiding my eyes, "I'm sorry, it's not that I don't want to give myself to you," she said, as she choked back her tears.

I cradled her in my arms and pressed my body close to hers. I whispered "Shhhhh" in her ear for a long time, rocking her beautiful body as her arms wrapped around my waist. I continued shushing, just like I would to get one of my babies to stop crying, until finally I felt her stiffness release. I placed my hand over her heart, feeling the slight outline of her breasts underneath, and out of nowhere I whispered, "I love you."

"I don't know why I haven't said the words before tonight. I'm so sorry for pressuring you. When I was with Jimmy's daddy, I thought if I loved him enough, he'd stop drinking so much. Stupid, I know, but I thought my love was the magic that would save him. This is different in a lot of ways," I said as she placed her hand over mine, still resting above her heart.

"There is nothing wrong with you and it's not that you aren't good enough just the way you are. In fact it's just the opposite. It makes me feel like I'm the one who's not good enough," I explained, trying to swallow away the pit in my throat.

Her tear-streaked face began to show a smile as she reached down and put my hands on the buckles of the harness.

"I love you too, baby," she said as she helped me remove it.

I guess Gram was right. The risk of a bruised heart far outweighs the isolation of keeping it boxed up all the time. I knew this moment was a precious gift. Just as I had with the first gift she gave me, again I found myself unraveling a stone.

To Fuck or Get Fucked

Rakelle Valencia

I like to fuck. In a fuck or get fucked world, I'm the girl, I'm supposed to get fucked. But like I said, I like to fuck.

Maybe it started with the butt boys. Oh, but it probably started before them. I'm not saying the boys were my first. Then again, I'm not saying they weren't. It was the butt boys who gave me the hunger to fuck, who showed me the power and desire of the fuck, who taught me to crave the undulation of bodies slamming and slapping in rhythm and against the rhythm. Boys just seem to know how to have fun, they know how to fuck. So yeah, it started with the butt boys.

Having someone bent over or writhing beneath me is all the same, gender-wise, and it's all very different. I'm not saying I would still do the boys, and I'm not saying I wouldn't. But the girls...girls know how to take it. A good chick likes to get fucked.

Now I know that callin' 'em chicks can sound derogatory, but it's not. I use *chick* with the highest regard. And the ones I call chicks probably call themselves chicks too. It takes a lot to stand up and say you're a chick. It takes a lot to get fucked like I'm talkin' about, and to be a good fuck.

Like this one chick, she couldn't wait for me to strap it on with her. In fact, she needed it so fast, she was always trying to get me to pack. But I don't pack. So she did the next best thing. And I'm telling you this chick was all-the-time crazy to get fucked. She made me a special strap-on. It was a beauty.

I still have it today, wouldn't be caught dead without it, and wouldn't trade it for the world. I'm talking no manufactured deal for this girl. I'm sold on this used-to-be one of a kind. The thing was pure genius with a touch of class and individualism. I like that, class and individualism.

I started callin' it The Snap-on Strap-on. The name stuck, I heard it the other day in that well-lit, frequented, women-owned, adult toy shop one block over from Main Street. My chick, she made up a bunch and they stocked 'em. Hot item too, 'cause it's not what she does for a livin', and she can only make so many, and I think girls are finding out that the personal touch with these beauties can be real handy.

What do I mean by that? Have you ever used 'em? Strap-ons? I mean, think on it. If you're not packin' then you're not ready. Do you warm her up first, then say, "Oh, excuse me dear while I step into this ugly, drab, black harness"? Then you know what happens. You fight with the damn thing, a tangled mess wrapped around a stiff backing that always seems to be on the wrong side until you work out all of the angles. That done, your next worry is gettin' into the contraption. Meanwhile your girl's coolin' off.

Worse than that, you jump off her bed to cram one foot at a time into the leg loops, and you end up fallin' over, eliciting whoops and hollers of laughter from above. I'm not unathletic, and I'm not saying I had been drinking or was on anything, you know? But if you're still thinking on it, you tell me how you've pulled off being suave with those manufactured strap-ons. Maybe something like, "excuse me a moment while I freshen up," as you make the mad dash elsewhere so you don't look like a fool. Like I said, your girl's coolin' off, you know?

Now let me tell you about these beauties, these Snap-on Strap-ons. Man, you can get these things on anywhere anyhow. You can get in 'em and out of 'em fast, real fast, in case you had to either way. I'm not saying I ever had to get out of one fast, I'm just saying it's an option. But I will say I've had to get into one fast.

Like that one time she had to have it, you know. We were in a memme mobile, a small sedan, and I wasn't gonna play Gumby, but she had to have a little somethin' somethin' and I was right there with her. I'm talking I was right there, wetter than a Slip 'n Slide at a family picnic on a hot July day. Nothing to worry about though, I had a Snap-on Strap-on and was ready for action in seconds.

This thing is as crazy as her. It has snaps on every strap, at every juncture. She took those beefy, plastic snaps, like you'd find on dog collars, and put one on either side of the waistband, and one on each leg strap, all in the back, off to the sides, adjustable too. In the front, a rubber ring, held in place with those silver, flat snaps that you'd find on denim jean jackets, and the works had no backing. No backing. I remember going into the toy store with her when she first presented her invention; the girl behind the counter was aghast, opening up her sweet, tiny mouth in horror, scrunching her baby-blues and freckled brow: "No backing? How does the dong stay in place?"

"YOU are the backing," came the reply. And it works, you know. No stiff, fussy, triangular-shaped piece of vinyl or leather to chafe the crease of your thighs to your pussy if you're a skinny drink like me. And the best part, the dildos are more easily exchangeable without breaking the action too long, if you know what I mean. With no backing, I've got it down one-handed, while the other hand stays busy in the slick and slippery.

But that's not what I was trying to tell you. It's not about the dick, it's about the fuck. It's about the chicks who like to get fucked. And I love to fuck. To fuck or to get fucked. Well, like I said, I'm supposed to get fucked, but I so like to fuck.

I like to crawl up between a pair of thighs and bury myself in their adjoining crevice, open, wet, and inviting. Maybe one leg is bent upward, hung over the crook of my elbow so I can grasp a fleshy thigh as I thrust in the missionary position, our torsos sopping with sweat, gliding over each other, nipples plucking at nipples.

Chicks are fascinating to fuck, and I like to be sunk home as any man does, as any boy needs, as any girl can do. Flip them over with some slap and tickle before greasing my silicone prick and hammering it home, watching her asscheeks ripple in response to my erotic pummeling. Smacking sounds of naked skin greeting naked skin, whimpers and moans entering in chorus, white knuckles gripping hip handles, and the body beneath, flushed and tensed in its buildup to release.

And I need this. I need to fuck. Sometimes the fuck is so alluring, so powerful in its promise that I beg to get off beforehand. "Get me done so I can last," as if I were a young, pubescent male ready to pop with the opening of the latest, coveted issue of *Penthouse*.

I'm not saying it's all like that, but I like to fuck for hours, where my knees get raw, my pubic bone believes that the dong is now embedded, calcified in, and muscles ache with the burn and twitch in exhaustion, and my clit is so hard that I know it would hurt to touch or that I'd pop off with the wafting of a mere breeze.

It's not about the dick, it's about the fuck. I like the fuck and I often come while doing it, in waves of spasms as she sits aloft, humping and pumping until she squirts her juices down my rubbery rod, over my flat, thin stomach, trickling past my hips and through my groin. The wetness like a salve soothes and softens the fierceness of my fuck, and it threatens to take me into a dizzying euphoria of a post-fuck snooze. But I don't want to go there, and wish she wouldn't let me. Some do. But not a chick, a chick likes to get fucked.

The Way She Does Me
Miriam R. Sachs Martín

she fucks me. she fucks me like a fist punching through
walls, like fury come down from up on high, like tenderness
turned to morning sunrise magenta-orange-gold fire inside
my cunt. she comes over late at night and though i know she
has to work early, though i know she needs her sleep, i wriggle
and slide up against her, hoping to get finished what was
started the day before when it was i who was exhausted and
late for work. she responds. she almost always responds,
these days. we've been together a while, and i'm getting her
well trained.

she fucks me like a farmer raping the land and reaping every
last grain that he sowed. she puts her hand inside me like a
blind person reading braille, hungry for knowledge, voracious.
she fucks me, her strong little arm like a piston in my cunt,
until she's trembling in exhaustion and fear from this much
love, and i'm trembling from the same fear, and from pain.
she rarely stops when i cry out in pain.

she fucks me until we're both high; giddy with our heady new drug, crazed from smelling so much pussy, and blood, and sweat; until i come and come, and orgasm again; the sheets are soaked with slippery stinky stains; my pussy breaks down and rips along the tight opening her knuckles are wedged into. she fucks me; she breaks my cunt in half, and then i sit on her face to get some more because I always need so much more from her. she says, "to give you all you need, I'd have to kill you."

she fucks me so that i cry hot salt tears, shimmy my ass shamelessly back and forth, bite green and black bruised arches into her arm for the pain she gives me. and for pleasure. she fucks me until i sigh helplessly into her neck, claw frantically down her back and buttocks, until i murmur her name over and over and say "beloved." she fucks me because i am the only one who can take every damn thing she has to give— and still love it all.

I am split open wide; a pomegranate sliced in two and dripping, and although i have given so much already, i say "what do you need?" and she says, "your heart on a little silver platter." she can't have that but she can have it fierce and ringed with thorns and ticking away merrily inside my ribs. and every time she eats me alive through her hand in my cunt she gets to touch it; velvety soft burgundy colored dangerous treasure. i tell her so. i say: "I can't give it to you, because you could take off with it, but you can touch it while you stay close." she stays so close to me.

and five years ago, i never would have thought that lesbian love could be like this; me impaled on her hand at four in the morning, crying in agony, coming for the seventeenth time, stretched full with all the pain and love; submission and violence; all the sensuality and pleasure in g-d's creation. i never thought another woman could take me like a man; piggish self-indulgence, intent on her own satisfaction. i didn't leave men because they know how to take, but now i know i came to women because they take *better.*

she fucks me with a vehemence, with a violence, with a total pleasure that i knew i could give, but i never knew anyone else could too. until i met her.

Penny, Laid
Kristina Wright

It was her ass they noticed. People stared; they even stopped
and turned for one more glimpse of the finest ass to walk the
Chicago streets. Whether she wore a miniskirt or sweats,
heads turned, pulses quickened, cocks hardened and cunts
moistened at the sight of her saucy, larger-than-life ass.

The rest of her wasn't so bad either. Long, wavy red hair
framed a heart-shaped face and cascaded down her back,
tapering to a V that pointed to the object of their desire. Full
breasts balanced full hips; shapely legs and delicate hands and
feet suggested she was sculpted by a master. She wasn't a traditional beauty: her hair was too dark, her skin was too pale,
her mouth a little too generous, but it didn't matter. The rest
of the package was just so much pretty wrapping. It was her
ass people noticed and she showed it off to best advantage.

Penny navigated Wacker on new, impossibly high fuck-me
pumps. She ducked into Rooster's Sports Bar and the din
nearly knocked her over. Three of her regulars were already at
one of the tables and she flashed them a killer smile. The joke
was on them; Penny didn't dig guys. But four nights a week

she served up wings and beer and a generous portion of fine
ass to those who appreciated it most.

"Penny for your thoughts, babe," Eric said. He was the
owner and bartender at Rooster's and as ass-hungry as they
came.

She made sure her butt came in direct contact with his
crotch as she sidled past him. "Penny's worth a lot more than
a penny."

His hard cock told her she could name her price. Eric knew
she was into girls, but he never stopped trying. It wouldn't
have mattered even if he was her type—Penny wouldn't sleep
with the boss.

She put a smile on her face and a wiggle in her walk as the
place really began to hop. She was the best waitress Rooster's
had ever had and generous tips had just about paid her way
through law school. One more semester and she'd graduate.
Not that any of these guys cared about her mind. Like the
good girl her mama had raised her to be, she gave them what
they wanted, and a side of fries, too.

Hours later, blisters forming on her toes, she was leaning
over the bar, tallying her tips. A voice purred near her ear:
"Nice...shoes."

She looked up into the sexiest cat-green eyes she'd ever
seen. She was tall, nearly eye level with Penny, but without the
benefit of four-inch heels. There was something a little intimidating about the way the woman leaned against the bar and
studied her.

Penny realized she'd seen her before. She'd been coming in
for a few weeks, always alone and never staying longer than it
took to drink a beer, maybe two. In her severe black pantsuit
and high-necked gray blouse, she looked like the female version of the workaholics that stopped by the bar before
heading home to the little woman. But this was no man. There
were generous curves beneath the hard lines of cat-girl's suit.

Her dusky skin and short dark hair were exotic, but it was the look in her heavy-lidded eyes that got to Penny. She had more on her mind tonight than work.

Penny blushed as if the woman could read her mind. They both knew she wasn't complimenting her shoes.

Penny looked back into those green eyes. "Thanks," she said, losing her carefully groomed composure.

"I'm Carla," the woman said, extending a hand with blunt, manicured red nails.

Penny shivered at the thought of what that hand could do to her. "Penny," she said, hearing the quiver of excitement in her voice.

"I know you're getting off," Carla said, pausing for effect as if she knew Penny was already creaming her panties. "I was wondering if you'd let me buy you a drink."

Some of Penny's confidence returned at that familiar refrain. "I work at a bar," she said, with just the right hint of sarcasm. "My drinks are free."

Carla arched an eyebrow as if accepting Penny's unspoken challenge. "Fine. Then maybe you'd like to come back to my place for a fuck."

This woman had her in a tailspin. She could use the same come-on Penny'd heard a thousand times from the male of the species, and it made her want to melt. Penny counted out twenty singles from her tips and exchanged them for a twenty-dollar bill from the register, conscious of Carla's gaze on her.

"It's late and I have to get up early," she said, though her wet pussy seemed to have a different opinion.

"Come home with me," Carla smirked. "I'll make it worth your while."

She should have said no. She had a midterm exam to study for. But she surprised herself by saying, "All right. Give me ten minutes."

Fifteen minutes later, she was snuggled into the passenger seat of Carla's sleek BMW, cruising the quiet streets of Chicago. They didn't speak, and Penny wondered what she'd gotten herself into. She fidgeted in the leather seat, trying to get comfortable, painfully aware of the wet spot between her legs. Carla's hand on her thigh stilled her.

"Relax, baby," Carla's soft voice soothed. "We're going to have fun."

City lights had disappeared by the time they pulled up in front of a townhouse in the 'burbs. Penny had suspected Carla was an overworked businesswoman, but this house was something else. The sudden suspicion that there might be a horny husband lurking behind the curtains made her stomach flip-flop.

"Come on, baby," Carla said, leading her up the steps to the front door.

The dim interior hinted at the well-heeled lifestyle Penny aspired to. Carla mounted the curving staircase without a word and Penny followed. The banister was cool under her damp palm. "Nice house," she murmured.

Carla didn't answer.

The master bedroom was straight out of a decorating magazine, lavishly furnished with antiques and dominated by an enormous mahogany sleigh bed. Layers of bed linens in pink, white, and sage invited rest, not sex. But Carla's grin suggested it would be a long time before Penny got to sleep.

Carla stripped off her jacket and no-nonsense business shoes. Her eyes never wavered from Penny's as she undid the buttons on her blouse. For her slender frame, her breasts were surprisingly large beneath the silk.

Penny swallowed, hard. Unsure whether she should take off her clothes, she stood there timidly, out of her element. This woman made her nervous. Nervous and hot as hell. She couldn't think, she could barely breathe. She just wanted. "Come here, baby," Carla said. "Let me get a look at you."

Penny took a few hesitant steps until they stood inches apart, breasts nearly touching. "I'm not sure—"

Carla laid her fingers across Penny's lips. "Shhh, little girl. It'll be okay." She stroked Penny's face. "So bright and beautiful. You have so much to offer."

Before Penny could question that comment, Carla was pulling her Rooster's T-shirt over her head. For a moment, her face hidden in her shirt, Penny forgot how nervous she was. Then the shirt was off and she was staring into Carla's green eyes. Cat eyes she wanted to fall into.... Then Carla leaned close and kissed her, her mouth wet, soft, sensual.

They came closer, breasts pressing together, and she could feel Carla's hard nipples through her blouse, grazing her own. She cradled Carla's face, kissing her over and over, while Carla's fingers found their way under her skirt and into her panties. She moaned against Carla's mouth, swirling her tongue inside the way Carla now swirled her finger around Penny's clit. Penny wondered what the other woman's cunt tasted like.

Carla pulled back, eyes sparkling, lipstick smeared. "You're so wet, baby girl," she said, showing Penny the evidence on her hand before popping her fingers in her mouth. "Mmm...I want to fuck you. Take your clothes off."

Penny trembled as she stripped. Bra, skirt, wet panties: they came off quickly, awkwardly. All but the shoes. She kept her sexy, slutty pumps on because she didn't want Carla to tower over her. She wanted to please this woman but she didn't want to feel smaller than her.

Carla cupped Penny's tits, raising them to her lips. She suckled the nipples hard, sending shockwaves straight to Penny's clit. Penny whimpered softly, pressing her tits into Carla's hands, wanting more. She tugged Carla's nipples through her blouse, enjoying the nubby feeling of them between her fingers.

Carla pulled her mouth from Penny's nipple, leaving it wet and standing tall. She put her hands on Penny's shoulders, pushing her down to her knees.

"Don't be shy, baby. Touch me."

Penny ran her hands up the heavy fabric of Carla's trousers to the waistband. She slipped the button and pulled the zipper down. Something brushed against her hand. Something large and hard. Carla wasn't wearing underwear and when her pants slipped down, Penny saw what she'd touched.

An enormous cock jutted from Carla's crotch. The kind sold in the back of adult magazines, the kind Penny had never felt inside her but had always wondered about. Bigger than any she'd seen in porn flicks, the cock strapped to this gorgeous, sexy woman looked like a six-shooter nestled in pubic hair as brown and silky as the hair on Carla's head.

Carla adjusted the dildo until it was pointing at Penny. The look of pleasure on her face made Penny realize that the broad, blunt end was pushing against Carla's cunt and clit.

"Go ahead, baby, suck it. Make it wet."

Penny grasped the thick cock and guided the tip to her mouth, never breaking eye contact with Carla. The tip popped between her lips and Carla groaned as if she could feel the sensation. Penny stretched her mouth around the giant dildo as Carla stripped off her blouse and bra. Her brown acorn-sized nipples made Penny's mouth water. At the same time, she wondered who this naked goddess was, standing before her wearing only a fake cock hung on a heavy black belt that crisscrossed her hips and thighs.

"Good Penny. Suck my big dick so I can fuck you with it."

It was Penny's turn to groan. The thought of this monster inside her had her trembling. She sucked the dildo as if it were the main course instead of the appetizer.

Carla pulled the dildo from her mouth and smacked it

against her cheeks. "God, you're hot. Over the bed now. Let me get a look at the rest of you."

Penny let Carla guide her to the bed. On hands and knees, she arched her back and thrust her bottom up, feeling cool air blow across her cunt and asshole.

"Baby, what a beautiful ass." Carla's hands caressed and molded the tight cheeks while Penny moaned against the sheets. "Nice little hole, too. I bet it gets fucked all the time, doesn't it?"

Penny shook her head. "No, never," she gasped as Carla's fingertips slid down her crack.

"I bet it does," Carla teased. "Who could resist this ass?"

Penny shook her head. "I've never—" Carla's hand cracked across her thigh and Penny jumped.

"We'll find out in good time what you have and haven't done," Carla said quietly.

Carla used fingers and tongue on Penny's wet slit, teasing and tormenting until Penny thought she'd scream. She wriggled under Carla's ministrations, imagining that huge cock inside her. Wanting it, needing it.

"Please, fuck me," she panted, rotating her hips as Carla tongue-fucked her cunt. "Fuck me with your big cock."

Carla chuckled. "Little girl wants her ass fucked, huh?"

"No. My cunt. Fuck my cunt."

Carla smacked her ass hard. "It's my dick. "I'll fuck you the way I want." Another smack. "Won't I?"

Penny nodded, hair swinging. Carla pulled away and she groaned. Waiting, breathless, Penny looked over her shoulder. Carla stood there, stroking the big cock between her legs. Penny whimpered, pushing her ass higher in the air.

Carla nestled the cock between Penny's asscheeks. "Everybody wants to fuck this ass, don't they?" she asked, giving Penny's bottom a sharp slap.

"Yes," Penny gasped.

"And you never let them, do you?"

Penny shook her head, unable to form words.

"But you want it fucked now, don't you?"

Penny groaned. "Yes! Fuck me!"

"Easy, baby," Carla said, climbing on the bed behind her. "I'm going to give you what you want. Soon."

Penny felt the dildo nudge her cunt. She reached down between her legs to grab it, but Carla pulled away and slapped it across her butt. Penny cried out in frustration and clutched the sheets.

Carla gently pushed the cock between the swollen lips of Penny's cunt. Penny pushed her hips back, wanting to feel it buried inside her. It slid farther in, bottoming out before she'd taken much more than half. She looked down between her legs and saw it sticking out of her, saw Carla's shapely legs and hips beyond it.

"Cock, Carla, cock," she chanted, fucking back against the hugeness inside her.

Carla thrust into her. "Baby wants more dick. Baby needs this dick in her cunt, up her ass."

Their rhythm was hard and fast, animal fucking, not gentle lovemaking. Penny wiggled on the cock inside her and Carla slapped the round globes of her ass, then thrust a finger past the tight ring of Penny's anus. Double-fucking her now, brutally, until Penny was screaming, "Cockcarlacockcarlacockcarla" over and over as orgasm after orgasm wracked her body.

In one swift motion, Carla pulled the cock out of Penny's wet, clenching cunt and thrust it into her ass. A sharp sting of pain was followed by sweet pleasure. Penny felt herself stretched, penetrated deeper than she'd ever thought she could handle. The orgasms didn't stop; they just went on as Carla pumped her ass methodically.

Penny reached to rub her clit, to keep the edge as Carla drove into her. Carla moaned, jackhammering into her ass so fast, Penny knew she must be coming too. Their damp flesh slapped together as Carla slammed into her, a fistful of Penny's long hair pulled up tight in her hand as she screamed out her orgasm. Penny collapsed under the onslaught, her knees sliding out from under her, Carla's full weight across her back and the dildo buried inside her. Her clit rubbed against the sheet and she cried out.

As suddenly as it had begun, the rough sex was over and Carla was cradling her, Penny's back pressed against her breasts and thighs. They were both panting, dripping with sweat. Carla stroked her, soothing her, the dildo still deep in her ass, moving slowly now, gently. For the first time in a long time, Penny closed her eyes and let herself be held by a lover.

"Sweet girl," Carla whispered, nipping her earlobe. "Sweet ass."

Penny woke the next morning to the smell of sex and the sounds of birds outside the window. Carla and the dildo were gone, but a delicious soreness remained. She reached for the note on the table beside the bed.

Sweet Penny, I knew your grades were impressive, but now you've dazzled me with your other charms. Give me a call later and we'll schedule a formal interview— and maybe dinner?
  Carla.

Penny wrinkled her brow. She had no idea what the note meant until she read the letterhead. The woman who'd fucked her silly the night before was none other than Carla Manning of Dunnet, Manning and Wight, Attorneys at Law. The law office she'd sent her transcript to a month ago. The same law office she would give her shoe collection to join after graduation. People complained about getting screwed by lawyers, but Penny had not only been screwed by one of the top attorneys in the state and enjoyed it, she'd been asked back for more.

Feeling like she'd been pulled apart and put back together again, she showered in Carla's enormous bathroom. Dressed, except for the panties that were now tucked in her purse, she took a tour of the townhouse and grabbed an apple from the kitchen on the way out. She strutted down the tree-lined street to the bus stop in her fuck-me pumps, a pleasant tenderness in her ass and cunt, contemplating the idea of fucking someone she worked for. Maybe it was time to amend her rule.

Tattoo
Fiona Zedde

My skin was itching for another tattoo. Three years ago, the thorny black rose blooming just above my shaved pubes was all I wanted. Now, I wanted more. I picked the place, a little shop in the neighborhood where I worked as a waitress, and made my way there late one Saturday afternoon.

Stung, the city's only twenty-four-hour tattoo joint, was packed. A shifting crowd of people was jockeying for space along the tattoo-covered wall. Others sat on the worn leather benches, nervously fiddling with their money or staring into space. A couple of leatherboys compared old tattoos, baring muscled backs and biceps to anyone who cared to look. I walked up to the woman at the front counter.

"How long is the wait?"

Her pierced eyebrow rose when she saw me. I knew what I must have looked like to her—a petite brown-skinned girl with wide, long-lashed eyes and rounded cheeks who seemed like she'd never seen the inside of a tattoo parlor, much less wanted a tattoo.

"At least three hours, maybe four," she finally said. "Why don't you come back later, around midnight when things are less crazy?" The girl glanced at the mob of people behind me. "Most of the crowd from the biker convention should be gone by then."

At 11:52 P.M. I was back at the nearly deserted studio, my design in one hand, the cash in the other, and a smile on my face. The woman I'd seen earlier was just getting ready to leave. She smiled at me as she grabbed her stuff. "Hey, I'm glad you came back," she said. "Our newbie is working the graveyard shift. She's real good, though." It really didn't matter who worked on me, as long as I got what I came for.

I handed over the money and my design, filled out the paperwork, then made myself comfortable on a reclining chair in a sterile back room. Except for a stool and a low leather-covered table that smelled like it had just been wiped down with antiseptic, the room was bare. With nothing else to do, I closed my eyes and waited.

"Is this what you want?" My eyes opened at the sound of the familiar voice.

Ria stood there looking yummy and fuckable in her baggy button-fly jeans and a tank top that shaped her full breasts like clay, offering them up to my eyes for inspection. After two years, she still had the same innocent baby face and cropped black curls. She didn't seem surprised to see me. Until now I had no idea that she was back in town.

She was my ex. The one who left me almost two years ago with my first and only broken heart. I gave her a small smile of recognition, then looked down at what she wanted to show me. In her hand was a thin piece of paper with the design I had copied and carried around with me for about a year. It was perfect. "Yes."

"Where do you want it?"

I stood up and showed her the place on the small of my back.

"All right. Take off your shirt and lie face down on the table. Straddle it." I did what I was told. My bare nipples hardened when they touched the cold leather. Ria arranged my hips at the very edge of the table, then touched my spread thighs once as if she couldn't help herself. She rolled the stool closer to the table and sat down.

My mind blanked as she tended to me, bathing my lower back with something that cooled my skin.

"Relax." Her breath shivered against that cool place.

I remembered that tone from years ago, how it had lulled me into trusting and yielding to her. It worked its magic on me now, softening my body, preparing me. *Did she treat all her clients this way?* Not that it mattered. We weren't together anymore.

With the touch of her gloved hand on my back I remembered what had drawn me to this girl. Her pierced labret made me wet the first time I saw her. All I could think about then was sitting on her face.

The first touch of the needle sent a shock wave of pain through my body. It made me remember how often she'd made me come just by touching me, once, then whispering a firm command in my ear.

The steady buzz increased the pain until I bathed in it. My teeth clenched.

"Relax. This is supposed to be fun, right?" I could imagine the ironic curve of her mouth—that sweet red thing—as she said that.

I'd worn pants that unzipped in the back, just in case taking my shirt off wouldn't be enough. I felt her hands on that zipper now, easing it down to bare the slope of my ass. Again, there was a coolness, then the heat of her hand on me. Just like I remembered, she was a furnace, all fire and stillness, inviting me to move under or over her. This time I stayed still, breathing slowly through my mouth.

The needle moved again over my flesh, startling pinpricks of sensation that pushed tears from my eyes. Pleasure came slowly, like a fever. It started under the needle, then spread to the point of contact between her skin and mine. Again, I wanted to move and ease the tension between my thighs, but I didn't. I couldn't.

The door was closed and we were alone. I could hear her breath, the needle, my breath, and the squeak of leather as I tried to relieve the ache in my nipples.

When she left me two years ago, I had been out of my mind with pain. I would have done anything to keep her. Except put up with her bullshit. She didn't want me; what she wanted was a toy to play with, then toss aside whenever her mood changed. And Ria almost had me like that. She was all I had ever wanted in a woman—clever, ambidextrous hands paired with a wicked imagination. We would have fuck sessions that kept me from concentrating on my work the next day, that left me raw and still wanting more.

The needle swept across my skin, drawing up pain and blood. I felt her hand wipe it away, gently. This was nothing new. Often, after long hours of feeding on each other, with blood near or on the surface of our skin, she would tend to me first, wiping me clean with a warm rag, then kissing my cheeks and forehead. At those times, she made me feel like the luckiest dyke in the world.

The vibrations from the needle held my whole body captive, drumming into my bones, the skin over my back and hips. We had long ago passed the stage of foreplay. My body was being tuned by her skillful hand, vibrating on the edge of fulfillment and release. And just when I thought I would fall over, she took the needle away and wiped my skin.

My body was drenched in sweat. My neck, the flesh between and under my breasts, my back. All wet.

"I don't think you're relaxed enough."

My breath was heavy. "I'll feel better after you finish."

Ria got up from the stool and came up closer behind me, her jeans brushing against my thighs. All the while the needle continued its dance over my flesh.

She hadn't been there when I got my first tattoo. But I had told her how it was, how my skin felt like it wanted to jump off my body and hide. Even my brother's hand clenched between mine hadn't been enough to stem the urge to take it all back.

As her body pressed against me, I could feel that she was packing. A quick breath hissed through my teeth.

The needle stopped and I felt her smooth something on the rawness at my lower back. Ria's hands settled on my hips, her fingers poised like question marks between my pants and my skin.

"Yes?" she asked from behind me.

"Uh-huh." I gasped my agreement through the droplets of sweat that clung to my mouth. Suddenly parched, I licked the saltiness away.

My hips rose up to allow Ria whatever she wanted. She took off my pants, then gently pushed me forward against the table. Tears of relief fell to the leather under my face. Her fingers found me first: wet, wanting. A low noise of protest scraped against my throat. I wanted Ria to fuck me, but not with her damn fingers.

"Open this." She pressed a plastic-wrapped condom against my mouth. I ripped the package open with my teeth, gasping as she teased my clit and rubbed her fingers through drenched pussy hairs to my clenched belly, then back down again. Behind me, I heard the buttons of her jeans pop open.

The first stroke made me gasp. This was a bigger dick than the one she packed when we were together. It filled me, sliding deep inside where I could feel it, squeeze it.

I remembered how Ria liked to lie on top of me, curling into my back like a child while her hips pistoned against my ass. She arched over me now, careful not to rub my new tattoo raw. I could smell her pussy. Fabric rustled behind me and I felt the hard points of her nipples against my back, the crush of her breasts. Ria pushed slowly into me, pulling a low moan from my throat and driving my fingers into the leather of the table. Her jeans were rough against the backs of my thighs. She pressed us together, keeping still. Her fingers brushed my nipples, feather light, leaving electric tingles in their wake.

"Do you really want this?"

I swallowed. "It's a little late to ask that question, don't you think?"

Above me, Ria laughed. She began to move with long, luxurious strokes, pushing deep inside me, then inching out, like she was pulling apart melting toffee. My back arched for her. I could feel the sweat gathering along my spine, trailing down the sharp valley of flesh that led to my tattoo. My breath released in a shuddering sigh. "Now. Please."

The table groaned under us as she rode me, building up her strength and speed with each stroke. I gasped and panted and pushed back into her, wanting more. Ria cradled my hips in hers, hands curved around my waist as she thrust into me.

"I missed you," she said, not meaning a word of it.

"Just shut up and fuck me."

Beyond thought, I spread myself wider to take more of her. I lost myself in the soft liquid suck of my pussy around Ria's dick, her low moans and the slide of my sweat-soaked skin under hers. Ria's hands covered my breasts, squeezing the nipples to the rhythm of her strokes. Beads of sweat, hers and mine, splashed against the table. The sensitivity of my back, the friction and pressure of her dick, the hands on my breasts were all pushing me toward the coming I craved. Wetness trailed down my trembling thighs.

"Do it now," I demanded.

Ria's breathless laughter poured over me as she lifted my hips to fit us even closer together. Her thighs slapped against mine. Faster. Pinpricks of heat flew from our contact point all over me, into me; my body was a ball of light, throbbing, waiting for the right signal to explode. Her gloved finger circled my clit, then finally, firmly, stroked the throbbing bundle of nerves. That was the signal my body was waiting for.

Her name ripped itself from my throat in a low, ragged moan. I pushed my face into the sweat-dampened leather, shuddering under her. The table shook as I collapsed against it. Behind me, I heard the sound of a condom being stripped off and tossed away.

"You're done," she said.

I licked my dry lips and took a deep shuddering breath. "I hope so."

"I meant your tattoo."

"Me too."

She gave me instructions on how to take care of my tattoo, looking away as I pulled my clothes back on.

"Thanks."

In the mirror, my tattoo was like a dream. A silhouette of the Goddess of Desire, a writhing, snake-haired woman with her long legs spread and arms open wide to embrace the universe. My own legs trembled as aftershocks of pleasure rippled through my body.

"Sure." She looked at me with a slight smile. "This tatt's on the house. Tell Shelly to give you the money back and I'll settle up with her later." This was as close to a real apology that I was going to get from her.

I nodded and kissed her soft, pouting mouth. "See you around." After one last lingering glance at her, I walked out, smiling and satisfied. Just like in old times, Ria had given me exactly what I wanted.

Look but Don't Touch
Sparky

You look down and see the bottle of whiskey lying in casual spills of cum.

You envy the boys for those quick joyous fountains.

It will take you much longer.

The walls are shiny from others before you: a glaze of sperm, sweat, other shoulders in leather jackets, and the strangely mouthwatering smell of cleaning solution.

Your shoulders are narrow. You fit neatly into this dark box.

There is no great mystery, you think, sliding a dollar into the glowing slot. Surrounded by darkness, you think of your mom, comforting you in the locker room: "We're all girls here."

But you smell like cool water for men and pomade, and you wear your most dapper boy clothes, black leather jacket and boots. Your hair is freshly cropped and no one can tell the tinge of lip liner. Your hair is carefully in its borrowed tranny boy flip. You are prepared for a mystery date. Who is behind the glass? That is the mystery.

A bar of light widens. The black window rises.

Five women in red-gold light are surrounded by mirrors. Dancing naked with their own lush bodies, with the mirrors reflecting silver and red flashes, girls upon girls, like the room is packed. One comes over to see you, dances before you. She has small, rounded breasts, rounded hips, catlike black-rimmed eyes and a ready, naughty smile, stands on tall vinyl stiletto boots. A black bob, a mini-version of Uma Thurman in *Pulp Fiction*.

Your face becomes hot. Your ears burn. Your expression is awe and wonderment. She grins down at you, pleased. Seductive. She shows you her breasts; their skin looks impossibly smooth and clean, with golden-rimmed, small nipples. You see the hollow of her throat, her collarbone, her little belly.

She is the loveliest being on the planet.

She is naked before you and you can do nothing but look and look.

You keep looking at her hips, peek at her pussy, and give long lustful looks to her boots.

"I bet that smile gets them every time," she purrs.

You realize you are grinning like a fool. You shake your head no but cannot stop the grin that is shy, nervous, awed.

She calls the others over. "Look how cute! Look at those dimples!"

Now you could not stop smiling if you tried.

Four of them peep in the window at you, pressing against it. They pretend to poke your dimples. "So cute!" Real smiles from them. You want to duck and you are blushing so hard but there's nowhere to go, the window's open, and your money is in there ticking away relentlessly.

They move to other open windows and you are left with little Uma Thurman. "I like your boots," you say.

You hear the click as she rests one high heel on the window ledge and bends over so you look up the spike heel and vinyl boot to her incredible round ass. She peeks at you from above her delicate pussy lips and asshole, smiling because, you think to yourself, now she knows. She knows how to get you. You feel tormented with need to be licking those boots.

She turns to face herself in the mirror and lowers herself below your window. She writhes back and forth. You realize with delight that she is fucking your imaginary cock. She's smiling sweet and wicked, as if she knows exactly how hard this gets your clit.

The black square of window lowers. She bends down to grin underneath, waving. You see the shiny toe of her boot, and are left in darkness.

You feel wired and keyed up, you've been here a long time and are likely to stay longer, not willing to jerk off like the others. You told yourself to come here for the experience but you will get yourself turned on until you want to climb the booths, kiss and claw at the glass, so near to those girls. Wanting to please them all.

The next booth smells salty and familiar. You realize it's freshly-pumped semen that glitters on the floor. You feel a sense of solidarity. You put twenty into the slot. You are in for the full ride.

The window rises. You lock eyes with a new dancer, across the carpeted, mirrored stage. This one has a cute black bob with little ponytails and bangs. She has little Cupid's-bow pouty lips and huge dark eyes with long lashes. She wears white thigh-high fishnets with bits of lace at the top and high-heeled sandals.

But most of all she has a body that is so lush and curvy, it looks familiar. It could be your own. She has a rounded tummy and her hips and thighs are buttery and luscious. With her black hair and sexy tummy, she reminds you of your first girlfriend. She is innocent and powerfully sexual. It is like the glass is gone.

She looks unimaginably soft and delicious. You want to roll around on top of her and feel her up, lick up and down her luxurious hips and belly.

She comes up and licks her lips, pouting and sexy, thrusting her heavy breasts, writhing her hips against the window. Her lips are trembling. You realize it's an effort for her to keep from cracking up. Soon she cannot stop smiling. Her eyes are half-lidded. She is everything lush and full, and you want to take her around the waist and wrap her legs around you. But she's behind the glass.

You ponder what to say. Poetry? Blank verse? "You are so cute," you say at last.

She smiles for real, her eyes lingering on you. "So are you!"

Her name is Persephone and that is not, she informs you, her real hair. She leans over to pull the wig a little. Her hair is blonde and cropped short, recently shaved.

The window closes and opens again, slowly revealing her white fishnets and finally the lace trim and her ass. She's talking to the other dancers. It's late now, and the catlike Uma Thurman dancer from earlier is stretched out against one wall, naked except for her boots, a lazy smile on her face. You are one of two people still watching. The dancers lounge around naked and hot under the lights, beautiful and untouched. It looks humid. You want to fan them with palm leaves. Suck on ice cubes and breathe mist into their lips. Wear your own outfit of gold sandals, and be their altar boy or temple acolyte....

Persephone does a silly dance, climbs up the pole and twists her way back down, does handstands for you. She comes back to your window and her eyes focus on you, serious, thinking. She undulates and smiles, showing you her ass, her tits, her shoes, her pussy, right at eye level. You cannot look away, you are enchanted. She is pink and luscious, sparkling, red-gold from the lights. She licks and bites her own nipple and you finally feel your clit so warm and hard the feeling has spread throughout your lower body, the urgency of this is unfuckingbearable.

You feel overwhelmed. You do not know what to do. How do guys deal with this? You look at the pools of semen with new understanding, but you're not about to do that here. Instead you feel wild, panicked, worshipful, at a standstill, spending more and more to keep seeing the girls deliciously naked and close enough to touch but you can't, and your breath is steaming up this little stinky booth.

The window lowers. The darkness is comforting after such staring at the light.

You walk outside into the San Francisco night. You turn and the lights of the Golden Gate Bridge stretch across the bay. They are shimmering in the fog. You think of the shimmering girls in their mirrored fishbowl dancing late into the night. The bridge and the girls: glittering, remote, and comforting all at once.

Never Say Never

Rachel Kramer Bussel

I can only come when my legs are spread apart as wide as possible. It doesn't matter what else is going on at the time; if my legs are spread, I come so hard I feel like a rocket about to be zoomed into space, wild and breathing fire and out of control. I like the way my legs stretch and pull apart and cause all sorts of divine sensations in my cunt. Even the tiniest movements make my insides quiver and quake; sometimes I feel on the verge of tears, the sensations are that intense. Nothing else can compare. All of my partners have been more than happy to oblige. It's really the only thing that works with me. At least, that's what I thought.

Until Jesse.

One night, I was at a play party, a pretty quiet and slow one, which was fine with me. I decided to attend because it was the only game in town and I didn't really want to be home all alone, but I wasn't in the most sociable mood. I was sitting alone, eating chips and gazing off into space, physically present—but mentally off in my own dream world.

"What are you into?"

Someone had just invaded my quiet little area, barging right up to me in such an aggressive way I had to look around to make sure we were at the same staid party that happens every month. We were, even though I almost never see women act so boldly there. They usually eye each other all night and make suggestive comments and then at the very last minute quickly ask if the other one wants to play, knowing that there's only time for the shortest of scenes.

I was impressed with her audacity. I knew her name, Jesse, because everyone knew her name. I'd never spoken to her and she'd never so much as glanced at me before that I could tell, but I guess she'd noticed me lurking around. Maybe she was more observant than I'd given her credit for. She didn't ask me first whether I was into her or wanted to play. I guess that was implied by the way I slouched against the wall, without trying to slink away or avert my eyes. Or maybe she was just one of those women filled with so much self-confidence that the idea of someone not wanting to play with her is completely foreign. In my case, her hunch was correct, but I didn't want to make myself seem that easy. I stood there staring coolly back at her. The body language of consent was all she was going to get.

"I said, what are you into?" she repeated, this time with an edge to her voice. I hadn't answered yet because I don't have a set answer, a one-size-fits-all play requirement; for me it really depends on the person, the setting, the context. It's an odd question to me too; how will I know what will work with her until I try it? So I gave her a broad but definite response.

"I don't know if this is what you're looking for, but I really like to come with my legs spread as far apart as they can be. That always works for me."

I didn't tell her it was the only thing that worked for me, didn't think I had to. She just looked at me; I couldn't read her gaze. She seemed slightly unpleased, but she just took my hand and led me into a room. She closed the door; I didn't look to see if she locked it, only half caring. I like my privacy too, even at a public play party.

"So I'm not quite sure I understand what you mean. Why don't you show me this fabulous way you like to come with your legs spread?"

I was sweating and my heart was pounding. She was acting friendly but I still felt intimidated, waiting for the other shoe to drop and her secretly nefarious intentions to be revealed. I was used to tops telling me what to do, not asking for things from me. Maybe in this case she was doing both. I liked her and was turned-on but wasn't sure if I could follow her instructions. It's one thing to come alone, twisting and turning into all sorts of bizarre contortions to reach that pinnacle of pleasure, but doing it in front of another person, especially one who's demanding it, was going to be a bit daunting.

I quietly asked if she had a vibrator. She handed me a small but powerful black plug-in one. I gripped it tightly, noting the controls, then closed my eyes, afraid seeing her would affect me too much. I lay down on my back, spreading my legs widely. Then I turned it to the highest speed possible, the sound drowning out her breathing, and pressed it against myself. I felt my clit light up, straining for more contact, and spread my legs wider. I love how flexible I get when I'm aroused. I had my legs as wide apart as I could get them, when she came over toward me. She leaned over me, put her hands on my feet and pressed hard. Now I was totally split apart, the pain streaking down my thighs, twisting my pussy and making the vibrations that much more intense. I was having trouble breathing, but I didn't mind. She kept pushing, staring down at me like some devious X-rated aerobics instructor. I could imagine her saying "Feel the burn," as she kept bearing down on me, my cunt utterly exposed to her powerful eyes. I started to rock back and forth slightly, really getting into it, knowing that she was safely holding me, when the power stopped. She'd unplugged it somehow; I was so lost in my thighs and clit that I didn't notice until it all came to a grinding halt. I stared up at her beseechingly. She couldn't be making me stop now, she just couldn't.

"That's enough of that for now, I just wanted to see what you like. Very good. Now we're going to try something new," she said briskly, like she was my boss giving me a challenging new assignment.

I wanted to protest, but there was no time. She pulled me up and had me stand with my hands over my head. My heart was still beating fast, and I had no idea what was about to happen. She shackled my wrists above my head, and while they didn't feel uncomfortable, I found myself starting to squirm. She pushed me toward the wall, facing it, and didn't have to tell me to stay there. I was turned-on but there was very little I could do about it besides pressing my cunt against the wall.

Then I felt her start to bind my ankles. I opened my mouth, but just held it open for a minute. What could I say? She obviously knew what she was doing and had a plan for me. It felt kind of good actually, the soft rope pressing into my taut ankles, yet I couldn't help wanting to spread my legs, even a little. All I could do at that point was rise up and down on my toes and wiggle fruitlessly against the ropes. When I tried that, she looked up at me with a severe expression, daring me to protest. When she'd finished with the last knot, she told me, "I think you'll change your mind, sweetheart, just wait and see." I had little choice on the waiting since I was now at her mercy.

I could feel myself getting wet, a liquid refutation of my wiggling protests. She leaned into my ear. "I'm going to spank you and whip you now, and you're going to like it, I can tell.

I've heard about you, you little slut, acting all quiet and shy but I know what you really want. And it'll be all the better because I'm gonna make you come with those pretty legs pressed together as tight as can be. I know you want to show off, you want everyone to see your nice, wet pussy, and how far you can spread those legs. You're good at that, I already told you. But I'm not gonna let you show off that pussy or move those thighs, not this time."

With that, she surprised me yet again, leaning me over a padded bar that reminded me of the kind I used to leap over during gymnastics class. With my head leaning forward, I could open my eyes, but the view wasn't all that spectacular: the dusty beige floor tiles were about all I could make out. In the silence, I listened for clues, sweating and breathing rapidly. I felt a movement behind me and then her hand coming down hard on my ass. I jolted, pressing myself more tightly against the padded surface. She spanked me again, and continued, keeping a rapid rhythm that was getting me wetter and wetter. At some point I felt something new. I knew that it was no longer her hand but something much stronger making contact with me. The pain was a rush but I knew that it alone wouldn't be enough for me.

The rope cut into my ankles as I pressed them as far apart as they would go, which wasn't very far at all. I could only rock back and forth, stick my ass out further, but my legs wouldn't stretch in the way that I love them to. I felt torn between enjoying the delicious sensations my ass was receiving and wanting to move my legs apart. I wanted her to see and feel just how wet I really was. And then I heard a knock at the door. I sighed, not wanting to stop. She left my side to answer the door, and I heard a whispered conversation that I couldn't make out.

She returned with someone else, a stranger. I didn't get to hear her introduce herself either. Jesse did the speaking for both of them. "M is going to take over now, because I have something else I need to do." She didn't ask me, just stated it simply. Her tone was totally calm, verging on disinterested, and it made me want to show off for her, impress her. Jesse lifted me up, then moved the bench away. I wanted that bench, wanted to have something to lean on, something to help me keep my composure, to prevent me from free-falling, literally and figuratively. But I had to trust that Jesse knew what she was doing; she certainly seemed to as she had me stand up straight, my ankles still bound, my wrists hanging together in front of me.

She placed herself in front of me, her hand covering my pussy. I pressed against her, wanting to feel more contact. I was relaxing into this new sensation when I felt the first smack. It came much harder than Jesse's, pressing me into Jesse's hand and sending its vibrations through my whole body. I opened my eyes and looked up at Jesse, pleadingly. With her hand on my cunt, I wanted to spread my legs and slide her hot fingers into me, but of course that was impossible. Her fingers started working my clit, as the beatings continued. I let out a little scream, wanting to move. "Oh, so you think you're going to come, do you? Is that possible, just from me playing with your nice juicy clit here, and M spanking you? Is it possible for you to come with those legs pressed so tightly together that it looks like you're trying to hold in your pee? I want you to press them even more tightly together, that's right." And with that she took her hand away and moved behind me. "Now, my dear, you are in for a little treat." I heard her open the door and let in our audience. I didn't mind, thinking maybe she'd undo my legs for this. But she had something else in mind.

"Now, my friends, here is Miss 'I-can-only-come-with-my-legs-spread-far-apart.' She prefers them spread all the way out, flung as far as they can go so her pretty little cunt is on display and she's taking up as much room as possible. She told me that's the only way she can come, but she agreed to let me play a little game to see if that's really true. You can place your bets with each other but I'm warning you now—I'm a sure thing." And then she sauntered back to me. "And just to make extra sure those legs stay put, I'm going to tie her up a bit more securely." And with that she slipped another piece of rope around me and tied me yet again, this time at the thighs. The rope pressed into that fleshy area, and I could barely stand it. Now I really couldn't move my legs and it was driving me mad. I wished she could at least tie me up with something between my legs to relieve some of this pressure she'd created.

She bent down to whisper in my ear, and for once her words were kind and soft, a surprise to me. "I'll make you come, sweetheart, don't you worry." And then she resumed her show for the crowd. "Now look at the way her legs are bound tight together, and yet she's still trying to spread them apart. See her pushing against them here, and here." She tapped me on the sides of my legs, Exhibits *A* and *B* of my struggle. "She thinks I can't make her come with her legs pressed so tightly against each other and her pussy all squeezed in there. Well, I've already told you who the odds are on." And then she took over where M had left off, and M took her position in front of me. I had little time to think as sharp, intense strokes fell on my ass, the pain of each settling in for only moments before another blow landed. I looked up at M to see her reaction but she stood there totally stoically, staring at me, like she was only there because Jesse had asked her to be. Her indifference maddened and excited me. Hers was the only face I could see, so I looked back at her. Then Jesse really started teasing me, using whatever had been sharply stinging my ass to do the same on the flesh right beneath it. I let out a long audible breath and scrunched up my face as I felt her move seemingly closer to my cunt with the whip, yet not close enough. I wanted something, anything, between my legs, or I was going to die right then and there. I was squirming and wet and by that point not even sure what I wanted. I struggled against the ropes just to feel any sensation other than the pinpoints of pain on the backs of my thighs.

And then M, still looking quite dispassionate, leaned down and began licking my clit. She started off softly, and I restrained myself from pushing her head harder against me, knowing that Jesse wouldn't stand for such insubordination. As it was, I just grunted. Both of them sped up their paces, the blows falling harder and harder on my ass, my thighs, my back. M used her tongue like a sword, cutting this way and that, no longer gently licking but forcefully beating my clit with her tongue. Then she sucked it into her mouth, as if it were my nipple, her lips and then teeth wrapping around it. The ropes dug deeply into my thighs as I rocked back and forth, left and right, any way I could. M grabbed my hip, digging her nails into my flesh, and I screamed, coming in such a flash of heat and power and liquid that I almost knocked us all over. Jesse and M stepped aside and moved me into a corner, leaving me to recover, gasping as I leaned against the wall.

"Okay, ladies, thank you for coming." With that, Jesse ushered our guests out the door, a few grumbles coming from the poor suckers who'd bet on me as they forked over their cash.

Then Jesse stood staring down at me, a pitying look on her face. "You're a smart girl but you have a big, bratty mouth. You should learn to watch that. If you've taken anything away from tonight, besides a sore ass and that greedy pussy of yours, I hope it's that you should never, ever, say never when it comes to the way you can and can't come. You just might surprise yourself."

As she leaned down to undo the knots that had held my legs together so well, I couldn't help but agree.

The Chick Magnet

Skian McGuire

It was only nine-thirty, and the Bijou was already packed. I was elbowing my way to the bar with ones and quarters when I felt a hand on my neck.

"Whatcha got?" The chain I was wearing jerked me backward. Shiv shouted over the din, "Poppers?"

I yanked it back and swapped Chris for the twenties she was waving at me before one of her customers could beat me to it.

"Jesus Christ, Shiv, what are you doing here?" I turned back around, stuffing the bills deep in a jeans pocket. "If Verlaine sees you, she's gonna throw you out."

Shiv ignored me, hauling at the small metal cylinder until we were nearly knocking skulls. "How do you open it?" She jammed it under her nose.

I pried it away from her. "It's Weegee's," I said, inspecting it in the light from the neon Budweiser sign to see what Shiv's busy little fingers might have done. It looked the same, as far as I could tell. I tucked it back in my shirt.

Shiv's eyebrows had disappeared under her bandanna. She took a step backward. Weegee may be an electronics wizard and self-made millionaire, but her hobby of inventing high-tech sex toys sometimes leads her down byways where no man has gone before, and from which many might run screaming.

"It's all right!" I told her. "It doesn't do anything."

Shiv eyed me suspiciously.

"It's just calibrating." I moved closer, trying to explain. Shiv backed into a statuesque blonde who shot her a look of icy disapproval. "Weegee wanted me to wear it into a crowd of lesbians. It's getting programmed for brain wave frequencies," I said.

"Brain what?" Shiv squinted at me. "What?"

"Brain wave frequencies! Weegee says it's a transceiver for sex vibes." Shiv shook her head and pointed to her ear. I cupped my hands around my mouth. "It's supposed to attract girls," I shouted into the silence as the music ended.

Chris stopped pouring. "What's the matter," she asked, "can't you get a date?"

Shiv snickered. I gave them a dirty look.

Behind Shiv, the blonde looked at me over the rim of her glass, her gaze unblinking. She lowered the drink as if in a trance and swayed. I wondered if I ought to tell Chris to stop serving her.

Cold fingers scrabbled under my collar. "So why doesn't Weegee wear it?" Shiv peered at the pendant. I grabbed it and tucked it back in my shirt.

I shrugged. "She said something about proximity. I didn't get it. Damn." My pager was vibrating. I unclipped it from my belt and tried to read the display.

"She needs it more than you do," Shiv muttered.

The office again. I sighed. What did the boss want this time? "Shiv, you better go back down to the Gorgons' Cave," I warned. The motorcycle club had rented their dingy, disgusting little basement space years before Verlaine bought the buildings for her bar. She knew that kicking them out would be bad PR in the dyke community. Evict the city's only lesbian bike gang? Uh-uh. Never mind that the Gorgons consisted of twelve largely out-of-work, substance abusing ne'er-do-wells, with only eight motorcycles between them. Lisette Verlaine did what she had to. She didn't have to like it.

"Better go back to your ca-ave," Shiv whined in an irritating little voice, mimicking me. "Go back to your ca-ave. Bad Shiv." She slapped herself. "Bad Shiv." She slapped herself again, harder.

"Oh, brother." I turned on my heel. The blonde stared after me. I was glad to lose her in the crowd.

"Well, hello, lover," a voice purred in my ear. I turned to the woman who tucked her arm in mine, drawing me up short in one smooth move. "I haven't seen you in *ages*." She reached up to plant a kiss on me that left me breathless. "Have you met my friend Charlie?" A tall butch with a coal-black buzz cut tilted her shades down and grinned, and I mumbled something inane, hardly taking my eyes off Moira.

She followed my gaze. "Oh, do you like my blouse?"

It was actually more like a silver lamé handkerchief with straps. She whirled a little to show it off, not letting go of my hand, and I glimpsed the curve of each gorgeous breast.

Moira giggled.

I leaned backward to try to regain the power of speech. I had, in fact, seen her just last week, but it certainly seemed that an age had gone by. Her long straight hair, formerly a fiery copper red, was now the color of raven's wings. She was wearing a tiny black leather skirt, and clunky shoes with ridiculously high platform soles gave her legs like a fashion model.

"We're dyed to match," she informed me, "in honor of the Morrigan."

She held Charlie's hand, and it seemed only natural for Charlie to take mine, closing the circle. When the music kicked into a dance tempo, Charlie lifted one eyebrow and shuffled around behind me, her sleek body perfect in a narrow-ribbed A-shirt and baggy camouflage cargo pants that did nothing to hide the muscularity of her thighs. Moira twirled, and I found myself sandwiched in a miniature conga line moving sinuously to the insistent beat. Charlie's strong square hands came to rest on my hipbones. Moira's deliciously round behind fitted itself against my crotch.

My pager went off.

I extricated myself reluctantly. "Duty calls," I told Charlie, who peered pleadingly at me over her shades. Moira placed a hand on either side of my face and drew me down for a lingering, voluptuous, turn-my-knees-to-jelly kiss. I was wondering how long it would take Verlaine to come looking for me, when the pager buzzed again.

From the lobby doorway, I turned to wave and smacked head-on into the tall blonde. She blinked down at me in the yellow glare from the coat-check booth.

"Do you come here often?" Her voice was pitched low and sultry. Her hand landed heavily on my shoulder like the claw in an arcade treasure machine.

I fled up the stairs.

"What took you so long?" Verlaine said when I flung open the office door, out of breath. "I was just about to..." She cocked her head quizzically and took three steps toward me. "Are you wearing a new cologne?"

"Cologne? You know I never..."

She crossed the floor, brushing the glossy mane of chestnut brown hair back from her face.

"Sam." She put her hands on her hips. "Have I told you lately how much I appreciate you?"

My jaw dropped.

"I couldn't run this place without you." She swung the door shut. "You know..." She stopped, her brow furrowed in concentration, and brought her hands up to adjust my collar. "Is that a new shirt?"

Her fingers brushed the chain around my neck.

I stepped backward so fast my shoulder blades slammed into the door behind me with a teeth-loosening thud. I groped for the knob. In one motion, I pulled the pendant over my head and pitched it out into the hall. "Verlaine," I squeaked, "what did you want me for?"

Verlaine blinked. She glanced at her watch. With a look of annoyance, she strode across the small room to her desk. "There's no water in the men's room." She thrust a piece of cardboard at me. "Hang this on the door. See if you can find the problem, will you?" She sat down and swiveled back to her computer. I heaved a sigh of relief. Then I looked at the Out of Order sign in my hand and got annoyed.

"You paged me for this?" I thought of Moira and Charlie. "Why don't you get Billy? He loves fixing things." Verlaine hired me as security, but she's never been above getting any odd jobs out of me that she can. Mostly, I don't mind. Everybody knows how I feel about Verlaine, even though it's been years since we were lovers. But I am not a plumber. I opened my mouth to tell her this.

"I tried." Verlaine scrolled down her spreadsheet. "The Gorgons are having a meeting. He can't come."

I let myself out. She didn't bother looking up.

I cradled Weegee's pendant in the palm of my hand and remembered the electricity of Verlaine's touch, the scent of her hair. Her breath on my skin. A wave of loss so old I'd nearly forgotten it swept over me. I wondered if Weegee could make another one, calibrated for just one set of brain waves.

I let the chain run through my fingers and, with a rueful laugh, stuffed it in my pocket.

Downstairs, I paused in front of the men's room, grumbling. Except when the Bijou is crowded, nobody uses it for anything but making out. I was going to hang the sign and not bother about the water; I remembered the jam-packed bar and thought again.

At the sound of the restroom door wheezing shut, two heads turned, their eyes fogged with lust. One head was close-cropped and coal-black, the other smooth as a raven's wing. They looked right through me and went back to what they were doing. Without a second thought, I pulled out the pendant and slipped it around my neck.

I cleared my throat. "Hey, Moira. Hey, Charlie."

Slowly, two heads turned back toward me.

"Sam," Moira breathed, "where ever have you been?"

Charlie tugged her pants up and staggered toward me, pitching the dark glasses into a sink as she passed. "Hey, hey, yourself," she said as she laid a shaky hand against my chest and started unbuttoning my shirt.

"Mmmm, yes," Moira murmured, pressing her breasts into my back. She reached around to open my fly.

In what seemed like only a moment, my jeans and sneakers lay in a heap beneath the urinals. I sagged against Moira, whose fingers expertly teased my nipples. My sports bra was rucked up under my armpits, nearly strangling me, but I didn't mind. Charlie's wet face looked up questioningly from my crotch.

"Now?"

"Oh, I should think so," Moira answered. "You don't mind getting fucked, do you, Sam?"

My groan was all the answer she needed.

"Over there," Moira directed. Charlie hoisted herself up onto a wide pedestal sink and pulled me up in front of her, her strong cammy-clad thighs squeezing my hips, the porcelain cold against my naked butt.

"Swing your knees up over mine," Charlie told me. Cool air hit my pussy. Charlie's hands cupped my tits and Moira leaned forward to kiss me, slow and deep and heart-stopping, as Charlie's lips found my ear.

We all broke off to draw ragged breaths.

In slow motion, Charlie's hands stroked their way down my flanks, pushed through the crinkly damp hair of my bush, and pulled my lips apart. The slight brush of her knuckle against my aching clit was enough to make my hips jerk forward.

"Patience, patience," Moira admonished. She flipped up the little black skirt and set loose an enormous purple dildo, already sheathed in a milky-colored latex safe.

"Oh, god," I groaned, regarding the monster through half-lidded eyes, "I don't know if I can..."

"Shhhh," Charlie whispered, "just relax." She guided its smooth round head to my wet hole, and I pushed toward it, starving for it. Moira pressed forward, and the dildo slipped inside me, slowly, as far as it would go. Charlie panted in my ear, matching me breath for breath.

I felt Moira's fingertips pressing gently but firmly under my chin. I opened my eyes.

"Look at me, darling," she said, "I want to see your face."

It was very hard. She pulled back and the dildo slid nearly out. I bit my lip.

"Look at me," she repeated, her thumb against the hollow of my jaw, throbbing with my pulse. Somebody squeezed cool lube down my pussy, and Moira pushed the slick dildo back in. My cunt seized it, pleasure running through my belly like a riptide. Then Charlie's fingertip stroked along the shaft of my clit, and the voltage of her touch surged through me. I threw my head back, past caring about the noise that came echoing back from the tiled walls.

Charlie's other arm tightened around my waist, and we were off. Moira guided the pumping dildo and gouged my thigh with her fingers; the effect of the toy pounding her pubic bone was evident on her face. Charlie drubbed my clit and ground her crotch against my tailbone, bucking and groaning. I rode the waves like a dory in heavy seas, coming hard enough to see stars.

We collapsed against each other in a sweaty tangle, letting our breaths slow, feeling more than listening to the deep thrumming bass from the distant dance floor through the porcelain and tile and empty pipes.

Charlie smacked her lips and worked her dry mouth free.

"What's that," she rasped.

"What?" I croaked.

"That."

We all held our breath. A faint buzzing noise suddenly ratcheted into a grating chatter, and I craned my neck to watch the pager skitter away from my wadded-up jeans in spastic, razzing jerks.

"That," Moira groaned, "is so rude."

"No kidding," I agreed.

I staggered out of the men's room into the arms of the tall blonde. My nose collided painfully with her collarbone. She didn't bat an eye. She held out a bubbly, ice-filled glass.

"Can I buy you a drink?"

I licked my sandpaper lips.

"I'm a Virgo," she said. "What's *your* sign?"

Halfway up the stairs, I stopped to gasp for breath and finally looked at the pager's display. I turned around, cursing. It was from the bar, not the office. The pager went off again.

"Hold your horses," I muttered. "Hold your goddamn horses."

The blonde was waiting at the bottom. She pressed a slip of paper into my hand as I dove past her. "That's my cell phone," she shouted as I ducked into the bar. "Call anytime."

Reaching out of the mass of bodies, Shiv grabbed my arm.

"You shirt is buttoned wrong," she chortled.

I yanked the pendant over my head and thrust it at her.

"Here," I told her, "undo whatever the hell you did before."

"Say *please*," she sang at my departing back. I flipped her the bird.

"Where the hell have you been?" Chris snapped at me. "I'm down to nickels and I'm running tabs for women I've never seen before in my life." She popped the caps off a row of Bud Lites and four hands snaked past me to grab them. "Can you get me some goddamn change?"

"Please," I muttered, pivoting back the way I'd come. "Can you get me some goddamn change, *please*."

I almost made it to the stairs.

"Sam!" An urgent voice called out behind me. "Can you give me a hand here?"

In front of her coat-check booth, Candy was staggering under the draped arm of a heavy-set woman. Something had soaked the front of the woman's T-shirt, and she was pressing her hand to her mouth.

"I think she's gonna do it again," Candy said, grimacing.

"Oh, Christ," I muttered, hurrying to get on her other side before she fell. "I don't need this."

By the time the ladies' room door swung shut behind me, twenty minutes had gone by. I flapped my damp shirt in front of me. I hoped I'd gotten it all out. With three hours to go till closing time, it would have to do. What I needed more than anything was a Coke.

The blonde was blocking my path.

"Please," I begged, "I can't deal with you right now."

She blinked at me. Her nose wrinkled as she sniffed the air around me. Her eyes cleared, as if she were coming out of hypnosis. "Well, excuse me!" She flounced off.

"Shit!" I gave myself a dope-slap and hurried to the bar. "Chris, I'm sorry, I forgot."

"That's all right, Sam," she said sweetly, popping limes into a pair of vodka tonics, "Shiv got my change for me."

"Whew, well, that's good, then. I got sidetracked with a..." It hit me. "Who got your change?" I must have heard her wrong.

"Shiv." She took a ten and deftly slid three ones across the bar to the woman beside me.

"Shiv? You sent Shiv up to Verlaine's office?"

"Sam," she shot me a hurt look as she fished a cherry out of the well for the whiskey sour she was building, "Shiv volunteered. She said it was all right."

"All right?" I repeated. Last time Shiv made an appearance at the Bijou, Verlaine wanted me to have the cops haul her ass to jail. "What do you mean, all right?"

"I don't *know*," Chris said peevishly, "She said they'd patched it up. She said she brought Verlaine flowers."

I took the stairs two at a time. As I waited outside the office door, trying to catch my breath, my ears picked up traces of a sound so alien to that place that I couldn't identify it. I turned the knob as quietly as I could.

Strains of something Viennese lilted out from a portable CD player on top of the filing cabinet. As I eased the door open, Shiv and Verlaine waltzed across the room, Verlaine's musical laughter tinkling out like little silver bells as they passed. Shiv's scrawniness suddenly seemed to pass for spare elegance, and I watched her erect form glide gracefully around the tiny circle, with Verlaine in delighted thrall.

I closed the door. I pinched myself. I opened it again, tapping gently as I pushed it ajar. Strauss played softly as it had before, tinny on the miniscule speakers. The two dancers turned toward me, faces aglow.

"Sam!" Verlaine beamed. "Come in!"

Shiv winked. A bit of chain glinted from the neckline of her threadbare Henley shirt.

"Look," Verlaine gushed, gesturing to a coffee mug full of tattered daisies and one wilted carnation. "Look what Shiv gave me. Wasn't that sweet?"

"Just lovely," I agreed. I turned to her companion.

"Shiv," I said, fixing her with a gimlet eye, "can I see you?" I asked Verlaine, "You'll excuse us, won't you?" Her face fell, and I assured her, "This won't take but a moment."

The door clicked shut behind us. I got hold of the chain and hauled Weegee's gadget over Shiv's head.

"Ow," she protested, "that's my ear!"

In the weak light from the hallway's overhead, I peered at the notched markings on the cylinder's knurled midsection and swore. I couldn't tell. I tried to turn it. I tried to pull it apart. Nothing moved.

"Here." I grabbed her hand and pushed the thing into it. "Put it back the way it was."

"Why should I?" Shiv smirked.

I glared. Her smile faltered.

"Oh, all right," she grudgingly allowed. She pushed the ends together and twisted. "Childproof caps," she said, and blew a raspberry.

I snatched it back and held it up to the light. The notches were different now.

"Whooo-weee." I let out a long, shuddering breath and hung the thing back around my neck.

"Thank you, Shiv," Shiv prompted.

I gave her a look. She tossed me a jaunty little wave and turned around to let herself back into the office.

"Are you sure you really want to do that?" I hooked my thumb around the chain and jingled it for her to see.

Her hand faltered on the knob.

"Here." I fumbled out my wallet and peeled off a five. "Why don't you go back to the Cave and buy yourself a beer?" She could buy herself five plastic cups of beer from the club keg for that, as she well knew. She eyed the bill.

"I can't," she grumbled. "We're having a goddamn meeting."

"It'll be good for you," I assured her. "You can share your wisdom and experience with your fellow Gorgons. They will heap laurels on your venerable brow."

"Huh?"

"Billy said they're gonna talk about getting one of those video poker machines." Instead of kicking him out, the Gorgons made Billy their mascot when he started his journey from F to M. He's the only one who always knows what's going on.

She brightened. "Really?" She released the doorknob and dusted off her paws. "Well, then. Say ciao to Verlaine for me."

She plucked the fin from my hand as she passed.

Verlaine barely glanced up from her screen as I stepped through the door. Madonna was warbling from the boombox, "Like a virgin, ooh, ooh."

"I almost forgot," she said, "the Board of Health is coming to check out the new setup on the balcony tomorrow. Can you get here early? Around two?"

"Sure."

"Great," she said. She typed a few words into the letter she was composing and noticed that I was still standing there. "Thanks," she said.

I was dismissed.

Moira and Charlie were gone from the men's room. The crowd was finally starting to thin. When I spotted them at last by the coat check, Charlie was helping Moira into a fluffy white fake fur jacket.

"I don't see nearly enough of you these days, darling," Moira said, her arm around my waist.

I squeezed back. "You saw most of me tonight, I think."

She swatted my arm. Charlie grabbed me for a bear hug, and I breathed in the smell of her bomber jacket.

"Come for our Samhain celebration," Moira said as Charlie kissed me, our tongues playing tag. "You don't work on Monday, do you?"

Charlie leaned back and winked at me. I shook my head. "That'd be great," I said, more than a little breathless.

I waved them good-night through the glass doors of the theater's old lobby, Jean-Louis Sol's bas-relief sun smiling down at me from on high. I sighed. Chalk one up for Weegee's new toy, anyway.

My pager went off.

I opened the office door expecting to find Verlaine's back to me as usual, her hands flying over her keyboard, but her chair was empty. It took my eyes a moment to find her, utterly still, smiling at the woebegone flowers.

I closed the door behind me. She shook her head. "Shiv," she sighed, as if that one word said it all. "I haven't waltzed since I was a Rainbow Girl." She noticed my expression and laughed. "I wonder where she learned to dance?"

I shrugged. Shiv might as well have sprung into the world full-grown, bandanna, biker jacket and all, for all anyone knew. Verlaine sighed again and shook her head to clear it, returning to the mundane present at last.

"Could you do me a favor? Candy didn't want to ask, since it's out of your way, but could you give her a ride to the El? Her car's broken down, and I hate to see her walking at that time of night."

"Sure," I told her. "If she'll wait till I take the deposit, I'll drive her home."

Verlaine's face lit up.

"Thanks, Sam." She hugged me. "I really do appreciate you. You know that, don't you?" She smiled up at me and my heart skipped a beat. I couldn't think of a thing to say. Her brow wrinkled.

"What's that smell?" Verlaine leaned back, sniffing. I looked down at the stain still faintly visible on my shirt.

My pager went off.

"I've got to get back downstairs." I glanced at my watch; it was nearly closing. "I'll tell you later."

Verlaine started to give me a peck on the cheek. I couldn't blame her when she drew away, but before I could head for the door, she pulled me back into her arms and kissed me full on the lips.

Downstairs, I made my rounds on shaky legs, turning up the lights. In the megawatt glare of the deserted dance floor, I pulled Weegee's gadget out for one more look. It was just as Shiv had left it: off. At least, as far as I could tell.

I took it back to Weegee the next day.

"Well," I told her, settling into her cushy executive arm-chair, "it certainly seems to work."

"Work?" She spared a quick glance up at me from the floor of her office, where she was putting together what looked like pieces from an Erector Set. "What do you mean, work?"

"It certainly seemed to attract women's attention." I pushed and pulled it, trying to turn the switch. Nothing moved. I handed it to my small friend.

She peered at it, frowning. "I hadn't thought it was that obtrusive. Didn't you tuck it into your shirt?"

"Well, yeah," I said, "but that didn't seem to block it."

"Block what?" Weegee asked, confused.

"The attraction vibes. You know. Whatever it was that made women fall at my feet." I thought of Charlie on her knees in the men's room and smiled.

Weegee regarded me curiously for a moment, then pulled a tiny tool out of a holster on her belt. In a flash, the cylinder was in two halves linked by an umbilicus of wire. She held it out.

"All it's got right now is the receiver," she said, "see? It was just supposed to be calibrating."

I scowled at it. As if I could tell.

She wore a peculiar smile. "I was afraid if I included the transmitter, you might be tempted to try it out."

"It wasn't me," I told her, my face burning, "Shiv…"

"I mean, knowing how you feel about Verlaine," Weegee explained, apologetically.

"…twisted the thing and turned it on without me knowing it." I finished as her words sank in. We stared at each other for a long moment. "Shit," I spat, "if that's what you thought, why didn't you just calibrate the fucking thing yourself?"

I heard her calling after me as I slammed the door behind me, but I didn't turn around.

I can't stay mad at Weegee. The next Friday, she showed up at the Bijou herself, peace offerings in hand.

"Weeg, you didn't have to do this," I told her as I tore the wrapping off the larger of the two packages.

Chris stopped wiping down the bar to watch. She burst out laughing.

"How to Pick Up Girls," I read from the book jacket. "Gee, thanks," I told Weegee.

"Open the other one," she prompted.

Out of crumpled tissue paper, I pulled a familiar-looking object on a chain.

"That's the one you calibrated last week. It's got a transmitter now," she said, smiling sheepishly. She nodded at the book. "You'll have to let me know which works better."

I grinned and shook my head. "Nah. Take it yourself, Weegee. Shiv says you need it more than I do."

She poked around under her turtleneck and hauled out a chain with an identical cylinder. "She's probably right," Weegee said seriously. "I wore this out to Kate Clinton's show last night to calibrate it. It's on now, but so far…"

Something nearly knocked me off my barstool.

"Hi," said the small dark head that popped up just under my elbow, "I'm Polly."

Another small head appeared beside the first. "And I'm Holly."

"Haven't we seen you somewhere before?"

They weren't talking to me.

"Oh, god," Chris groaned. "The Tiny Twins. They're friends of Shiv's."

The two very short women, exquisitely dressed in matching silk suits, had already cut Weegee out of the pack and were herding her like a brace of perfectly coordinated Border collies.

"The first time they came in here, I carded them," Chris told me, watching the group recede into a dark corner beyond the dance floor. "Boy, was that a mistake."

"I've never seen them before." I stared after them. "How tall are they?"

"Not as tall as Weegee," Chris observed.

I started to laugh. "Proximity!" I told Chris. "That's what she meant."

Someone pushed past me to get to the bar, and I turned to look. The tall blonde was looking down at me. She sniffed experimentally, then smiled.

"Well, hi there," she said, "long time no see."

Halfway across the dance floor, I turned back to see the blonde setting my barstool back on its feet. In the shadowy far corner, Weegee's head turned from one twin to the other like a spectator at a tennis match. The speakers were pounding out something Latin. Around me, the space began to fill with gyrating bodies, and I felt a hand slide down my back.

"Hey, hey," said a voice in my ear. Charlie caught me by the shoulder for a bone-crunching squeeze. Moira appeared out of the throng to hook a finger in the neckline of my shirt and pull me down for a kiss. She was wearing a leather corset and a leather thong, thigh-high boots with stiletto heels and elbow-length gloves of supple black kid.

"For Badb," Charlie explained, smiling fondly at Moira, "the bitch goddess."

I pointed my chin at the riding crop Moira was bouncing against her shoulder.

"She know how to use that thing?" I asked Charlie with a sidelong look.

Charlie regarded me over the top of her shades, as if to say, *Are you kidding?*

Someone tapped my arm and pointed toward the bar.

"Hey," Chris called, "don't you want these?" She was waving the book and dangling the chick magnet by its chain. The blonde was staring at her like a dog watching burgers being flipped.

"Nah," I shouted back, "Hold on to them for me, will you?"

Charlie's hip nudged mine to a salsa beat.

"You can take a little break," Moira said, stroking my cheek lightly with the braided handle of the crop, "and dance with us, can't you, Sam?"

My eyes lingered on her stunning décolletage. Charlie grinned.

The pager buzzed. I swore and looked around. The tall blonde was draped halfway across the polished wood of the bar, and Chris was backed up against the rear counter. She held up the pendant, gesturing frantically. Across the room, the twins had closed in, and Weegee's head vanished from sight.

I looked at Charlie and Moira.

"Modern technology—who needs it?" I asked, shaking my head.

I turned the pager off.

Wire

Elspeth Potter

Harrah elbow-crawls through oily black mud on a planet called Swan Aleph. There are two giant people-eating turtles having sex fifty meters to her left, skidding and squelching away. Harrah watches, hidden in plain sight. They're kind of sexy. She likes the way whatever they're feeling makes their beaks snap open and closed and their tiny tails flutter.

She's wearing *mecha,* a sleek silver suit needling into her body via nanoprobes. Her mecha keeps the turtles from sensing her, if she's careful to stay out of their direct line of sight. The mecha also hides her from sensors around Swan Aleph's prison compound, the only structure on the whole planet. Harrah takes advantage of the enhanced strength and agility mecha provides her and scales the first wall inconspicuously as an ant. She creeps across an open area that someone is supposed to be watching but isn't. Then she scales a mundane fence and pops neatly into the back door of the prison.

Prisons really shouldn't have back doors like that.

There's a soldier from the Other Side in the prison. Her name is Riesel Flood. Harrah escaped from her custody once, which is why Flood is here. Harrah has decided to get Flood out. Rescue her enemy from her enemy. It's a fun vacation.

Flood will be surprised to see her.

There aren't any guards because everything is remote. Harrah suspects nobody really watches. There are no executions, but if the prisoners get out, the turtles eat them. The Other Side isn't sorry if that happens.

Still, she takes precautions. Harrah's mecha blurs the sensors in here, too. Anybody watching would just see glitches.

There aren't any cells. There are just tables, spaced out, with prisoners strapped to them, one per. The prisoners don't know Harrah's there because they're hooked up with wire. Harrah takes her time, ambling along the rows of naked bodies. She's not much interested in the men with their flaccid little dingles—but the women, well.

She sees Flood. Flood's hair has grown out some; small black curls, each ribboned with silver, cling to her scalp. Her dark skin looks more sallow, but that might be the light, which is poor; the hood sensors in Harrah's mecha amplify available light or she wouldn't be able to see at all. Flood still looks strong, though, and her arms and legs have muscle tone. Harrah isn't too late.

The next trick is to get the wire out. Mecha soldiers all have a little port behind one ear or the other, where the original wetware download happens. After Initializing, soldiers stick plugs into the ports, made out of gold or platinum, or sometimes diamond, for decoration. But when a soldier's mecha is taken away, the plug comes out and wire goes in.

Wire puts a brain on hold. The bad thing is you *know* you're on hold. Not fun.

Harrah commands her hands and the mecha ripples like a disturbed pool of mercury until tools form over her fingers. The table straps will have to be enough to hold Flood still.

Harrah sets to work. She has to stop when Flood's body twists in pain, then she resumes.

The wire smells burned as she finally withdraws it from Flood's port. The smell is illusion, her mecha letting her know the job's done. She lets the wire slither to the floor and steps on it while her gloves go back to normal. With her mecha, she's able to crush the wire to dust.

Flood's face muscles twitch ever so slightly. Harrah is pretty sure Flood is awake; she makes a decision and peels back her hood. She can barely see now, but she can smell again: bitter tang of metal, and greenish scent of disinfectant mist overlying human skin. Harrah says, "Hey, Flood! I am here to rescue you. You are remembering me?"

It's comical, the way her eyes fly open. "You," Flood says. "Fuck you."

Harrah laughs. "You are not getting deadbrained, then."

"Dream." Flood's voice is stronger now.

"No. You are not getting so lucky." Harrah reshapes her mecha gloves and rips open the table straps. "Time to move. I am wanting to get out of this nasty place."

"Turtles. Mecha. I don't—"

"You are talking too slow, almost deadbrained. Have a see."

Harrah springs up to the table and sinks to her knees, straddling Flood's waist. She's a little person and isn't afraid of crushing her. She takes Flood's left hand and places it on her waist, then the right. Flood's hands tighten automatically.

Harrah opens her mecha's pubic flap. She's depilated bare as metal beneath. She can tell that Flood has no idea why she's doing this and it makes her grin. It's strange to grin without feeling her mecha stretch over her face. Harrah says, "I am not going to all this nuisance so turtles can eat you." Flood looks confused. "I am having mecha. For you."

Flood asks, "Where?" Her fingers are digging into Harrah's hips. If it weren't for the mecha, Harrah might get bruised.

Harrah sighs. "I am showing you." She uses both hands to hold open her own cunt lips and rubs her clit with her thumbs. She says, "Mecha is rolling up small, you know?"

Flood laughs. Harrah feels it shake her belly. Flood says, "Crazy." Her eyes roll to the cameras that stud the ceiling.

Harrah says, "If anyone watches, it will be taking them only seven months to reach Swan Aleph." She looks down and is distracted for a minute by Flood's big tits. Harrah likes them naked and spread out below her. She reaches down and plays with Flood's right nipple. It stiffens up quickly. That's still working, then. But Harrah has other things to do. She continues, "No other way of carrying mecha hidden. And sex will loosen you up so you can be walking out of this nasty place. Two birdies, one rock." She stops and takes a breath.

"Crazy," Flood says, but her skin temperature rises a few degrees; Harrah feels a rush of warmth along her skin as her mecha translates. Then Flood's big hands slide around and cover Harrah's, and her breathing changes.

Harrah wishes her hands were naked. Too bad there's no time for that. She can peel her hood back without much trouble, and the pubic flap where there are no nanoprobes, but everything else is more complicated. She settles for pressing the backs of her hands against Flood's palms before she pulls free.

Flood's thumbs take over where Harrah's left off. Her hands are hot and the whorls of her skin still have that slight roughness mecha soldiers get. It's been a long time since Harrah's had any sex, especially skin to skin. Her clit is so sensitive it feels like the top layer of skin was ripped away. Three swirls of thumbs across her clit and Harrah's chest is heaving and she's forgotten she meant to stroke Flood's breasts while her ass grinds into Flood's mons.

The little sealed cylinder inside her passage feels unyielding, unliving. Harrah wants fingers inside her instead. She works her suited fingers into her cunt and teases out the package, letting it drop onto the table. The impermeable wrapping is wet with her own fluids and smells like sex. In case Flood gets the idea they're done, Harrah says, "Keep going."

"What about my mecha?"

"Shit!" Harrah yells. She picks up the cylinder and fumbles it before she can unseal the seam. Silver spills out, expanding, rippling onto the floor. "Satisfied?" Harrah says.

"Not yet, but soon." Flood grins. Harrah realizes she's never seen Flood grin. It's startling. Flood must be reading Harrah's mind because she grins bigger, showing sharp canines.

Harrah wants more action, and now. She drops forward and presses her whole self to Flood and does a thing with her mecha that isn't in the manual, brushing Flood with a hot furry brush, all over, all at once. Flood makes a sound like *nngh* and hooks one leg up around Harrah's ass. This is more the thing. Harrah grabs Flood by her shoulder and waist, shifting them over onto their sides in one easy movement because she's as strong as six people with her mecha on. Then she grabs Flood's arm from where it's pinned between them and puts it where she wants.

Flood's shaking because Harrah hasn't let up with the furry brushes thing. Her finger finds the mark anyway, sliding in and curling and pressing. Another finger goes in just as quickly and then a third one. Flood's stroking forward and Harrah feels it deep inside like Flood's pulling something out of her. Something's not enough and she doesn't know what until one of them stretches her neck and Harrah's mouth touches Flood's. Harrah's trying to suck in someone else's air; she's kissing her enemy. Flood's tongue swoops in like her fingers and that's all it takes to make Harrah come.

Harrah didn't mean to do any of that. It's too late now. They turn onto their backs and Flood kisses her neck while she pants in aftershocks and Harrah remembers she meant to get Flood's muscles working. That's her excuse for doing what she wants to do anyway. She pulls away and slides down Flood's body. Harrah thinks about finger-fucking but ends up licking around Flood's lower lips instead, using just her tongue-tip, like she's marking referent data points. Harrah wants to touch Flood with something other than mecha, and if that's not what Harrah expected to want, she's not going to think about it now.

Harrah uses her hands to smooth down Flood's thighs while she eats her, being careful not to hurt her with enhanced strength. Flood isn't talking and her body undulates with each stroke. When Harrah nips at her belly now and again, she can see Flood's jaw is clenched tight. Once the back of her head hits the table, *thunk*. Harrah thinks she could maybe go on forever like this. Except then they'd never get the hell out of this place.

Harrah finds Flood's clit. It juts enough so Harrah can swirl her tongue around and around while she presses Flood's cunt lips open and kneads the insides of her thighs. That pushes Flood over; she comes in a series of deep groans from the belly and Harrah wonders if she could make her ejaculate sometime. The idea makes Harrah hot all over again but it's smarter to get the hell out of this prison right now.

Flood's still gasping when Harrah rolls off the table and pulls her hood on. She seals the neck and her pubic flap, sealing off the warmth in the air and the smell of their sex. She scoops the mecha off the floor and drapes it over Flood's waist. "Put it on," she says.

The mecha slithers out of Flood's grip but she grabs it on the second try. There are no sonics to clean her off; neither of them mentions it; Flood will just have to clean the dead skin cells out of the mecha later.

Harrah ambles out of the prison with Flood at her side. Flood's an old soldier and moves in the mecha like it's her own skin, and she's pragmatic enough not to look at any of the wired soldiers they're leaving behind. Harrah admires that. Maybe that's why she came here, because Flood wouldn't expect it in a million years. Flood probably forgot about *her* as soon as the court-martial was over.

They climb the fence and crawl around giant people-eating turtles having a party, or at least banging their shells together and churning up more mud. Harrah almost swims through a few places, but then they are out of range of anything worrisome and she leads Flood to her shuttle at a lope. Wearing mecha, it's not much of a trek.

Flood doesn't ask where they are going. That's good, because Harrah doesn't know, not in the ultimate sense. Not that Flood seems like a person to ask about ultimates. She's a soldier and she lives in the now.

Right now, Harrah has to go back to her ship. They won't like what she's bringing with her. Flood's their enemy. But Harrah wants to keep her around, and Harrah's in charge. She'll have to tell Flood that one of these weeks. Maybe after they've had another adventure like this one. Harrah could live with that. She has a feeling Flood won't mind, either, and if she does, there's always the wire. It's fucking perfect.

Educating Billie

Betty Blue

She had a voice like Judy Holliday's, and a body to match. Not that Billie would have known what the hell Whit was talking about if she tried that as a line. Probably wouldn't even get the allusion to the "Billie" character. Maybe it was the name that had gotten Whit thinking about Holliday, but from the moment Billie had shown up (it was billiards night at the local dive and Billie had just dropped herself into the game with a smile), Whitney was hooked. She hadn't intended to go along when the group decided to go dancing, but Billie had wheedled her with that voice, and she'd just spent half the evening watching Billie perch against the pool table to take her shots, that amazing ass in the air.

Whit felt too old to be dancing here at Red, and definitely too old to be ogling Billie. It wasn't as if she'd seen *Born Yesterday* on the big screen (she had to keep reminding herself of that; she wasn't old enough to be Billie's mother, not quite—at least not for a "good girl" where Whit had grown up); she just had a weakness for '50s Hollywood femmes. But her other weakness was for sweet kids like Billie that nearly *were* born yesterday. There weren't a lot of twenty-year-olds these days built like Rita Hayworth or Kim Novak; low-rise would never make it on a pair of hips like those. But Billie— holy shit, Billie stopped Whit dead in her tracks.

From the safety of the bar, she watched Billie dance, hips hopping up in little twists to the backbeats. God, it was painful.

Billie caught her eye and grinned and came hopping her way, spinning as she reached the bar and falling back with her elbows propped against it. The gorgeous ass scooted back on the red vinyl stool and nearly missed and Billie laughed and threw her head back, sweat dripping a dangerous trail from her throat into the cleavage of her tight, cropped tee.

"God, I *love* dancing! Why aren't you out there, Whit? Come on!" The high-low voice wouldn't have worked for anyone but Billie; it came out like a sexy little croon, starting soprano and ending up alto.

Whit shrugged and tipped her bottle of beer. "I don't really dance."

"Oh, please," said Billie, rolling her eyes. "Gimme a break." She grabbed Whit's free hand and started pulling her away from the bar, and when Whit hesitated, Billie took the half-empty beer out of her hand and slid it across the bar.

"Hey!" protested Whit, but Billie was tugging her out onto the dance floor, already swaying and bouncing to the next song. "I don't really—this isn't my—"

Billie had sidled up to her, sweat-slick belly pressed against Whit's; with the bottom button of her cotton shirt undone, Whit could feel the warm skin, and she put her arm around Billie's waist involuntarily. Billie hooked into her, letting Whit's hand slip down and rest at the top of her Holliday ass. The slick red lips were saying something, but it was lost in the throbbing house music, and Whit was lost in the disco-ball glints off the blue points of Billie's cropped, bleach-blonde hair, and the wrinkle of her nose as she smiled. The black, baggy jeans pressed in closer to Whit's leg, and Billie began to rock against her thigh in a smooth, deliberate stroke. Her wide grin was glowing ultraviolet.

She said something else, leaning close so that her tightly cupped breasts mashed into Whit's. Whit shook her head with a questioning look, still unable to hear her; she probably wouldn't have been able to understand if she *could* hear her. Billie smelled so good and felt so soft that Whit couldn't even think.

Then Billie had grabbed her hand and was threading through the crowd, Whit stumbling along after her, wondering if she'd had too much to drink and was just imagining that Billie was sending signals.

Billie dragged her into the dark, cramped bathroom meant for one, letting the door with its heavy layers of red club paint slam behind them. It opened inward, and Billie was pressing Whit against it and sliding the bolt.

"Billie, I—"

"You talk too much," said Billie in that lazy inflection that managed to be in both high and low cadences at once. "I think you should kiss me."

"You think so, huh?"

Billie rolled her eyes and made a mocking pucker at her, lips black in the red light of the bathroom. Whit pulled the warm hips in close and Billie dug her hands into Whit's hair and offered up the lips in earnest. They were soft and tasted like watermelon gloss and Billie was making a tiny humming noise against Whit's mouth.

Whit let one hand slip from Billie's hips up over the tight crop-top to squeeze her breast lightly through the fabric. She could feel the nipple stiffen through the bra.

"Yeah," breathed Billie against her lips, and wriggled closer.

"So I guess you—"

"Geezus, Whit, shut *up!*" Billie insisted, quickly working her way down the row of buttons on Whit's top. She pushed the sleeves back against Whit's shoulders and tugged down one bra strap and dove in, dragging the nipple into her mouth with a rough tug that made Whit's knees buckle.

Yeah, this looked like a good sign.

Whit stopped wasting time and tunneled her hand underneath the white crop-top and black bra, pinching the tight nipple, earning a squeal from Billie, who somehow managed it without opening her mouth. Billie was yanking Whit's belt from its buckle, and Whit gasped as the cold paint of the door met her skin at a quick nudge of her pants from Billie. Billie moved them out of her way just enough to get her fingers between Whit's legs, and burrowed in.

Whit was bucking in time to the muffled beat from outside the bathroom as Billie's fingers spread her lips.

"Geezus, you're wet," said Billie as she snapped her mouth away from the captive breast and dropped down to a crouch to press it into the spot her fingers had opened up for her. She was working her fingers as fast as her tongue, making those tiny humming sounds again like she was drinking a really great chocolate shake and didn't want to let go of the straw.

Whit moaned and pressed into the warm mouth, faster as the music picked up steam, and Billie's fingers with it. The bass was pumping heavily against the door and Whit's ass. Whit was about to come and she wanted to prolong the moment.

"Come here," she gasped, tugging on Billie's blue spikes.

Billie obliged and stood up, slipping her slick tongue sweet with Whit into Whit's mouth without missing a beat with her fingers. Whit reached blindly and tugged the bra and crop-top free, earning more little Billie-squeals as one breast spilled into her hand. With her other hand, she snaked into the loose waistband of Billie's pants and found her cunt damp and trembling.

"Yeah! Yeah!" breathed Billie between kissing and squealing, thumping out her own beat against the insides of Whit until the two were in harmony, hips grinding against fingers against hips.

Whit opened her eyes and saw the moon-curves of Billie's unbelievable ass in the mirror, her muscles pumping as she snaked against Whit, and it was all Whit could take. She shuddered and twisted against Billie's fingers, groaning as she tightened against them and fucking Billie at the same time with swift strokes that matched her own body's rhythm. The feel of Billie's fingers slippery with her made Whit pump her own fingers even harder.

Billie's knees went slack, letting the hot weight of her cunt bounce to the beat with Whit's hand supporting her as Whit fell back against the door, breathing in a crescendo of softer and softer sighs until it was all she could do to keep hold of Billie and not slip to the floor. As Whit's body relaxed, Billie let go and braced a hand on either side of her against the door, thrusting into Whit's fingers in a slick *slap-slap-slap,* making high, tiny sounds with each stroke, her eyes wide and her face flushed, her tits spanking against Whit's.

Whit dipped down and caught one of the hot, hard nipples in her mouth, cupping the other breast with her free hand, thinking incongruously of how it felt like holding a perfectly risen yeast bread in her hand. Her thumb was stroking automatically against the soft hood of Billie's clit, her hand warm and wet with Billie, and then Billie was gasping "*fuckfuckfuckfuckfuck!*" and bouncing against her on each syllable, beating out her climax against the door with one hand.

She collapsed against Whit at last, breathing hard, and sweating harder, and Whit, watching her in the mirror again, couldn't resist running her hands down the back of the loose jeans to cup the perfect ass.

That was when they noticed the complete lack of muffled bass coming from the other side of the door. Whit looked down; the crack of light from the club was no longer strobing ultraviolet, but a dull yellow-pink.

They scrambled to pull things back into place, buttoning, shoving, tucking, smoothing back hair, and Billie gave Whit one last kiss of watermelon and honey-musk before they opened the door and tried to act cool.

It was last call and a small line of club goers were waiting to use the john.

"Get a room," said somebody.

"Nice song," smirked a soft butch by the door. "It's got a good beat, and you can dance to it."

Whit ducked her head down, but couldn't hide the canary-eating grin. Billie slipped her arm around Whit's waist and sauntered cool-as-you-please past the line and out to the open air of the exit at the end of the hall. She leaned into Whit's shoulder, her spiked hair damp against it, as she waved down a cab.

"I thought you said you didn't dance," said Billie with a wink as they flopped into the backseat. There was a distinct lack of accent to her otherwise still-soft voice and Whit squinted at her suspiciously.

Billie's grin was smug, leaning back against the seat with her hands hooked behind her head. "What?" she said. "You didn't think I could keep that up all night, did you? Never fails. Girls always fall for it. It's a Judy Holliday thing. She's my favorite '50s movie star."

Whit glared, folding her arms, but her cunt gave a warm little jump at the fact that Billie knew the movie, and well enough to perfect that accent. "So I suppose your name isn't Billie, either."

"Huh," Billie laughed, back in the voice. "Whaddaya think, I was born yesterday?"

The Lost Blackjack King in My Eyes / El Perdido Rey del Tahúr en Mis Ojos

Tina Cristina Maria D'Elia

Where did it all start? And to where did it go...? This was really the beginning. After two and a half years of not making it back to the Southwest deserts, I, Cristina Rivera, realized my body craved—ached for—the sand, *las arenas,* the brown earth and vast skies meeting and intertwined as eternal lovers. I packed full one large duffel bag and reserved two nights at the Luxor. I rented, for an edge, a 2003 silver Jetta with cruise control. I threw on a black spring dress with red strapless pumps and took off at dawn. I drove from my apartment in San Francisco, to my destination of fallen angels, empty dreams, overfilled cups of diamonds and clubs, sparkling silver-midnight-rhinestone-moonbeam white. Timeless, this city of sin, Las Vegas. *La ciudad del pecado.* Perhaps to reveal my own? Espresso in hand, I needed a change....

In silver exterior and black leather interior my skin stuck like leather-seated skirt to a bare ass, getting a good slap to raw skin. My sweat lubricating the back of my knees, moving inside my thighs. I pass another exit, sliding in my desire crowding into two streams coming into a cannon. Collecting at the darkness in dampness of my thin silk ruby thong's edge. My body, my spirit exhales long and sweet as I cross the Nevada border into the Southwestern precious golden-brown landscape.

I then pull off the road and trade in the Jetta, yuppster mobile, for a shiny pink convertible classic Mustang. *Mi Chica Femme* mobile, *ummm, sí Cristina*, one gas guzzler replaced by another...well, hell.

Now with the top down, without covers, my human spirit touches endless landscape—the mahogany-reddened bronze brilliant, smooth, and peeking into jagged rocks all around. Each dark nook I pass instigating another erotic reason for me to turn off the road and meet myself beneath the sun upon the rocky surface. *Aquí*, is where my mixed *Mexicana* heritage ancestral oculars saw through their own eyes. *Aquí, donde los Indios Nativos Norteamericanos* have loved and lived and fought hard—silent inside these landscape stories, spiritually alive.

Algún día mi corazón will be closer to the flat brown beauty of it all. Be closer to *mis días, mi Diosa, a La Vírgen, a la Mija,* magenta crimson fuchsia sky and *Madre rojo*—orange-brown earth similar to the skin tones of all that came to this earth before Rivera.

Valle to the Luxor and then to an unfinished, unsolved mystery that curled me inside it. I could deny no longer. I had heard like myth, like folktale, like film noir—all in one—of the infamous *Mexicano y* Native American Indian *Macha*, The Transgender King of Blackjack, Jesús Antonio Gitano.

Jesús es the one whom genderqueer, folks of color, every flashy fag and glitter queen, Zoot Suit *Macha*, and Nightclub

Rumba *y* Femme Fatale would move in and hover around to see his steaming table after midnight to taste what his next move would be. Who could take down the Champ, the King of *Tahúr, el Rey*, if only for a night? Who would be *la bonita, elejida,* if only for *una noche*? This quest was both illogical *y* methodical—odds of one in a hundred that a stranger could catch a shark's eye.

My bets were on the quintessential *La Bryja Salvadoreña*, the visionary, Esperanza Margarita Aguilera. A tango starlet in her youth, *ella* could fill a room of *deseo*/desire, all would worship her. Esperanza could know of a journey before it reached your own consciousness.

I get into Vegas after five P.M. Enough time for a quick shower at the hotel and then *el rojo y negro* outfit. A deep low-cut V-necked sleeveless dress. A long scooped open bare back revealing my light brown skin. With my black open cha-cha heels and the dress just above my knees, a black Spanish shawl from *mi Abuela,* I finish by grabbing a small black sparkling-beaded purse and deep crimson lipstick. I proceed to the Bellagio to pursue the inclinations of Esperanza. The purse will catch the light of my silver Navajo necklace and *sus ojos.*

I end up walking seven blocks and enter, a little in disarray, and immediately see a group of mixed-race gender-queer players hitting the floor.

"Hola Señor, dónde esta Señorita Epseranza Aguilera?"

I feel my *corazón* pounding. *El señor dice, "allá"* and points to a second floor dinning room. I approach her with honor and sweat on my brow.

A mortal to a spiritual guide...she is speaking to *un amante*, a lover, I believe.

"*Un momento, por favor, mi querida,*" she whispers.

Her Butch kisses *la Bruja's* hand and touches her face before exiting.

She is stunning in an ivory gown, with a turquoise stone resting near her fine breasts. The most exquisite, dark skin and long black hair, like *la Reina*, a Goddess *hombres y mujeres* kill to be near. Suddenly she looks deep into my eyes.

"*Sí*, what is it you search for, *mija?*"

I exhale. My breathing is still coming off a little rapid.

"Jesús...Jesús Antonio Gitano."

She raises her right eyebrow.

"I see. Tonight he's at Caesar's Palace. He may need your help."

I push my hair back.

"*Dónde?* Ah, Caesar's Palace...*muy bien. Ah, muchas gracias, muchas gracias Esperanza.*" I start to turn away...

"Table 84, *y...le gusta el rojo.* He likes red."

I'm running...now...sprinting actually, to a taxi. Entering through the crowds of Caesar's Palace, a basic tourist nightmare, and I'm sweating profusely at this point. I chant, "Table eighty-four, eighty-four, no, sixty-seven, no, thirty-four..."

I notice there's a back section I must check. *Nada*...hmm.

Upstairs...*sí*. As I enter the lounge I can hear the reverberation of Luscious Jackson playing.

Take your hand in mine...
Mi corazón starts to beat faster
We will travel to another time
Subo the stairs and turn the corner
If you look inside my Gypsy eyes

I stare across the room and there flashes the top dog pool table.

I'm gonna take you away

Then just beyond it, the Blackjack table, crowded with tension.

Oh yeah, I'm gonna take you away...

Then I approach a table filled with andro/femme/butch/ transgender mixed-race boys and girls in gowns/trousers/ boas and false diamond watches, glitter necklaces and smoking jackets. I see a drop-dead gorgeous transsexual *señorita* who looks at me, then glances toward the table. I move in and see Jesús, and as this happens, *señorita's ojos* meet Jesús'. Either light hits me, or instinctively and instantly, Jesús looks at me.

I overhear a butch *pinoy* Frank Sinatra say that after a losing streak, Jesús' luck has turned.

Jesús gives me his arm, and escorts me out. I look at him— he is ancient—and he looks at me like a myth.

"*Cómo te llamas, hermosa?*"

"*Cristina Rivera.*"

As we step out into the night, Jesús takes a deep breath.

"Cristina, you have done more than cause me to end a losing streak and win the worst hand I could have landed in Blackjack. I came out a hero. And you in that *vestido rojo*, red dress, hmm, you don't even know."

I unlock the door to my hotel room and Jesús whispers in my ear.

"Every part of you—I will take tonight."

Smirking, we go inside.

I see him try to light each tender candle. I see how he moves, butch-trans-top-proud Latino. I move around the room lighting my two Virgin candles. Bringing one near the window.

Us smiling. I, feeling his eyes upon me. I see—I feel my awakening heart—like the pulsating volume of my body consuming the room, wet *y muy caliente*. Holding both sides of the bureau, I take him in, and he gazes back into me, massaging his hand against his hard stomach.

"Do I cause this stirring?" He steps out of the shadow and meets me face to face.

I am a foolish maze, a panting creature of femme-fatale flesh.

"The effect doesn't wear off for days, *mija*, I hate to break it to you."

His right hand leans next to mine.

"Now, who told you red is my favorite color," he says and touches the straps, his fingers tightening into my arms.

"I know."

"Do you...*mijo?*"

"Sí."

"Midnight is shining inside you. Goddess, *tú*, you are shining inside of me *esta noche.*"

I breathe out.

Immediately his grasp dominates all thoughts. Jesús pulls my entire body against the wall. I am off my heels and he holds me hard, our strength is ripping eroticism off the walls like the immensity of the deep magenta-blue sky edged with rough crimson penetrating fuchsia clouds, godlike, hard on my inner thighs.

Our kisses move everywhere. He and I tearing off his white button-down shirt...

"Like the sky possessing the sun I am making love to you."

"Oh, is that a sincere promise?"

I, orange golden-garnet blood burning beauteous, am taken over. He lifts me by my waist and hips. My legs and heels come together around his waist and he thrusts us up against the next wall.

"Hold on to me, tighter!"

"Is that an order?"

We begin bucking into each corner from desk to bureau again to the bed to the chair.

His hands up my dress and ripping down the straps grabbing each breast. I moan faster as he groans, hunger through hands and tongue biting and working sliding inside me. *"Ay Dios..."*

"Mi Angel!"

"Sí, mijo?"

"I want to fuck every inch of you..."

He unzips, rips off my underwear, and tosses them to the floor.

"I have wanted to worship you this way since I first felt your stare." Jesús, speaking and spreading my legs, holds them open with his thighs, and takes my face and hair.

"Every part of you—I will take tonight—you, Cristina my sweetest Angel."

"I want..."

"Yeah, I know," and he holds his cock against me.

"I want your cock so deep inside me I forget all but this moment." And our eyes meet, as he pushes, sliding fast, then pausing, then moving faster inside of me.

I am moaning and listening and suddenly our words cannot make sentences:

"Here/ move/ fuck/ harder/ me/ oh/ *sí*/ ah/ listen/ hmm *sí sí sí*/ I'm/ tell me/ going to/ oh/ yeah"

We can only say one or two words at a time.

"Oh *si*, take this off/ oh this way/ me/ move/ tighter/ yeah/ no hmm/ yeah yeah/ more/ hmm / uh/ I'm taking you/ bend over/ you're mine/ ffffffffuckkkk/ I'm yours/ oh/ fuckkkkk/ NOW!/ oh/ yes/ I want it/ aaaaaaaahhaaaa/ What do you want?/ Yeah, you like it, don't you?"

He whispers to me, "*Orale pues mami…*"

"Don't you/ you know I do/ tell me/ *dígame*/ what do you feel/ *dígame*/ what you feel."

With my legs above his shoulders, he pounds into me.

"I'm inside of you, fucking you soo deeply like this…*la Macha* you've only met six hours ago!" We laugh, getting more heated.

"That's right, I always get *mi hombre*." I shudder, my body shifting into building breaths.

"Oh yeah, you think so?"

"That's why we're—" I start to tighten my body, "—here." And this continues for another three hours.

Jesús making me cum and cum all night.

"Aaah…"

"Uuhhh…"

"*Querida!*"

"*Sí, querido*, again."

"Aah!"

"Uh!"

"I love watching you *mi bonita*." At five A.M. I find myself washing my face, almost asleep, brushing my teeth, leaning into the sink. We sleep touching, and every second our bodies move closer. When I awake, Jesús says in his fine voice, "*Buenas días*, you like a coffee?" I turned and my eyes close for a few more minutes, then I hear a door close and silence. I turn to stare at the door, knowing he's left. I crawl out of bed and find my coffee steaming with a short-stemmed budding red rose. He also wrote:

Gracias, gracious Phantom goddess of my darkest hours
Alas, must I wait for another lifetime to see you again?
You and I are on separate journeys, verdad.
Perhaps our paths will cross another time?
Besos, Jesús

I must admit I entered the shower redone. His words crooning mixed twisting together in my mind. *I am fucking each part of you like the sky takes the sun.* Exhausted, intoxicated, overwhelmed, dazed, and from the heat of water beating down and soothing my head, my hair, my skin. I become undone, and I start to sob, not knowing of my tears, not knowing if my tears were more for me or for him.

The next day I feel solemn, knowing I will not find him. Try my own luck at gambling, win a round and lose two, miserably. I looked for Esperanza but when I'd come near her casino, I feel overtaken with shame. As though I have told my secrets to the spell, and now it is broken.

The third day I knew I'd be leaving by daybreak.

I stare at the sun. He stands behind me as masculine moon/feminine sun and pushes my legs apart. My ass feels his pressure, he's ready, hard, packed, and the moment shudders. He pulls up my shirt in back and with one hand, unsnaps my bra. His brown strong hands pull me by the waist, grazing my stomach, my brown skin against his. I feel his breath, his body tensing, increasing in muscle and emotion, and I am the desert's lost rain, coming down my thighs. I feel...I am begging.

He reaches to pull up my skirt, I am breath to landscape, his finger reaching for my clit. This rain of pussy this rain of cum through skirt to rocks I feel his Latin rhythm enter his hips and I respond as I'm led to his fist. His left hand has found my breasts, tightened my nipples to points. I must feel the rhythm of his lips, for his native tongue that's speaking down my spine, down the cloudless sky of crystal blue to violet pink to welcome a deeper force of twilight deep purple. Like a burning emotion of want and wait, his right hand feels *mi corazón* and the air is a guitar of deep sighing. We must be screaming into the skies—I don't even know the song we could become—it hasn't been written, but is felt in our eternal human existence. His left hand moves to his side as warrior. We are in offering. We are offering ourselves, our sexuality, our cultural pride, our ancestral complexities, our desire/ *deseo* to madre earth/ to *Mija* sky/ to *Mijo* stars/ to padre moon/ and to the blessed mountains of blood-orange-dipped twilight.

Upon this moment and breath, I am panting as though there is a rigorous, intoxicating climb inside. We are climbing. He is pulling off my shirt and turning us, as in salsa, grasping my right hand and gripping me harder. Jesús kissing and licking my back, as I turn, licking down his brown muscular arms. He moves to my back, to my ass, and toward my shoulders before instinctively, we are in eye contact again. He is now drawn to me: Goddess, La Femme *Latina*, ultimate *Vírgen*/Whore, am I. Jesús, *él estes mi Dios,* the lost warrior, the last Gypsy, and the unstoppable Blackjack King. We worship each touch, submitting to taste of what mortal lips can offer. For I am beyond the poetess, the high-ranking Courtesan, the *Puta* men wish to save, the Latin Amazon from the East/ West/ North/ South. *Nosotros,* we, are prayer. And I am now the next mystery, *la Vírgin* he invoked to absolve and purify his body and replenish his soul anew. *Mi alma,* enhanced and washed, my body appeased, massaged and sore. I am at one with him and this panorama. No longer is my heart aching. *Nosotros*/we, enraptured and enwrapped as *dos amantes morenos,* entwined like ancient *Mexicano* constellations, shining beautifully, below the Southwestern sapphire skies and upon the rocky brown desert landscape, tanned reddened glorious shifted, until the next time.

Carving a Woman
Jewel Blackfeather Welter

Have you ever thought about how you would describe tasting salt for the first time to someone who never had the opportunity to scrape salt crystals away from a piece of pizza and feel the granules almost burning the tongue with a flavor that is neither sweet nor sour? What about a way to explain why the moon in full face drives some people to spin beneath the milky light and wish on stars and newborn babies, torn comic book covers and broken glass, metal soda can tabs and glittering Mardi Gras beads? Trying to express these things is like translating the language of the heart, which speaks in sparrow-pecks and wild canary trills; like detailing how the human form became a marvel that walks on two legs after years of evolution.

The only way you can even think to touch the feeling behind the words is to call it magic. People say magic is dead, but they lie. They are jaded with the milk of death in their eyes while they dream awake. Go ahead and laugh if you must when I speak of magic. That is what my roommate Lalita did the day we walked into a room as friends unacquainted with the love of our gender and exited with girl-juice on our lips and the sweat of pomegranates and tangerines along the creases of our thighs. She laughed at me constantly, but her laughter was not the laughter born of scorn and derision.

Lalita's laughter was like coyotes dancing in the desert and she wore the scent of sun-dried wood on her skin from her main job of making cabinets. On weekends, she carved animals out of logs for spare cash. Many nights, she walked deeply into the woods near our house and cut faces into tree bark so that anyone else who wandered through the woods saw that the trees, like rocks, had faces. She loved drawing the human eye to the personality of each tree. During the week and on the weekends, the rich odor of wood surrounded Lalita, an odor so real inhaling it was like walking barefoot in the grass at midnight.

I liked waiting until she returned from work, just to be near the wood smell. She came home in her faded jeans and cotton apron, her hair pinned on her head in long coils that reminded me of crow nests. Straddling a kitchen chair, Lalita took the pins from the back of her head and slowly shook the black strands forward. Shavings fell from Lalita's hair. After she unlaced her utility boots, her feet pressed the curls of pine, oak, and cedar into the carpet. Chuckling, she told me the lewd jokes the men at her workstation told her, about the teenage boys in a convertible she flashed at a stoplight when they gawked at her, and the painted Sioux ponies she saw behind barbed-wire fences on her way home. I tried to concentrate on Lalita's words, but all I could see were her long, lean legs wrapped around the legs of the chair and the white curve of her incisors against her lower lip when she smiled.

She was sex-voodoo, that woman with Taxco silver on her wrists and my heart in her palm. At the time, I did not think Lalita was aware of my affections. Now, after having impaled her with my tongue and been impaled by her tongue and teeth, I know she understood all along, maybe had planned the seduction from the first time we spoke. I did not know. My eyes were half-closed to what was alchemy: her. She opened my eyes with her tongue and laughter, with the inclination of her head to kiss my throat and her fingers bowed around my hips as she held me like a piece of wood she planned to carve. And carve me she did, casting a spell of fingernails and cunt-muscles and the fragrance of her that was like the inside of a sacred forest, untouched by human hands.

The day we shared a tryst that led to our eventual relationship was the same as any other day, except for the magic that drifted through the air, on Lalita, and in me—a magic I did not acknowledge until she smiled as fiercely as I ever saw her smile and told me I was her heart. "You're my heart, Shawnee Blue," she sang, thumping her fingertips against her breastbone, "my heart, heart, heart. A sleepyhead, but still my heart." Although I had an Indian name, Lalita was the true Indian: strong hips and the kind of high, sloping cheekbones that seemed formed from desert rock. Her eyes saw far into the future and her hands knew how to shuffle the Mexican tarot cards that were a staple in her heritage. She was half Indian, half Mexican, and all woman.

My response was to throw a pillow at Lalita and burrow deeper beneath the blankets. The warm cocoon smelled of cedar chips and wildflowers with a hint of Lalita's musk and cinnamon spice. She dodged the pillow, flashing her teeth at me like a she-wolf searching for a mate. I nursed a terrible hangover from a night of drinking tequila and Salsa dancing. Lalita had held my hair back from my face while I vomited the contents of my stomach into a toilet and then, a trash can. She slept in the bed with me, bent around my drunken form, her warmth so good and real, so close and true.

"You shouldn't have drunk so much last night, Shawnee," she stated seriously. Lalita stroked baby tendrils of light hair away from my face. I leaned into her touch because she radiated intensity and summer sweat born from the work she did honestly with her hands. Her wicked nature belied the strange tenderness she showed for me, as if she were protecting me and I was a member of her wolf pack that she needed to keep safe. Sometimes, I fantasized about being a wolf cub that needed to crawl up onto her body and nurse milk from her teats. Other times, I envisioned us as lionesses, tonguing impurities from each other's bodies. Most of the time, I watched Lalita, my fingers itching to trace her skin and hair. Something inside of me burned and trembled for her.

"Call it a forgetting," I mumbled. "Instead of a haunting, it was a forgetting. I needed to forget."

"Yeah," she breathed. Her dark eyes seemed darker, more liquid in the slanting morning light that played across her features. Ordinarily, Lalita's irises were a deep brown that turned to amber when certain types of light played over her face—like the fluid, burnished gold of an autumnal afternoon. "We all need to forget sometimes. You, more than most." She adjusted the pillows on the bed and settled onto the floor, cross-legged and straight spined, looking like an Aztec princess.

"Yeah," I agreed. I was a young thing, but I had seen enough betrayal to sharpen my perspective and turn my blue eyes gray. "I don't understand it all, Lala. I gave him everything and still, it wasn't enough for him. I don't know how many times I can keep rebuilding myself and rising from the ashes someone has left of my life before I just…" Unable to continue, I paused and rubbed at my eyes.

"But you rise. Your instinct knows more than your heart." Her eyes lingered on my small hands, inches from hers on the edge of the bed. "Your hands were born to fight." She patted my hand, and a wild animal stirred in my heart. When she drew her hand away from mine, I was more than a little regretful, but I pretended not to care.

"I don't have hands like yours, Lalita. Your hands do things. You create with your hands." As I spoke to her, I looked at the folding of her fingers on the white sheet, her skin like new sage leaves and dark as a farmer's egg. My lips lowered to press a kiss to the knob of a knuckle before I could stop myself.

"Your hands can do things, too, Shawnee," she laughed, raspy and low.

"You could carve a woman with those hands, could cut tracks into flesh with your fingernails." Her full little mouth was so close—too close—and rather than resist the gravitational force that emanated from somewhere at Lalita's core, I kissed her soundly on the mouth, just a touch of lip to lip, a slight grazing of teeth.

"I want to hew you the way you carve your wood," I whispered. "I want to carve you with my hands." Silence lingered between us, heated by the breath escaping our lips, tickling our throats, and flaring our nostrils. I was almost afraid I had made a serious mistake until she let out a small snarl and curled her fingertips across my jaw line, forcing my gaze to meet hers.

"Then, you should," Lalita purred. It was a delicious torture to have her finally in my grasp and to be uncertain of how to first stroke her. I had never made love to a woman before Lalita. Now that I've seduced and been seduced by her hundreds of times, my fingers deep in Lalita's cunt and tongue twisting with hers, I cannot imagine being penetrated or captured by anyone but Lalita. She said I was her heart, but she is my life.

So, on that morning, I looked at Lalita's pink, flushed cheeks and felt desire rising from the tips of my toes to my hips. Instead of asking why or how, I let my eyelids fall shut and learned about loving Lalita with my bare hands. My palms trembled along the flat of her chin, the proud line of her shoulders, and the curve of her belly that was girl-soft and woman-firm to the touch. She did not melt into my caresses, and met my fingers with lips, thighs, and the hardened pebble of a nipple that ached and arched against my fingertips. I rolled the second nipple with my other hand and listened to her pant when I tightened my hold on her.

"I want to see you, really see you," I whispered, biting her earlobe and snapping at her lower lip. I drew her cotton T-shirt up higher until I exposed her large, dark areolas and swollen nipples. Since Lalita had been sleeping, she wore no bra to fetter the fullness of her breasts or provide a barrier to my curious hands.

Her restless spirit did not quiet itself as she pulled and clawed at the sheets covering me and then removed me from the battered sweatshirt and bikini panties I sported. Cool air swirled across my torso. I huddled under the quilt Lalita's *abuela* knitted for me the Christmas before. Lalita's eyes dissected me. She told me that she wanted to fuck me in full sunlight and eat fruit from the dip of my navel and the hollow of my sex. Then, she said I was magic and yanked me from beneath the blankets and onto the sun-dappled living room floor. Patches of the wooden floor were worn from the pressure of our heels when we taught each other how to Salsa and hopped from one foot to the next after biting fresh *habañero* peppers from the garden behind the house.

I was tempted to tug her into the backyard and roll around the endless vines of the tomato plants, thrust my thumb into Lalita's pussy amidst the orange sorbet–colored blooms sprouting from the squash, and sink my teeth into the ripe tissue of a peach toasted by Lalita's hands. There was a world of possibility that unfolded when we fell upon the floor and on each other, tongues flickering serpent-like in the half-light of an afternoon just beginning. When I fluttered my forefinger along the slight decline of her clavicles and felt the ridges of her ribs floating just beneath the milky caramel of her abdomen, I wanted to plunge deeper into her, wanted to see if she tasted like cardamom and honey, like prickly pear cactus fruit and deep August monsoon rainfall.

I cooed as she straddled my face and let me produce the hungry slurping sounds that I needed to emit against her, my Spanish lover. Lalita rode my stabbing tongue and showed me that her taste was deeper, more primeval than anything I'd imagined. She was an ancient earth goddess reincarnated in a mortal's succulent body. Raven-black hair curled to protect the tender lips that my teeth liked gnawing at, just because it caused her to shiver, stretch the delicate musculature at the small of her back, and spread her thighs. Intoxicated, I stared at Lalita, waxing and waning for her luscious body, sweat-slicked vulva, and the exquisite little growling sounds she made low in her throat the quicker I washed my tongue across her clitoris. I could tell by the way she tilted her pelvis that she wanted me to dig my fingers into her folds and immerse myself in her clear to the knuckles. I did not give Lalita what she needed, not just yet. We had years for the culmination of our lust and only that one moment to savor and remember the tracks in the snow and across sand that led us to discover each other this way.

Desire radiated from Lalita and I wanted to love her, fuck her, and violate her, just to let her know how long she'd been beneath my skin and sinking into the marrow of my bones, a magic only explained by carving a woman from passion and perspiration, oxygen and heartwood that looked like heaven and the soul of love on Lalita's tongue when she murmured that she loved me. Rather than do any of those things, I held her in my arms, pinned her like a butterfly, and watched her gaze intensify when I uttered her name and knew that I'd be saying her name for many years, just as I suckled at her tits and lapped moisture from the sweet sex that was never more beautiful than it was magic.

Class Struggle
María Helena Dolan

Ah, *such* a lovely evening. The sky is that spectacular autumnal azure, with the sun just starting to ribbon across in long twilight gold and rust and purple rays. Ain't Nature grand? Me, I'm sitting on the raised dais of the Front Desk, face phosphorescently aglow from the triple bank of monitors, wearing a .38 and a natty blue uniform, complete with military-style tie and cop-style hat.

Oh yeah, lest we forget the *personal* touch: my first initial and last name are stitched in discreetly contrasting thread over my left breast. Here I am: the few, the proud, the underpaid.

It's a full employment economy, doncha know? That means full scut work too, for liberal arts graduates with no particular skills and no particular connections and no particular wish to be hassled about being too goddam butch.

So I'm "guarding" a high-tech facility with lots of big-time hush-hush genetic researchers. (I guess on some jobs, you *want* a weight-lifting, tough-assed Latina dyke—so maybe thievin' competitors think twice about rushing a place guarded by a gun-totin' *marimacha* who tops out at 5'10" and 220, with formidable shoulders and killer thighs.)

Hey, it's a living—barely. I've worked off the books for a long time, though, and I'm trying to get some legal time in.

So, I'm here as a Guardling to watch monitors, sign people in and out, make two rounds a night to ensure nothing's been forced or blown up, handle any petty bullshit that comes up. And Guardlings *are not* permitted to read, watch TV or make personal phone calls. Oh the distraction! Oh the humanity!

Not that most of these *pinchones* think of *us* as human. Basically, they don't think about us, period. We're the brown faces in blue uniforms sitting at the front as they plod or trod in. We're "Security" after all; *they're* scientists, doctors, Big Shots with tons of research money and Names to make.

So why would they know ours? A few of the "staffers" do; the ones who're smart enough to realize that they're really only one rung above us, so they know better than to give attitude.

Those are the ones who aren't blind to that fact that if their key cards malfunction or the toilets don't flush automatically or a gadget goes missing, they dial one set of four digits.

And the Voice on the other end answers, "Front Desk." We're troubleshooters as well as keeping the bad guys away from the lab rats—that's what everybody in Security calls these gen-mod geniuses. (And Front Desk can either come through promptly on a call, or take fuck-all sweet time; how do you think that determination gets made? Mr. Asshole So Big I Can't Even See You or Miss Is Your Mother's Cold Any Better? Gosh, wonder which gets a better response time?)

Now, I could obsess about the cultural and class unfairness of how I came to be here on this dais. But, I actually sort of like it. There's a kind of power in sitting here raised slightly above the crowd, with my gun.

In fact, we could have bigger caliber semi-autos; the company even supplies them if we want. But I like the feel of this baby in my palm, and I like the way she lays just right on my side. So as long as they furnish the hollow point, I'll keep my first love with me, thank you very much.

It's not as if I ever have call to pull her. No no. We don't even get *borrachónes* or homeless from the street. The lines of this place are way too severe, and it fends them off in a sterile feng shui sort of way.

Given the lack of stimulation, there are blocks of time I have to fill. For amusement between the rounds, I give myself little exercises. Yeah, I have hand grips and leg weights. But I have to be sort of discreet, keeping that shit under the desk for later. So instead, I have to do more *subtle* things to keep from going shit-screaming stir-crazy, or totally postal.

Like, I'll see how many times I can fully extend my tongue and retract it in one minute. And then, counting silently, I do 100 tongue rolls to the left, 100 rolls to the right, and then 100 center waves, with a little back flip of the tip. I even brought in a hefty baby rattle to do lifts with: fold the tip under and around the bar, lift for 20 reps, then rest, then 20 more, rest, finish with 30. Shit, I can about do *push-ups* with this thing. Man, I should have this baby registered or something, maybe like for Guinness.

And this is all genetically controlled, ya know. Actually, I *do* know, because I studied genetics and biology in college. But hey, would any of these "professionals" take *me* for a college grad, or even a person with half a brain? After all, I wear a shirt with my name on it....

Come mierda; most of them don't even look at me when they enter. A few make nice, and a couple of secretaries have slipped me their phone numbers. But man, only a *pendeja* shits where she eats, huh? I figure all that good pussy can wait. I got a girlfriend, and she's so ultrafine, I don't even *want* to play around. And ooo, she's been *muy gratificado* with this *desarollo*, too.

Hey, when it's late and quiet and the corridors are empty, sometimes I get this makeup mirror out to check how I'm doing. Yes, you have to possess the right code sequences to do *this* move: a back flip *and* roll. Or *this* one, where I punctuate sticking it out about an inch and pulling both sides up to create a trough, by pinching in the tip so it looks a little like a clit. Hey, an artist has gotta admire her work. My natural endowment, my experience and hard-won champion artistry, plus the sheer stamina I've acquired from all these nocturnal workouts…they all enter into it.

I tell ya, the Old Lady's been *thrilled*….

But that ain't *all* the lowly servitor does during her shift, no *señor*. Not after I got to be buds with Wild Davy. Man, he was the shit; sold killer-assed, drive-yo-*Mama*-blind primo weed to a quarter of the lab rats for *locura* prices; and laid it on his fellow Guardlings for practically *nada*. Wild Davy sold so much he retired behind it after like two years. But not before that techno freak sleepless fuck seamed into every friggin' cam and computer in the building, tying them all into this little zoom box I got strapped under the console.

Wooo! I sit here and spy on *all* the stinkin' docs and their gofers and ferrets, now that everything's rigged and totally accessible. They have no idea Big Sistah is watching!

Hey—you wouldn't believe how many of them jack off in their "research rooms." Or how many have call girls come in at lunch time. Now I *know* they can't *possibly* realize how ludicrous they look when they're only wearing socks, a watch, a T-shirt, and a condom on a half-mast little dick.

Never mind all the quickies and blow jobs amongst the fuckin' staff. And FORGET the downloaded porn! Jesus H. Christ! Talk about your tax dollars at work! Woo-hoo!

In the face of all this ridiculous-assed stuff, I thank the Goddess and whatever gods there are that I was born queer. Whew!

Needless to say, I spend a lot of evening shifts in between rounds trying to amuse myself in ways other than by watching bad reruns of this same old shit—which is where the tongue laps really come in handy. Say, what if someone catches you *en medius*, and asks "What are you *doing?*" "Nothing" doesn't permit much beyond that perimeter, even for someone with a brain. I mean, what does it look like you're doing? Wiping peanut butter off your lips? Shee-it, man. Can they really scope out Sapphic Artistry in the ring?

Speaking of which—I've been noticing that damn Dr. Roberta Russell. Okay, I admit it, I find brains awfully sexy in a woman. And not only does she have doctoral degrees out the wazoo, but she's got curves that should come with warning signs—they damn sure look dangerous from *here.*

Plus she's got plenty of at-ti-*tude.* I saw her coldcock a flirting lab rat at ten paces just a week ago. He thought he had a smooth line and he was hitting on it. But he was hittin' on *nothing*—a fact she made demonstrably clear with one line and a slight raise of an eyebrow. The dickless wonder tucked and limped away....

She's coming in late again, I note as La Doctora approaches my desk around ten. The denizens have to sign in and key the elevator with their cards anytime after six.

"Good evening, Doctor. More after-hours research?" I inquire pleasantly. She looks right at me, in a very...direct sort of way.

"Yes. In fact, when you make your rounds at eleven, I'd appreciate it if you'd stop by my office. I'll require some assistance at that time, Sergeant Rivera."

"Any way I can help you, Doctor, I am only too happy. You just need to ask."

"Yes, I've observed you being helpful to other women, so I'm *counting* on that. Um, I don't think I've ever been told your first name."

"My first name?" (Whoa! Where'd that come from?) "People don't use it much around here, at least, not the docs. But, it's, well, it's rather long, and friends just call me Lu. With a *U*."

"Lu? Lu Rivera—has kind of a ring, eh?"

I look at her pretty closely to see if she's bustin' on me or not, but she just looks as though she's mulling it over.

"Well Lu, see you later. And you can call me Bobbie." She smiles, a big red splash across her face, with some nice white showing between.

Bobbie, huh? Wonder what she needs help with. Well I'll be damned—she's walking to that elevator like she's *hot*. You know, like she needs to be careful with how those legs move across each other, cuz the friction might ignite her middle in an awful powerful fire. You don't think...*me... ai no...¡ai cunyo!*

Eleven o'clock, and all's well. Except for me. While I'm prowling the halls with the requisite *macha* swagger and attention to door details, I'm also shaking like a grade school girl at her first dance—not to mention sweating like a *puerca* looking over at the *chicharrón* stand, wondering what the hell to expect next. And whatever it is, it's coming up. Because this is her office.

Well, here's the door. *The* door. Of course I took the liberty of looking in on the good doc before rounds. She was just staring at her computer screen, which faces away from the cam so I've No Clue, Lu. Since she doesn't wear glasses, I can't even get a reflection there. What's up with this woman?

Knock-knock, tembladora calling. "Dr. Russell? It's Security."

"Yes Lu, come in."

So I wipe my sweaty palm on my shaky thigh and turn the knob. And pause to adjust from the hyper-lit hallway to the sudden half-gloom. It seems like about the only light is a line along a worktable. Wait, what're those, *candles?* Man, open flames are *so* against regs! And they smell like musk or something.

Where's the Doctora...¡*Ai Madre*, she's standing right there, wearing only a black slip and a big smile!

Like a jerk, I just squeak, "Doctor Russell!"

"I'd hoped you'd call me Bobbie, Lu."

"Yes, Bobbie, of course," I stumble. "You wanted me to help you?"

"Indeed I did. It seems that the recent late nights allowed me to see an entirely different side of you. I always thought you cut a handsome figure in that uniform. But those baby rattle exercises *definitely* caught my eye."

Shit! She *saw* me!! Oh *shit!*

Whoa, she's walking toward me, all hot and determined. Pulling on my tie and roping me close to her, she says, "As a scientist and a woman, I want to investigate just how developed that organ has become."

I can feel the heat rising off her and smell the estrogen in the air—she's completely ready. When her mouth reaches mine, that's it, I'm gone. I toss off my hat and undo the tie while she watches, real close up. I unfasten a few buttons, but we begin to embrace. And it's instantly exciting. She's a skilled kisser, and her flesh trembles with life at my slightest fingertip touch. Her nipples swell and push against the slip—and into me.

I pull her closer to me, breast to breast, lip to lip, hip to hip. I slip a hand down to the hem of the slip, touching nylon and her own smooth silk. Her hips roll and I slide up further, and then further still, meeting a little rill of wetness. ¡*Que mujer!* ¡*Que boca, que tetas, que chocha!* I want to fuck her brains out right there on the floor, suck the clit right off of her! Arrrrrrr!!

Ah, but I have to hold on just a minute. I won't sweet talk, no, I'll go medical on the doc while I work my hands over her.

"Ooh Bobbie, I want to slide my tongue up into your Grafenberg spot and trill on it. Then I want to back out slowly from your vaginal opening, and slide up one inner vaginal lip to your urethral opening and then down the opposite side and on further to the perineum...."

"No no no!! No clinical terms! Just give it to me *raw*. Pisshole, cunt lips, pussy, ass," Dr. Russell cries as she pulls my head down and right *into* her cunt, finally roaring, "Come on!"

So I do. No talking, no nothing, *sin los previos*, just my face planted up under her slip. Licking away, I put my hands under her ass, lift her up, and ease her down onto the thick pile rug. Still licking, I roll her over and prop her up so that she straddles my face as I lie on my back.

Once she's on top, I wrap my tongue around the hood of that clit, and rock her from side to side so fast and so smooth you can't even tell when my thumb pushes back and up on the hood, and my tongue drills on the seed pearl like a sapsucker drilling for the sweetest spot. She just starts moaning and shaking and groaning, and whispering, "It's good, oh, it's *g-o-o-d,* oh, oh yeah, oh!"

Hell, I'm just getting started. Whoo, honey, I work her like I'm on the Grand Tour and her pussy holds *all* the stops. And I keep on until she says she can't stand it and then keep on until she's begging for more. And don't worry baby, there's plenty to go around, because I've been honing it for decades and I *live* to have my head between those legs and my mouth on those juicy pussy lips.

And when she can't speak and she damn sure can't come any more, I suck out every drop from her gushing cunt hole, and lightly kiss her lips.

After quite a long moment, she gasps, "Oh, Lu, I needed that."

"Evidently. And I'm happy to be of service," I say as I stand, straightening articles of clothing as I proceed from prone to upright. One kiss on the face lips, and I start to walk away.

Shaking a bit, she pulls herself up on one elbow, legs and slip still askew, and asks: "Wait, where're you going?"

"Back to work."

"What? You...you can't just *leave*!"

"I have to finish my rounds. Otherwise, how should I explain the time gap in the Log? 'Conference with Dr. Russell?'"

I finish tying my tie, adjust my holster, set my cap at the right angle, and head out into the hallway.

A Tangle of Vines
Cheyenne Blue

Marianne lived in a house surrounded by sunflowers. Sunflowers, wheat, and vines, symbols of abundance, of the good life, of fecundity and indulgence and lazy summer days.

It had been four years since I'd seen her last; long enough that she'd produced a son, the heir that her husband demanded. Long enough that she had settled into her life in rural France, shouldering her way uncompromisingly into the community, talking French with her strong American accent—French to the villagers who shrugged with Gallic nonchalance and pretended not to understand; English to her son, who would only answer in French.

I arrived in a hire car to a flurry of laughter, hugs bursting out onto the stone driveway, a reunion under the pale blue sunwashed shutters, a meeting that rolled back the years to when we were young, and stupid and drunk on what we might become.

Marianne screamed her joy, and there were tears in her eyes as she hugged me. "Suzie! *Merde,* it's good to see you!" she said, when the euphoria had subsided enough that we could speak coherently. "Come in and have a beer!"

The farmhouse was cool and disorganized: a stone flagged kitchen, with a haphazard collection of children's toys and empty wine bottles by the door; a playpen under the stairs; a ripe, oozing farmhouse cheese collecting flies on the counter. She pulled glasses from the cupboard, a bottle of Picon, small bottles of lager, crackers, the cheese, and then we were outside on the uneven patio, sitting on the wooden bench, raising our glasses to friendships old and renewed. Her husband, a military man, was away again, this time a peacekeeping tour of duty in a foreign country that maintained an uneasy truce with its neighbor; a parry here, a thrust there, the bluster and ever-present threat of chemical weapons or nuclear attack.

"When he's home," she said, "my heart rejoices, for oh...about three weeks. Then I count the days until he leaves."

We toasted her husband, her reason for being here, in the country, by the estuary, the salted air encrusting on her washing, coating her vegetables, coarsening her hair. We toasted her child, a precocious darling with a funny little voice, a child of two cultures and none.

We sat, the two of us, and drank and talked, letting the sun lower itself into the sea. The beer ran out, so we opened a bottle of wine, then another. Her boy ran around us, in and out of the vines, bringing us small treasures for admiration—a perfect curled young green vine leaf, a favorite picture book, a ripe tomato from the vegetable garden.

The long twilight drifted into dusk, and dusk into night. The stars rose, silhouetting the tangled rows of vines, washing the farmhouse in a surreal light. The buzz of small insects shrilled into the soft night, as we sat and drank and talked and drank and laughed. Marianne's son gave up trying to capture our attention and fell asleep on the couch in the untidy lounge, curled up in a knot with the sun-bleached sheets, taken in from the clothesline.

We talked on, and the talk gave way to drink-induced euphoria. Marianne put on some Latin rhythms, and returned through the doors, her hips twitching, long russet hair streaming behind her as she salsaed her way out into the night.

She sat again, and we clasped hands over the armrests in that unspoken communion that women sometimes share. She poured more wine, sloshing it over the rim of the tumblers so that it puddled like blood on the wooden table, then pulled me into a hug, tight, close, so that my head rested down on her shoulder, short blonde hair to long fox hair. I turned my cheek so that I could feel the pulse in her neck, warm against my skin, and slipped my arms around her waist. We stayed like that, rocking together for a moment, before she pulled away, standing unsteadily, and moving inside.

I waited, with a faint sense of disappointment. She was tired, she had gone to crash, and I was not ready for the night to end. I laid my head back against the stone wall of the farmhouse and closed my eyes. Then the music blared again, and she was back, pulling me to my feet, slipping off her shoes.

"Let's dance, Suz!" she cried, and the moonlight glossed her cheekbones as she threw her head back, highlighting her face with an edgy beauty.

I allowed myself to be pulled to my feet and obediently followed her stumbling lead, into the garden, past the raspberry canes fallen in drunken profusion, out past the end of the orderly part, down through the waist-high weeds, to where the sunflowers and vines met in a tangle of muddled cultivation. A step, step, hop, a stumble, a laugh as we blundered our way along, the gasps of hysterical laughter wafting away, bouncing off the solid walls of the farmhouse, floating over the nodding heads of the sunflowers, down to the estuary, down to the sea, over the ocean. Who knows how far our laughter traveled that night? A glance back at the house to chart the familiar, then Marianne was tugging me forward, into the vines, where the leaves curled out from their strings, tendrils of entanglement and enticement.

I held her waist, and followed her lead, a step and hop and kick, down the rows we salsaed, following the music in our heads as we moved between the lines, brushing off the curling green leaves. The loamy dirt pushed between our toes, bare feet sinking slightly into the soft earth. Our dance disintegrated into a shuffle, then an amble, and finally we just relaxed into the night, our arms around each other's waists, as we stopped midway along a row of the vines.

My senses burgeoned, a combination of wine and moonlight, loam under my feet and the fresh smell of new growth, the distant tang of salt sea air. Marianne turned her head, and I saw her lips, softly parted, before she came closer, kissing me softly, on the side of my mouth, then, when I didn't resist, on the lips.

We had never done this before, she and I, never shared experimental explorations as younger women. I had gone straight to male lovers, and she, I assumed, had done the same. But over the years, the boundaries defined by gender, by sexuality, and acceptability had blurred to a faint line, and her kiss wasn't shocking or unwelcome. It just was.

We kissed, hesitantly at first, then with increasing ardor, but with such tenderness, such a simple extension of our friendship that it grew in intensity as naturally as the vines around us bore grapes. When she stroked my hair, when I ran my hands along her shoulder blades, when she pressed soft kisses to my eyelids, there was no decision to be made, it just was.

Her hand slipped under the hem of my T-shirt, stroking the skin above my waistband with a soft touch, each finger imprinting itself on me. It dragged slowly up toward my breast, and when she cupped it, stroking a careful thumb over my nipple, the die was cast. It was just Marianne and I moving further along the line to love.

I pushed my hands into her hair and continued to kiss her. Slow languorous kisses, deep drowning falling kisses, where we moved and melted into each other. There was no hurry; unlike our frenzied laughter of before, now our movements had a slow gliding quality. The advance and retreat of tongues, mating and withdrawing, had the ritualistic well-honed precision of a ballet.

She pulled her T-shirt over her head, allowing me to explore her breasts. I did so slowly, carefully, tracing a fine blue line with my tongue, examining the fine hairs around her nipples, chocolate-drop mother's nipples. Her body intrigued me; long arms, wiry muscles and bumpy elbows, and I put my mouth to the splatter of freckles on her shoulder, opening over them, scraping gently with my teeth. Her long hair drifted over my face, coarse from the salt and the soap she used to wash it, tickling my nose. I kissed my way up to her neck, burying my face in the curve of neck and shoulder. She stiffened slightly as I breathed over her, the ridge of muscle pushing into my face, then relaxed again, humming and sighing in an undulating pitch, as I stroked her skin with my tongue.

I don't know which of us made the move to take it further. To progress beyond the stroking gliding caresses, to take it into a more physical realm, but Marianne's skirt slid to the earth, my shorts lowered to join it. And then her fingers were underneath my cotton panties, feeling, exploring, pushing, and then a concentrated pressure on the side of my clit, the wonderful friction dance.

I swayed, closed my eyes, let her fingers push me to the edge, and swayed some more, the wine, the night, the darkness all combining to disorient me. So much so that when, on the outer edge of orgasm, I opened my eyes and saw stars, I didn't know if it was the wide swath of the French night, or they were purely behind my eyes.

Marianne withdrew her fingers, and I shuddered at the loss. I kissed her again, let my own hand trail down her body, down to the thatch of curls between her legs. She shifted slightly, trying to balance her legs apart. I was taller than she, and the dynamics were wrong.

Behind her, the trailing arms of the vines stretched their way along the strings. Every so often there was a post, rough-hewn and sturdy. We shuffled back, until Marianne rested against the post. She stretched her arms along the strings, spread her legs, and threw back her head. Such a picture of wantonness, of earthiness, of need. For a moment I just watched her, saw how the pale fingers of new growth tickled up between her fingers, how the shoots caught in her back-swept hair, as if somehow she was becoming part of the living earth. The fancy was sudden, but I saw her merging into the ground, her toes turned to roots, gnarled and clinging, her fingers pale and green, slim filaments of vines, inching along the strings. It seemed as if a tendril of leaf curled inward over her thigh, but that was surely an illusion.

Dropping to my knees in the soft, yielding ground, I parted her with gentle fingers, moving the insidious green shoot to one side. Marianne's head was now bent forward watching me, her hair falling over her face. Through the disarrayed curtain I saw her eyes; slitted, glittering with pleasure. She hissed in anticipation, and held my head there, as she swayed back and forth on her heels; back, so that the vines brushed over her skin, forward in intoxication, so that her toes dug, prehensile, into the dirt to keep her balance.

The air curled in moist salt eddies around my face, and her pubic hair tickled my nose. She tasted of the sea, but strangely sweet, different from me. And it was natural to kiss her, and swoop my tongue around and over her, gauging her response, until her breathing quickened and I thought she would come.

She did. Her upper body jerked, her pelvis pushing into my hands, her head thrown back to the stars as she arched in bowstring tautness up, up into the sky, a long lupine howl of satisfaction and completion. She slumped back down to earth with an abruptness that made me stagger back a pace, as her weight slumped forward. I rose, and turned her in my arms and we embraced. She slid her arms around my waist and we sighed into each other's necks, soft exhalations of pleasure.

We slept together that night, sprawled over her big bed in a tangle of damp limbs. And later still, when the birds sang the oh-so-early French morning into existence, Marianne and I rose and silently shared a cup of strong dark coffee, drunk from bright, chipped pottery bowls. Her son staggered in rubbing his eyes, and she scooped him up onto her lap, murmuring to him in English.

We walked outside, she and I, with her son between us using our hands as a swing. We walked down to the end of the garden, to where the tangle of vines began. Far off, the muted sunlight reflected off the distant estuary, and the taste of salt was in the air. The vines trembled in the light breeze.

Marianne slung an arm around my waist. "It's not so bad here, really," she said.

Paisley Comes Back
Kyle Walker

The last time Sallie had seen Paisley was in tenth grade. That was the year Paisley's family moved away. Sallie was bereft for months. She hadn't realized until Paisley left just how much fun they had, how she'd enjoyed their late-night talks and overnights. High school just wasn't the same after that.

Sallie was voted "Most Dependable" in their class. Paisley hung out with the art crowd: for middle-of-nowhere Schuyler, which had just gotten cable TV, they were wild. They were the kids who wore paint-streaked clothes, sassed the teachers, and cut class and smoked pot and cigarettes. They listened to weird music and the jocks sometimes tried to mess with them.

Even so, Paisley had ended up at Sallie's house a couple nights a week to study or watch a movie. After her family left, they stayed in touch through letters, and later email. In college, Sallie found herself with less and less to say to Paisley, and sometimes didn't hear from her for months. Now Paisley was in Boston, doing a master's degree in art. Sallie was in New York City, and had just found out something very important about herself.

As she waited for Paisley's bus to arrive, Sallie nursed a coffee and remembered things she'd conveniently pushed aside for a while. Their friendship had begun in eighth grade, when the junior high boys stopped pushing them down, and started asking to walk them home. The boys used to chase Paisley around the schoolyard, and she was the first one in their grade to go into the woods with them after school. One day, Billy Henson called her a slut at lunch, and she dumped her tray on his head. Billy tried to hit her, but Sallie stuck her foot out and tripped him. When the assistant principal asked what all the fuss was, Sallie told him that Billy started it. He got detention, and Paisley asked if she wanted to come over after school.

In Paisley's rec room, they looked at some books Paisley took from her parents' private stash: *Fanny Hill, Delta of Venus, Once Is Not Enough*. Paisley knew where the sex scenes were, and Sallie had never read anything like them. Her mother had given her a talk when she started her period the year before, and she'd heard there'd be a film the boys and girls would see separately when they got to ninth grade. But since she had no older siblings, and mostly hung around with a tame crowd, she'd never been able to find out what actually went on between men and women. And women and women, as it turned out.

"Isn't it cool?" Paisley asked, as they looked through the books. "This is what we can do when we're grown up!"

"People don't *really* do this, do they?" Sallie asked, feeling uncomfortable, and something else. It was kind of like an itch, but more of a tickle. She felt Paisley's breath on her, as the other girl leaned over to point out some particular detail.

"Of course they do! Maybe even your parents," Paisley said.

"I'm...I'm not ready for this..." she told Paisley, shutting the book. Paisley took it, and the others, and put them back in their hiding place.

"Maybe not now, but one day we're going to be old enough to do this stuff...and *want* to do it. I think it's just a matter of getting used to it. Getting good at it."

"I can't imagine doing *this* with any of the boys we know," Sallie told her. "I can't imagine *liking* it."

"That's why you have to practice," Paisley replied. "You have to learn how to do it right, enjoy it."

"Is that why you go with so many boys?" Sallie asked. Paisley glowered at her.

"Do *you* think I'm a slut, too?" she snapped.

"No...but you have to be careful, or the girls will hate you and the boys won't respect you." To herself, Sallie had to admit that she admired Paisley's take-no-prisoners approach. "I hate it when the kids say mean things to you. That's why I tripped Billy."

"And of course, they believed *you* when you stood up for me. Because you're Sallie Girl Scout. I was so surprised...."

"You might try a little harder to fit in," Sallie said. "People treat you better."

"I don't think I'm ever going to fit in. I just feel...different from the rest of you." Paisley turned away, her arms folded. Sallie put her arm around Paisley.

"I bet you go the furthest of anyone in our class," Sallie said. "One day you'll be famous, and all of us here in Schuyler will say we knew you when..."

Paisley turned with a shy smile. "You really think so?"

"Why, you're the best artist in school, and even though a lot of the kids pretend to ignore you, they all watch and see what you're going to do next." Sallie was one of them.

"I kiss the boys because I want to make love to a lot of people when I grow up," Paisley announced. "What about you?"

"Um..." Sallie said. "I guess I'll learn when I get a boyfriend. And I guess when I get married, I'll do it with my husband."

"What if you get a boyfriend who's not a good kisser? You'll have to show him!"

Paisley was right, Sallie realized.

"How can I learn?" she asked, worried.

"It's easy," Paisley assured her. "Just take it slow and soft...." She pulled Sallie into her arms. "Mmmm...follow my lead...." *Just like dancing lessons*, Sallie thought. Paisley's lips were soft and at first she kissed lightly, just brushing Sallie's face. Sallie felt her breath quicken. The feeling she'd had when she was reading the books came back. Paisley leaned her back on the couch, and they lay with their arms around each other.

"This is how Billy Henson kisses," she said, slipping her tongue between Sallie's lips. Sallie was surprised, but she liked it. Paisley kissed her slowly and expertly, letting her tongue wander into Sallie's mouth, then pulling it out again. Sallie's mouth opened, too, and soon their tongues met. It was wonderful, it was heaven. They kissed for a while, then Paisley drew Sallie's head onto her chest. Sallie wanted to do more, but she had no idea what.

"Do the boys hold you like this?" she asked.

"No, they just wipe their mouths and go home," Paisley said sadly. "They miss the nicest parts."

"Do you let them touch you?" Sallie asked.

"Only over my blouse," Paisley said. "They squeeze so hard, I don't want their hands on my bare boob."

"I wouldn't squeeze hard," Sallie said. Paisley looked at her and seemed to be considering. Then her mom called them up to dinner, and they both jumped a mile.

They were friends after that, and even though they hung out with completely different groups in high school, they never stopped seeing each other. Paisley still went out with a lot of boys, but she developed a steely persona that cut them loose when they got too rude, or too mushy. Sometimes, after a date, she'd go to Sallie's house, and they'd talk about what was wrong with the boys Paisley dated, and Paisley would show Sallie what the boys tried to do.

Sallie didn't have a boyfriend until junior year, after Paisley left. Evan was a very nice boy, and a decent kisser, but somehow she never got as excited with him as she had with Paisley.

Seven years later, far away from Schuyler, Sallie had finally realized why no boy could ever take her to those heights. Now, any minute, Paisley would be getting off the bus from Boston. Paisley had never mentioned a boyfriend in her sporadic communications over the years. She hadn't mentioned a girlfriend either. What if she'd left her practice kissing behind, in Schuyler? What if she had some serious, sensitive artist beau who made up for the rough, ignorant small-town boys?

The bus pulled in, and Sallie scanned the passengers' faces as they streamed into the Port Authority. Then someone who was light-years away from the high school sophomore Sallie had last seen, but definitely Paisley, burst through the door. She'd always had an abrupt energy, but now it was of laser intensity. Paisley's gaze darted around the dingy concourse, her ice-blue eyes taking in everything. It was a few seconds before she spotted Sallie, who let out a quick sigh of admiration. Paisley wore her straight, dark-brown hair in a razor-cut bob, letting it fall long at an angle across her face, highlighted by a single bright red streak. She was still bird-thin and small. Sallie felt massive next to her.

Paisley wore an all-black outfit, including pointy black vinyl boots, under a coat with a velvet collar. Sallie noted that her nails were painted different colors. Then Paisley looked at her, and as their gazes locked, Sallie also knew that along with being cool, Paisley was also very hot. She grinned at the memory of all the practice kissing, and felt the same feelings course through her...and now she knew what they were.

Sallie wanted to run right up to her and show Paisley how well she'd learned to kiss, right there at the bus station. But she didn't, because it would have taken even more courage than she had in her newfound supply of the stuff. What if Paisley took the next bus back to Boston? What if she gave Sallie that look of pity and disgust Sallie had once tossed over her own shoulder at the queers?

Still, they had to hug, didn't they? And Sallie was gratified at how tightly Paisley held her, and how warm and soft her lips were as they shared a friendly peck. Paisley kept her hand on Sallie's arm as they snaked their way through the crowds.

"Where do you want to go?" Sallie asked. "We can drop your stuff off at my place, but that's a good hour away. I have passes to MoMA, if you want to do that first."

"Let me catch up with you," Paisley told her. "MoMA will still be there, and I haven't had a good look at you yet." So they went to the bowling alley at the Port Authority, and Sallie had a hot dog and Paisley, who was vegetarian, had fries, and they both had a beer, even if it was just past noon.

"This is cool, very retro," Paisley said approvingly. Sallie nodded. She'd figured out that some old-fashioned things were retro, which was good; while others were just old-fashioned, which was bad; but she had a hard time telling the difference.

"How's school?" she asked.

"I'm not one to brag...oh, who am I kidding? I've always tooted my own horn. It's going pretty well," Paisley said. "I've gotten some attention in the student art shows. I'm lucky. I have a mentor...one of my teachers. She'll take care of me with fellowships and help me find teaching positions. Introduce me to gallery owners. She's got pull, and that's what you need to get ahead."

"That's so great!" Sallie told her. "I always said you'd be famous."

"It's...not what I expected," Paisley said with a shrug. "I

didn't know how...complicated it is to establish yourself. But I'm sure it'll all be worth it in the end."

"Oh, you were always a hard worker," Sallie agreed. "And I thought you were an excellent teacher," she added. Their eyes met and Paisley let herself smile a little.

"That's because I was passionate about what I was teaching," she told Sallie. There was a moment when either of them could have said something, but they let it go by.

"Are you seeing anyone?" Sallie asked. Again, Paisley shrugged.

"Yeah...yeah," she finally answered. "It's a good thing... we're happy," she told Sallie. "It's just a little overwhelming, sometimes. I'm really glad you invited me down this weekend. It feels weird telling you about it...but good. I mean, this isn't high school anymore, and I'm not coming by after a date to complain."

Sallie took Paisley's hand, which was cold. She'd always had cold hands. Sallie rubbed it between her own two.

"Now I remember why I came by your house," Paisley told her. "It's a shame things didn't turn out differently...." She put a little distance between herself and Sallie. "So, how's— what's-his-name? your fiancé?"

"We broke it off," Sallie told her. Paisley perked up.

"Oh really?" she asked. "How come? Did you find someone you liked better?"

"Yes...," Sallie said, feeling herself blushing.

"Come on! I want details," Paisley told her. She put her hand on Sallie's arm, and Sallie had to restrain herself from *showing* Paisley what had happened for her to lose interest in Larry. Paisley was wearing lipstick that matched the streak in her hair, and had a full, sensuous mouth. "Are you with someone now?" Paisley continued.

"Uh, no...," Sallie muttered. "But it was an experience that made me realize that...Larry was definitely not the one."

"So what does that mean?" Paisley asked quietly.

"I guess it means I need more practice," Sallie said, letting at least one shoe drop.

Paisley seemed to think about it for a minute. She laid her arm across the top of the banquette, almost but not quite touching Sallie's shoulders.

"You know, I, uh, messed around with a lot of boys in high school," Paisley said. Sallie gave her a "tell me something I don't know" look. Paisley continued. "I didn't really feel that...invested in it, but I felt like I had to do it." Sallie waited. "As long as I had boys following me, and boys wanting to do me, and did some things with them, I was safe."

"Well, except for possibly getting pregnant, and picking up a disease," Sallie pointed out. Paisley gave her a "tell me something I don't know" look.

"See, if I messed around with Billy Henson, or Matthew McGonnigle, then what I was doing with you didn't count." Sallie's heart lurched. "If I kissed a boy, it didn't matter if I kissed a girl. Boy, was I fucked."

"In many ways," Sallie agreed, and they laughed.

"I suppose I'm lucky I didn't get knocked up; and I'm lucky I finally figured out that I didn't have to fuck boys to prove I was normal," Paisley told her. "So college had a purpose after all. What sucks, though, is how much more I wanted you than any of those boys, and I couldn't have you."

"Not *then*," Sallie said. Paisley cocked her head, as though she hadn't quite caught what Sallie said. She started to say something, then stopped. Such a look of longing passed over her that Sallie couldn't help herself. She took Paisley's face in her hands and gave her a long, sweet kiss that so loosened her hold on the present that for a minute she could almost smell Paisley's basement rec room.

"That's how Sallie Gardiner kisses," she told Paisley.

They went back to Sallie's place, which she had to herself, since one of her roommates was out of town, and the other spent weekends with her boyfriend.

They held hands on the subway, and kept bursting into giggles as they looked at each other. Sallie felt like a sophomore again, and not the good one she used to be, but one of the ones who broke the rules. They caught a few surprised and rude stares on the train, but also some looks that Sallie was beginning to realize were of quiet recognition.

"I can't believe it," Paisley said to her in a low voice as they headed for her house. "When did you finally realize? Is that why you moved to New York?"

"Um...well, it wasn't consciously why," Sallie said, wondering if her unconscious had been smarter than the rest of her. "It was...uh, very recently. Um. Last weekend."

"No!" said Paisley, stopping in the middle of the sidewalk.

"Yes," muttered Sallie, pulling her along.

"And the first thing you did was get in touch with me," Paisley grinned. "You *knew*, you just didn't know."

"I guess...," Sallie said. She'd never liked to be teased.

"Hey...hey," Paisley said, catching her arm. "I'm thrilled... and flattered...."

"I just got started...I don't know anything yet! And I kept remembering you."

They were at her building, and she fumbled with her keys, concentrating on getting the door open. They didn't speak in the elevator, as they rode up with an older woman and her grocery cart, and a young mother and her little boy.

Paisley rested her hand on Sallie's back as she opened the door.

"It's not much, but..." Paisley stopped her with a kiss.

It was a great, wonderful kiss, filled with all the things they hadn't known or wanted to know as teenagers. Still kissing, they began to take off each other's and their own clothes.

Coats, gloves, shoes, socks, blouses, panties, bras littered the floor around them in far less time than Sallie would have thought possible. Still, they were standing there, clutching each other, touching, rubbing, exploring, biting, sucking, grasping.

"Do you want to sit down?" Sallie whispered.

"NO!" Paisley hissed back, sliding her finger into Sallie's very wet pussy. She fixed her lips on Sallie's left nipple and sucked hard, while she pushed first one, then two, then three fingers in and out of Sallie's cunt. Sallie thrust herself on Paisley's hand. Her old friend's fingers were strong and sure.

"Give me...everything...everything you wanted...," Sallie gasped.

"Really? Really?" Paisley asked.

Sallie bit her hard on the neck and jammed herself onto Paisley's hand, as she squeezed Paisley's nipples. She felt as though Paisley could crawl up inside her, and Sallie wanted her deep inside her womb; she wished Paisley could come inside her.

Paisley rode her hard and expertly, and moans of satisfaction escaped her when she took her lips off Sallie's breasts. Paisley knew right where Sallie's G-spot was, and her middle finger rubbed at it hard and exquisitely. The now-familiar sensation, like water pulling back from the beach before the wave hits, began, and Sallie knew she was about to come. She felt the cry build and Paisley increased the intensity of her stroking. From a low moan, her orgasm grew in volume and intensity, and she let out a shout that she knew the people in the next apartment could probably hear, but she didn't care. She almost collapsed on Paisley, who was small, but strong.

Sweating and shivering, Sallie realized she was cold, and still standing, when the thing she wanted most was to be snug under the covers with Paisley. They didn't bother to pick up their clothes, but went right into her room.

The sheets were smooth and gentle on their skin; and Sallie pulled one of her mother's quilts over them. The radiator let out a quiet hiss as they twined themselves together, looking at each other and laughing with surprise. Sallie looked at Paisley's naked body, gently stroking her taut breasts, feeling her fine, pale skin grow warm. She was small, hard and muscular. Paisley shaved her pussy, and Sallie liked the feel of its nakedness, its wetness leaking onto Paisley's thighs.

She felt soft and undefined next to Paisley, but the other woman seemed to like her form. She squeezed Sallie's breasts, and ran her hands down to Sallie's buttocks and cupped them.

"Do you know how much I wanted to do this when we were younger?" Paisley asked her, gently kissing Sallie's shoulder. "Do you know what it felt like to lie next to you at night when we had sleepovers?"

"Was it all you thought it would be?" Sallie hoped she hadn't disappointed.

"Do you have to ask?" Paisley said, with a delighted laugh. Her eyes sparkled, and the tight, passive mask she'd made of her face was gone. She was alive and sparkling, her breath deep and even, her voice full. "Sallie, I'd forgotten what it's like to be desperately in love and sixteen years old, and you just brought back the good parts."

"I'm glad...for both of us," Sallie told her. She was ready to make love to Paisley, who suddenly sat up and listened.

"Oh...I think I hear my phone in the other room...," she began. She scampered into the living room for her bag. When Paisley didn't come back right away, Sallie pulled on a T-shirt and grabbed the quilt off the bed. She found Paisley sitting on the sofa, naked, curled up into herself as she spoke.

"No...I *said* I'm sorry, Magda! I said I'd call in the afternoon...it's still the afternoon...." Sallie sat on the sofa next to Paisley, and drew the quilt around both of them. Paisley didn't seem to notice. "Yes, I did think about what we talked about...but isn't it reasonable for me to...Magda? Stop talking over me...." Paisley sounded so miserable that Sallie wrapped her arms around the smaller girl. She quietly kissed Paisley's shoulders and her forehead, began to rock her slightly. "I just don't know...yes, I want *you* to be happy, too. I want there to be an *us*, but we both have to want the same things...." She started to cry again. "I'm sorry...I can't...no, I'm not trying to manipulate you...don't call me that... hello? Hello?" She turned to Sallie. "She hung up...."

"Come back to bed, Paisley," Sallie told her.

"I love her so much...," Paisley said miserably. "I *need* her. Not just for the fellowships and teaching jobs.... She's taught me so much, taken me so many places, but sometimes I just wish she'd stop taking it out on me...somehow it's always my fault: whether she sleeps with someone else, or doesn't get her grades in on time, or gets drunk and misses a class."

"I'm glad I've never been in love like that," Sallie said.

"That was mean," Paisley told Sallie.

"I guess it was," Sallie replied. "But you shouldn't be with someone who just cuts you off. That's wrong. And *she's* your teacher? That's only wrong in about a dozen ways."

"She's very talented. And famous. You don't know her!" Paisley started.

"I don't want to," Sallie replied. "I don't care how many good things she does for you. Fuck her if she treats you wrong." Paisley gasped. Sallie *never* swore. "What happened to the Paisley who cut them loose when they got to be too much trouble?"

"I just can't let go...," Paisley began. "I'd lose so much. Her, and all the *things*.... I have a career to think about, you know. And I'd be all alone."

"Maybe alone isn't all bad," Sallie thought aloud. "Can't you get what you want without someone giving it all to you?"

"I don't know...," Paisley said quietly. "I don't know what I'd be by myself. Suppose I don't have what it takes to make it by myself?"

"Wouldn't you rather know?" Sallie asked. Paisley was silent a long time. She snuggled close to Sallie, still shivering, still breathing hard.

"Yes," she whispered.

"You always did whatever it took to find out what you needed to know," Sallie reminded her. "Even when it didn't turn out well. When you ended up in the principal's office, or got grounded for teaching yourself how to drive."

"But you were always there to pick me up after," Paisley said.

"Did she ever sit in your rec room and read the dirty parts of novels?" Sallie said softly, taking Paisley's phone from her. She put it back in her bag, and pulled them both up off the sofa. They walked with the quilt around them. "Did she practice kissing with you? Did she listen to you pour your heart out? Because back then, neither of us knew what we were doing, but we did know how to take care of each other."

"We did," Paisley admitted.

"You could at least expect her to treat you as well as your junior high girlfriend," Sallie said as they crawled back into her bed. "She was a good kid."

"Still is," Paisley said. "I mean, a good woman."

"So let's just be as good to each other now as we were then, Paisley," Sallie said.

"I don't know how it's going to...I mean, I can't promise or expect..."

"Shhhh," Sallie told her. "We're not the girls we were in Schuyler. We're here right now, and this time, you're not going to have to lie next to me wishing."

"You're right," Paisley said, wiping away the last of her tears.

"If you want, we can go to MoMA tomorrow," Sallie told her.

"Maybe next time...," Paisley said. "We have a lot of catching up to do."

The Devil's Dew
Abbe Ireland

Orange flame spread swiftly through sheet after sheet of crinkling letterhead, wickedly dissolving logos from the best publishing houses and biggest agencies into wispy black ash and curling smoke. I lit another side of the large paper mound filling a round metal barbecue in my dime-size backyard, causing more fire shafts to burst paper membranes in a fiery *fuck you* to every gnome assistant who'd gleefully stuffed 878 rejection slips into 14 years of my virgin SASEs. Sniggering the whole time, I assumed, and without ever reading a single word, I was certain.

I stepped back and watched the conflagration turn the conical paper stack into Lady Liberty's torch—I first thought, before realizing it reminded me more of a giant fire tit with a blue nipple flickering on top, dancing like a hot lascivious tongue. Perfect. I liked that better. I grinned, watching the Flaming Tit of Rejection collapse into a smoldering ash heap, feeling lighter but not entirely good.

For years, I'd tried everything to sell my writing—large and small publishers, agents, contests in weekly newspapers. I'd written novels and short stories experimenting with every genre. I'd tried different names, different genders, even a different sexual orientation. Nothing worked. About the only thing I hadn't tried was selling my soul to the Devil, a fad that had peaked with *Faust* in the nineteenth century but had seriously declined in favor with intellectuals ever since, despite being the current rage with CEOs and accountants. Now it was astrology's turn. My horoscope that morning urged me to unburden past failure in order to open myself to future possibilities. It wasn't the first time I'd received such enlightened advice from the stars. It was, however, the first time I experienced an epiphany about my distinctive letterhead collection. What was I doing hoarding 878 rejection slips anyway? I'd been dutifully packing and moving them time and time again as if they were precious treasures or some pet albatross I shouldn't leave behind. Ritually burning them seemed a better idea the more I thought about it. As a final gesture of release, I also decided to sprinkle the ashes with holy water. Holy water I'd transport inside my gold Cross pen, I concluded. The symbolism would be perfect.

I passed the Church of the Blessed Sacrament every day on my way home, four blocks before my preferred neighborhood watering hole—The Devil's Detour. I spent enough time there to order "the usual" whenever I walked in, day or night. I liked the bar's casual seedy atmosphere, mixed clientele, and walking proximity to my slum studio behind O'Henry's Cashbox Pawn and Jewelry. I especially loved the divine irony and devilish wit of the bar's name apropos of the Blessed Sacrament. Once the bonfire tit completely self-immolated and I'd doused it with the holy water, I planned to walk back three city blocks for some elbow genuflection to toast my newfound freedom.

Earlier that day, after pulling in front of the cathedral, I'd sat in my car deciding if I really wanted to do it. Although my lapsed Catholic parents believed Catholic theology was a Big Crock in an Einsteinian universe, they'd also taught me to respect other people's beliefs. I really didn't want to offend anyone, but I also really wanted the water. Fortunately, when I did finally duck through a massive wooden door set between two Gothic stone spires, no one was around. I quickly dunked my gutted pen into the holy water grotto, covered both ends with fingers, and hurried back to my car, driving the rest of the way home one-handed.

It was perfect—the perfect instrument for anointing ash. I wielded my mighty gold pen as a magic wand flicking holy water against a huge nemesis, making the smoldering ash pop and sizzle in a satisfying way. Ritual complete, I reassembled my magic pen and headed to the bar.

I'd just started my third drink when she slid onto the stool next to me, barely dressed in a light-blue halter top tied by a string behind her back. Blown-out, faded jeans with shredded holes front and back revealed natural cotton tights that hugged her butt with soft, sensual suggestion. In front, the jeans cut below a navel pierced with a silver stud. Dressed so provocatively, she sat straddling the metal barstool, legs wide, feet tucked under the rungs, bare back arched, right hand holding a cold sweaty margarita, two slender fingers on her left playing with a red plastic straw. Her hair was raven black, long and wavy; her eyes, dark and beguiling.

Seeing what I was drinking—a Bombay martini with three olives—she offered to make me the best martini I'd ever tasted. At first I wasn't sure I was up to the obvious sizzle. On the other hand, I informed myself, gulping another fiery blast of cold gin, how often do you run into so much fire aimed straight at you like a heat-seeking missile? Besides, the whole point of my earlier ritual was opening myself to something new. What else could I do but accept?

We left the downtown bar and drove through the city to an imposing stone castle high on a hill. Cloistered among towering trees, the amazing stone anachronism sat barely visible above an encroaching swell of urban sprawl, its turrets, stone archways, gardens, and glass-domed atriums sequestered from the tide of modern development by a massive, twelve-foot stone wall along the bottom edge of its sloping property.

We drove up a long winding driveway to the castle's entrance and parked. A pair of heavy wooden doors similar to the Blessed Sacrament's opened as we approached them, climbing a broad stone staircase guarded by two carved griffins. The doors closed silently behind us and I instantly felt a delicious sense of removal from the noisy ugliness of modern life outside. My peace, however, was immediately challenged by a black panther prowling the marble foyer, its cold, gold eyes burning straight at me. The large sleek cat growled once before gliding away down a shadowy hall lit by oil lamps flickering in black metal sconces.

"Nice pet," I commented.

"There's more," she said calmly. "They add something, don't you think?"

Oh, certainly a free-roaming black panther added something: the distinctive aura of animal strength and speed, raw chthonic power tinged with the possibility, even certainty, of danger. I began wondering who my hostess was beyond her sleek, attractive appearance.

Undaunted, however, I floated after the creamy insinuation of her ass working through torn jeans to a room that duplicated the bar we'd just left. Totally familiar reflections of liquor bottles, bar glasses and neon beer signs glittered in a long mirror behind the bar. It was a perfect copy of Home Sweet Home—The Detour.

She moved behind the bar to fix my martini.

"So why the heavy medicine?" she asked, dark eyes staring as she placed a chilled glass of clear, cold heat in front of me. "The forlorn look? Sagging shoulders? What's wrong?"

I took a fortifying sip of the best martini I'd ever tasted and launched into my entire Pitiful Writer Story, the complete No-Luck Saga, the whole unabridged tale of Hovel-Dwelling and Suffering for Art's Sake.

"So it's success you want? Success as a writer?"

"Sure. I've been slamming against that wall for years now."

"Maybe I can help."

Considering the size of her hovel, she no doubt had resources.

"Want to read something?"

"No, thank you. You need something fresh. A unique point of view. For instance...how would you like to make love with the Devil?"

Sucking an olive, I inhaled sharply and almost choked. Fortunately, it dislodged on my first cough.

"What? The ugly dude with horns? No! No, I don't think so, thank you. Not my type. Sorry. No way. You, on the other hand..." I paused to lift my glass, toasting her. "You, I'd consider.... Hell! I'd more than consider, I'd be thrilled!"

"What if I told you I *am* the Devil?"

"But I thought he was a guy."

"Common misconception."

"And really ugly."

"I leave that to your opinion."

"With eyes flashing fire."

"Oh, I can manage eye flashing just fine. Most people consider it sexy. How about you?"

I checked her eyes. Dark. Intense. Flashing a hot smoldering heat. It was definitely sexy.

"Cloven hooves?"

She held up both hands and stretched her long, slender fingers, several with silver rings on them.

"Just these."

"How about the tail?"

She turned around and bent over. Cotton tights visibly stretched tighter through two large holes below both buttcheeks. It was a lovely ass—shapely, sculpted to perfection. The female ass—enticing, delicious, delectable, the most tender rump of revelry and redemption: All in One.

"Oh, my! No tail there!" I admired. "You sure you're the Devil?"

"I'll let you decide. More gin?"

I'd already guzzled her perfect martini unusually fast and almost said yes. But what if I *was* talking to the Devil? What if I had, in fact, unknowingly mixed ritual metaphors and inadvertently sent up unintended smoke signals? When I declined, she glanced at me quickly, then smiled.

"Shall we move on then?"

I grinned, feeling heat between my legs throbbing hard where you notice most, just watching the sizzle behind the bar, sensing the implied power and sex in every flick of her wrist, waist bend, hair toss, cigarette pull, and pursing of her lips as she sucked tequila through a red straw.

"Sure.... Let's move on."

We continued down the long hall, walking past endless closed doors with muffled, barely audible music playing inside, until we reached a large atrium. My hostess led me inside a lush paradise of tropical trees and exotic flowering plants. Perpetually trickling water created a sense of energy and tranquility both. Haunting, hypnotic flute music played softly in the background.

I followed her along a sandy path to a stone grotto of clear water with white mist steaming from its calm, shiny surface. She leaned against a large rock near the grotto's edge.

"Shall we?"

She began unlacing her shoes. I did the same with mine. Then she slowly unbuttoned her jeans...peeling away her creamy tights...releasing the halter top. Damn! What a sight!

Winding her hair behind her head, she secured it with a wooden barrette that appeared suddenly in her hand. A strand of curly hair escaped the restriction and hung down her left temple. Spectacularly nude, she eased down natural stone steps into the water and stood waist-deep, slowly spooning water over her neck and shoulders, scooping it with cupped palms, trickling it down her arms and breasts. Smiling back over the curve of her bare shoulder, she invited me to join her.

"It's wonderful. Come on in."

It looked wonderful. Thrilling, in fact. I'd never imagined the Devil looking so goddamned beautiful, so radiantly irresistible, naked in the steamy semi-dark.

Removing my clothes, I stepped down into the water. The temperature was perfect. Fine sand tickled the bottom of my feet and squished through my toes. I couldn't help smiling as I waded toward her.

"Feel good?" she asked, turning toward me.

"It's perfect."

She began spooning water over my shoulders and arms, watching with a faintly wicked smile, eyes hooded, as it trickled over breasts and nipples that instantly puckered and swelled. Stepping closer, she traced her fingertips across both collarbones, slid down both armpit curves to my tits, caressing them with watery palms before dialing hard engorged nipples gently between thumbs and forefingers, dialing for home, dialing for down under.

I inhaled sharply and arched back, barely able to stand the intense ache surging through my body. Enjoying the sensations, I opened my mouth and released whatever sounds—mostly soft laughter—wanted to escape. When I felt her lips kiss the side of my neck, I gasped.

"We could make a deal, you know," she whispered in my ear.

"What kind of deal?" I whispered back, fighting the jellying weakness in my knees.

"I could tell you stories."

"What kind of stories?"

"The kind that sell. You'll have all the success you want."

She was kissing the other side of my neck, sending shivers down my back.

"What'll it cost me?"

Moving along my chin, soft lips traveled to my lips.

"Your soul, of course."

She was kissing me so sweetly, it was hard to imagine I was kissing the Devil.

"My soul."

Her tongue lightly touched my lips, requesting entrance. Eagerly, I took her inside, tongue meeting tongue, sucking in and pushing out with mounting hunger and desire.

"Your soul," she repeated, stepping closer until our bodies touched, tit to tit, pelvis to pelvis, submerged pubic hair tickling thighs, slipping toward V-groove heat.

It was a novel experience: selling my soul to the Devil. An incredible experience. Electrifying. I tilted my head farther back and purred like a cat—one happy pussy—rocking my crotch on her thigh as she kissed and nuzzled under my chin, down my neck.

Taking my hand, she led me further into the grotto toward where the sound of falling water got stronger, to a rocky waterfall behind a dense patch of tall ferns. Smoky torches flickered among trees as we approached the falls, creating long shadows in feathery mist still rising off the water.

When we reached the ferns, the Devil smiled coyly and said, "I've reinvented the waterbed. Care to see?"

"Love to," I mumbled.

"Slide in on your stomach. It's more fun that way."

She took one step up. Water cascaded down exposed buttcheek curves and the hot slit between them. Silently I whistled at the incredible sight that vanished too quickly inside the lacy ferns. Within the shadowy dimness, I heard splashing water and the Devil calling: "Come on! You'll love it! I promise!"

I plunged head first, sliding on my stomach across sheeting water over soft chamois cloth, water spraying my face, laughing with surprise as I glided toward my hostess. The Devil lay on her back, both hands holding her hair, elbows in the air, water splashing her head and lovely shoulder curves, covering tits and jutting hipbones that rose from streaming water like four lost islands in need of discovery. Tilting her head back made water rush over her face, eyes closed, mouth open, gurgling, spitting, laughing. Long, wet, black hair swirled around her shoulders. The sight was totally awesome and beautiful. I paddled toward to her.

Opening her eyes, grinning, she said, "What do you think?"

"It's fabulous! I want one!"

"You've got one...right here...forever."

She reached out a long arm and pulled me down, kissing me hard but playfully, laughing, before rolling me over into the water, soaking my hair. Still kissing, we rolled again, back and forth, over and under, slipping, sliding, splashing, laughing until our breath came short and fast, and the energy inside the fern fort crackled with sex and intensity.

Ending on top, I parted her legs with my thigh, slid slowly down her long body, kissing her stomach, dipping inside a watery, studded navel before continuing to her pubic mound, where black hair waved underwater like moss in a gentle tide. It was so dark, mysterious and hypnotically beckoning, I took a deep breath and plunged head first into deep-sea diving. *Vive* Calypso!

Nibbling and sucking, my mouth the mouth of an angelfish, I darted my tongue through wavy moss to nuzzle and tease, releasing air bubbles on her swollen clit until she yelled.

"Oh, my God!" the Devil exclaimed.

Still nuzzling, I slid my arms around her butt and rocked back on my knees, pulling her to my mouth, resting her ass on my tits.

"Je-sus!" she exclaimed again. "I haven't done it like this lately! Wait!" A pile of purple pillows appeared from nowhere to support her back. "That's better. Continue. Please!" she urged, eyes hooded with pleasure as she rocked her pelvis in rhythm to unseen drums that beat louder and faster, accompanied by louder gasps and moans.

Cupping my hands in water, I sprinkled her hot, red, cunt mouth with rainbow-colored drops like tiny gems that glistened in her short wet hairs. Pale moonlight beamed through a high glass ceiling overhead as I began retrieving those gems with my tongue, exploring slippery vulva crevasses before plunging as far inside the Devil's Sinkhole as my tongue could reach.

"Oh, myGod myGod myGod!" chanted the Devil.

Lapping droplets of dew—the Devil's Dew—hot, silky, creamy smooth, I sucked mouthfuls, tongue probing, hands massaging double circles in soaked bush, pressing her clit, doing abracadabra magic until the trick worked and the Devil spasmed, arched, and exploded: "JesusHolyHellthat's—too— good!"

Totally aroused, I came myself just hearing her. I had to yell too, I was so thrilled, and the night was just beginning.

"Watch...the water flow changes," the Devil said minutes later as we lay side by side, hot bodies touching in warm water that poured down the rock wall at the bed's head; it stopped suddenly as waves began surging upward in a tidal rhythm that echoed through the grotto.

"Whoa! *From Here to Eternity!*" I laughed as a wave flooded between my legs, swept over my stomach and breasts to my neck, then retreated, thousands of watery fingertips slipping down my body before a new wave surged, covering us again.

She rolled over, smiled her same wicked smile, and slid on top of me. Pleasure shocks ricocheted through my body, matching the surf pounding over us. She stared into my eyes, radiating an intense hypnotic heat that took my breath away, serious for a change.

"You can reconsider, you know."

"Reconsider what?" I asked faintly, not wanting to think.

"Our bargain. It's not final yet."

"Oh... When's it final?"

"You'll know."

She began sucking and tonguing a nipple. I moaned and grabbed her head in my hands as she teased the other. I opened wide, wanting her whole body between my legs, wanting her to fuck me. Absolutely. Totally. It was exactly what I wanted, what my body ached for as she continued kissing and licking everywhere through the rushing water.

"I—uh..."

"What?" she stopped and looked up at me, smiling, knowing.

"I—uh..."

"Go ahead. Say it. Tell me. I like hearing it."

Another wave crashed against the graceful slope of her bare back, rocking her body against mine, pushing her pelvic bone against my crotch. My eyes closed, heavy with desire. Another wave. More rocking. I opened wider, wanting her badly, hands sliding to her shoulders, pulling her closer.

"Fuck me! Please!" I shouted, laughing, running my toes up the watery back of her legs.

"You sure?"

Another wave rocked her against me.

"Oh, yeah!" I answered, tightening my legs, pressing up against her.

Instantly, I felt a hard jelly tip teasing inside me on the next surge in, jazzing my G-spot. I splayed my legs wide as she rocked farther making my cunt spasm and grab. I slid my hands the length of her body, feeling the leather strap across the hollow of her lower back before grabbing her cheeks and pulling her in hard, rocking, fucking in the tide and moonlight. Drums pounded. Want and fire intensified inside as she rocked, pushing faster in and out.

I dug my fingers into her butt as I arched up to slam against her before rolling over so I could ride on top, stroking cunt and clit simultaneously. I continued banging up and down until I yelled then laughed and giggled, gasped, then yelled some more, loving it—the fucking—bucking on and on! Ahhhhhhhhhhhhhhh—Yes!

I thought the next morning I'd feel terrible, having drunk martinis, fucked with the Devil, and sold my soul the previous night. Surely, I'd be paralyzed by some wretched emotion: shame, guilt, horror, dread, panic. But no. I felt remarkably well, replete, satisfied, happy, luxuriously stretching in the warm sunlight that dappled me through a lacy canopy of tall ferns, listening to water trickle melodiously throughout the grotto.

When I found my hostess later, sipping champagne, reclined on a red velvet divan under a massive oak branch on a grassy slope outside, I asked about the bad part.

"What bad part?"

"The bad part that comes from selling your soul."

"Why? You starting to worry?"

"No. Surprisingly. Not yet. I feel too good to worry. I like it here."

"I thought you might."

So far, the Devil has kept her promise. Every time we make love, I find myself afterward wandering to the same room—a medieval chamber lit with large candles dripping molten wax puddles. Dusty books line tall dark walls surrounding strange ornate symbols on a polished wooden floor. I sit in the same chair always, straight-backed with ornately carved arms, upholstered in royal blue. A shiny black raven appears as soon as I enter, flying through a high window to perch by my shoulder while I write without effort, seemingly entranced, pen flying, story after story.

For this I made my Faustian deal with the Dark One, waiting for the day when the horrible bill comes due, when a profound evil, cruelty, deception, or unkindness is finally revealed to my utter horror and dismay. So far, however, my tantalizing hostess remains beguiling, whimsical, ever surprising, and, at her very worst, devilishly elusive.

Thus I live, remaining at the Devil's beck and call, anytime day or night. Even now I hear her in the Zen garden with its sweet, pink cherry blossoms and natural steam bath. Or perhaps she's in the Turkish room of giant pillows, scented oils, and suggestive music beginning a slow, sinuous, sexy rise to dervish climax. Or she's stark naked and picnicking in a wooded glen as in a Manet painting, blades of tender grass tickling the backs of her knees and gently insinuating between her legs, waiting for me to find her. Very soon now, I must leave my high turret window to answer her call wherever she may be—I have no choice—and the soft, singing crack of her eternal whip. Poor me. Poor, poor me....

Last Pan of the Season
Debra Hyde

I hate mornings like this, mornings when you wake up so horny that if your cunt was a hand, it'd be a clenched fist. I hate it because I can't relieve myself of the tension, even rising early the way I do. I can't afford to. I can't lose time to the sun.

So I throw on some clothes, grab socks and my work boots, and quietly steal into the kitchen. I don't want to wake Annie; she can sleep for a time yet. What needs to be done can start with me.

A quick breakfast of toast and coffee, and I'm out the door and down the stairs. Our shop is a stone's throw away, the walk-in basement under our old Pennsylvania German row house. Good thing it's close—time's fleeting. Today's our last chance to work meat magic.

Magic, that's what I feel every time I jiggle the key free of the lock and step into our shop. The white plaster walls, the glass-front refrigerators and deli display cases: I've known them all my life. They haven't changed an iota. But what has changed is that it's mine. All mine. Finally.

I go into our workroom and run the tap. Water sputters and the pipes rattle, and as I wash my hands I know I'll have to call the plumber soon. We were lucky we made it through the winter with just air in the pipes.

Later, though. That can wait until later. I've got pots to boil, pans to rinse and meat to grind, and I've got to get it done before the chill of the morning fades.

I fill two big pots with water—it's the first step to the last pan of the season—and while I wait for it to boil, I wash loaf pans. Not bread loaf sized, but longer, long enough that a "half a panhaas" would roughly match your average banana bread.

At the sink, I think about our meats. Do we have meats! Dinner sausage, plump and filling. Smoked sausage, perfect for stews. Sweet bologna and Lebanon bologna, lunchmeats fermented to a rich, smoky perfection. Ring bologna so good you'll never again eat that crap they try to pass off as meat at that kiosk in the mall.

I think about how busy this weekend will be. Everyone knows the weather's warming fast, bringing scrapple season to its annual end. I've planned a third more meat than usual, anticipating the demand.

While the pots work their way to the boiling point, I clean shop, sweeping the floor and wiping countertops. It's mindless work, so mindless that my thoughts wander to Annie. Sweet, luscious Annie.

I think about how her slip-of-a-willow body bows before my trunk of a butch body; about the softness of her breasts, their petite fullness, their always-ready-to-respond nipples, nipples that I know have gone hard when I've not yet touched them just by the way Annie moans. Then there's that soft, sparse tuft of hair between her legs and the sweet cleft that leads me to her delicious wetness. I think about the bud of joy that perches there, waiting for me to coax Annie's pleasure.

God, she's beautiful. From head to toe and everything in between, Annie is beautiful. I never tire of wanting her.

And I want her so badly that it's all I can do to put the pig's knuckles to the pot when the water finally boils, Then I dash to the house, climb back into bed, and slip my arms around her. By the time I start to roam her body, the crotch of my jeans has grown downright damp.

Later, when I pack and tuck myself back together, I think of my wet jeans. I tell myself we'll have a lot more than just the smell of cooking meat rising in our midst. I pat my crotch and smile, already set for more.

Making scrapple is a long process. After the meat boils for a couple of hours, you have to remove it from the water and let it cool thoroughly. You set the water aside—it's now a reserve broth—and you find other stuff to do. Typically, I work in the smokehouse while Annie contacts various farmer families for goods that today's younger generations don't have time to make from scratch anymore: chowchow, pickled red beet eggs, pepper cabbage, and shoofly pies (dry- or wet-bottomed, but let's not go there).

It's late morning before Annie and I actually get things going, but once the meat's cool, we swing into action. I strip the pig's knuckles and chop up lots of lean pork shoulder. Annie measures and mixes the cornmeal and spices, paying special attention to the pepper. With our recipe, it all comes down to the pepper.

I struggle to concentrate on my work. It's not easy with Annie so close. I'm aware of every nuance of her body as she moves. Her breasts dance as she stirs the dry measures and the cool air of our shop keeps her nipples enticingly erect. Even the dress she wears tempts me, clinging suggestively in all the right spots. I'm all too aware that I'm only three steps away. It wouldn't take much for me to come behind her, stick my hand under that hem, and find a lush, warm paradise.

Annie's so magically distracting that I almost cut the wrong species of knuckle. But not a moment too soon, I finish my chopping and return the meat to the broth. Impishly, I wonder if Grandpa Nonnie ever felt distracted by Grandma Nonnie when they made meat here in the shop in their younger days. Did he ever drop his work to cop a feel? It's a little hard to imagine, what with their conservative Lutheran mores, but then they were married for over sixty years and Grandpa never lost that twinkle in his eyes for his wife.

We're generations apart, Grandpa Nonnie and me, and that distance made it hard for me to become a butcher. I had to convince him that a woman could do the job. Especially a woman like me—stout and butch, and pigheaded as any man.

Well, stout and pigheaded, anyway. See, with Grandpa's generation, it does no good to mention the butch part.

But butchering: Why, butchering was men's work. Grandma was only a helpmate until enough male offspring could pull their weight in the business. And my working for Grandpa Nonnie only happened because I nagged him into it after my last brother left for college. Eventually, I got the store, but only by default: no man in the family ever stepped forward to take over; Grandpa finally became too frail to keep going; time ran its course.

Annie turns the burners down a notch, ready to add the dry mixture to the broth. I lift the bowl over the pot while she pushes the contents in. It's close work and I can smell her hair from here. Its florals mingle with the dry scent of peppered cornmeal and the rising steam of meat, merging into an enticing aroma of promise. It's as if her body promises one thing while the meat mixture promises another. I become hungry for both.

But I must curb my appetites for a few minutes more. We must watch over this newly-mixed brew like shepherds tending their flock.

This is the delicate stage of making meat.

We stir, turning the heat lower and lower still, striving for the right temperature. We'll know it when we reach it: the mixture will slow cook on its own without scorching.

When it reaches the correct low heat, we cover the pots. I reach for Annie and take her in my arms. We have twenty minutes.

I kiss Annie roughly, hurriedly. I want to get to the good stuff quickly, but I move slowly enough to appreciate how her slender tongue flickers against the flat of my broad beast of a tongue. I pull her shirt up as I kiss her, stuffing it under her armpits to free her breasts. Her breath catches in her mouth as the air hits them, she moans when my hands cup them and caress them. All the while, we kiss.

God, her tits are wonderful. They fit perfectly in my hands, their flesh just soft enough to give under my fingers, each nipple so hard that I'm tormented with deciding whether to keep kissing Annie's mouth or move to those rosy tips.

The nipples win out and I'm greedy when I latch on. I suck one hard, hungrily, while teasing the other with mischievous pinching. Annie moans and her hands go to my hair. She tries to run her fingers through it, wants to wrap it around her grip, but it's too short. I'm too butch.

Annie presses in as close as she can get to my hunched-over body. She wants to grind against me, she's so horny, but I'm sucking and pinching and I want to feel her writhe a little while longer before I go lower. I torment the other nipple with nibbles that progress toward biting.

"Oh, please!" she pleads, barely able to speak, she's so ripe!

I pull away from her nipple. "Is that *Oh please you want more?* Or *Oh please make me come?*"

Annie whimpers. It's too hard a choice.

I make it for her. I slide down her torso, lifting her skirt as I travel. As I kneel before her, her sweet cleft greets me. Full and inviting, it's swollen with fleshy desire.

My own cunt pulses at the sight of Annie's arousal and as I put my tongue to her clit, her wet aroma overtakes my senses, mixing with the wafting smell of meat that simmers to perfection.

I slip two fingers into Annie as I tongue her and find that she's simmering to perfection as well. Her slit is slippery, welcoming, and her clit rises hard against my tongue. I work my fingers steadily and she opens wide for me. I slip a third finger in, filling her, all the while savoring the smell of her, of scrapple, of all things cooking.

Annie pants heavily, and I know I'll being able to bring her off quickly. My fingers are a steady pressure inside her. My tongue on her clit is like a hummingbird at a flower.

Then it happens—Annie comes. And when Annie comes, my whole world stops.

I hold my breath as she pitches over the edge, her cunt grabbing at my fingers, her legs shaking and weakening, her voice shrill with surrender. I keep my tongue busy to prolong her orgasm. Sometimes, if I do it right, I can make her throb inside and quiver outside for what seems like forever—times like now.

When she's done, when I've pulled the last contraction from her, I rise up and take my dear Annie in my arms. I kiss her again, bringing a taste of her success to her lips.

While she savors it, I reach for the stove and turn off the burners. It's time to let everything cool. But only slightly.

Now the busiest part of the meat making happens. We have to spoon the thickened slop into the pans. Because our pots are large, we can't simply pour it out the way you might with a small, home-cooked batch. Because we don't use preservatives—and this is why we can't do scrapple year-round—we have to ladle quickly and cool the scrapple before it can spoil.

For all the heat we cooked up between us in the kitchen, now we set about this task as if we hadn't had a libidinous thought in our heads all day. Silently, we work as a team, efficiently ladling spoonful after spoonful from our pots until each pan holds the requisite amount of meat mixture. It's like pouring concrete in microcosm.

When we've filled a dozen pans, we "bounce" them. We slam each pan a couple of times against the countertop to get the air out, to help the scrapple settle into the thick brick it's meant to become. Bouncing is a noisy process—more of a pounding really—but when you see the scrapple close ranks around a busted air pocket, you know a good pan is in the making.

We pour and bounce three times before we're done and, just before we start cleaning up, I stick the last pan of scrapple into the fridge.

"Why are you doing that?" Annie asks.

"You'll see."

I say no more and Annie knows me well enough to guess I have something up my sleeve. Well, something up somewhere, that is.

We do the dishes. Annie scrubs, I dry and set away. That way, I can ogle her while she concentrates on the spic-and-span of cleanup. I admire how her lean arms flex as she scours, how her breasts jiggle while she works. I love how that dress of hers sculpts the curves of her body, accentuating her finest features. I love how hot she looks in the kitchen, even when she wipes the sweat from her brow.

Especially when she wipes the sweat from her brow.

God, I'm right back where I was when I was stripping meat off the bone and, again, I want to interrupt her. I want to take her eyes off her work and put them on me. I want to see them flutter shut when I play with her nipple, when I press my thigh between her legs. I want to kiss and caress her into an arousal so obvious that she'll beg for relief.

But I can't. Not yet. I have something else in mind. Patience, I tell myself, is a virtue.

But one that, soon enough, I can turn to vice. Annie finishes washing and empties the sink of soapy water. I check the cooling pans. They're almost ready for the refrigerator, which means the solitary pan I stashed there should be far enough along. Good thing, too, because I'm ready. I can't wait another minute. I take the pan from the fridge and, bringing it to the countertop, inspect it. It's cool, it can't burn, and its contents haven't fully set either.

Perfect.

"Come here, baby."

The words are telling. Annie furrows her eyebrows as she complies. She knows I'm about to initiate something.

"Whatever are you—?"

She doesn't finish her question because I grab her by the hair and drag her over to the pan.

"Put your hands in it," I tell her.

"Huh?"

"Like the Hollywood Walk of Fame."

"Oh."

Perplexed, surprised, Annie complies. She puts her hands into the pan, then giggles, "It's squishy!"

"Just like you're going to be, baby," I predict from behind her.

Annie sighs when she hears me unzip my pants. As she awaits what I'm packing, I raise her dress up and push her panties to one side. Deftly, I slip it to her. Eagerly, she takes it and within a few strokes, she fulfills my prediction.

God, I love fucking Annie. The wet sounds of her cunt as it slobbers all over my big dick, the way she squirms and squeals when I grind my meat—damn, if it doesn't make me feel beastly.

But good lover that I am, I reach around and find her clit. I match my strokes, hand and dick, so they work in tandem. I want to bring her off big-time and, when I'm done, I'll make her kneel and suck my cock. I'll enjoy watching her mouth at work. I'll let her burrow her scrapple-covered fingers under the harness, find my clit, and do me one better.

Such thoughts make me lose it and I ram Annie, hard and fast. She squirms as if it's too much for her.

"Come on, baby. Take it," I urge.

Banging her this hard, it's difficult to do her clit just the way she likes it, but the rhythm has its own reward: it's so wild, it can make Annie come. Guttural sounds escape her now, and I know that with a touch more intensity, she'll come.

I reach for her hair. I get just enough in my hand to pull her head back, to bend her back toward me. She's pinned now, between my hands and my dick. It's rough. It strains her, I can tell.

That's when the most wonderful thing happens: Annie's entire body shudders. Orgasm rakes her—not her clit or her hole, but her entire body. The strain is so intense, so overwhelming that she has nowhere to go with it except into orgasm. As much as she can, Annie bucks beneath me.

All the while, her hands are still in the pan.

As her orgasm subsides, I slow my pace. I let my grip go and allow Annie to relax. I watch my dick work back and forth. Juice covered, it glistens magnificently. It's all so leisurely now.

My mind drifts, and next thing I know I'm thinking about stomach casings. Yes, stomach casings. Now that scrapple season's ending, folks will want their natural casings. They'll want to cook their meat and mashed potatoes in them to make what we call Pig's Stomach. If we're being honest, that is. When we're serving it up to squeamish guests, we fake it and call it French Turkey.

Stomach casings. I can't believe I'm thinking about stomach casing. I shake the thought away. After all, it's still scrapple season and I have Annie quivering before me. I want to enjoy the last pan of the season—and all who come with it.

A Bushy Tale

Jean Roberta

Louanne and Thomasina (who could stand being called Tommy but not Tommy-girl) were getting acquainted over leisurely cups of coffee on the patio of Café Mocha. They had been introduced by their mutual friend Mick, a dyke DJ who enjoyed watching women on a crowded dance floor, and occasionally tried to match them up. The spring weather was bright and breezy, coaxing all the trees and plants in the neighborhood into showing their first trusting leaves.

"Do you like your job?" Louanne asked Tommy, whose arm muscles impressed her. Louanne imagined being wrestled to the floor, and it made her blush. She had been told about Tommy's sexual tastes, but decided to stick to safe topics.

"Oh, yes," Tommy smiled. She was noticing the way sunlight brought out the reddish-gold highlights in the wood-brown hair that brushed Louanne's shoulders. Tommy wanted to stroke it, gather it up in one hand, and pull it to bring Louanne's mouth closer to hers. She decided to focus on the conversation.

"I work for the Humane Society, you know. When we get complaints about animal abuse, I go check them out. If I find that, uh, the animals show signs of abuse, I bring them back to the shelter and we take care of them. I like watching them recover."

Louanne beamed, and Tommy gave her an answering smile. "I know what you mean," Louanne assured her, even though she seriously doubted whether anyone really knew what anyone else meant. "I've been a volunteer counselor on the sexual assault and abuse line for a few years. Dealing with women who've been abused is hard, but it's good to see them getting their lives back, little by little."

"You sound like a good counselor," remarked Tommy, thinking that some delicate flirting would not be taken amiss. She noticed that Louanne's face was classically beautiful, and almost innocent of makeup.

Louanne looked charmingly abashed. "I just listen," she explained modestly. "That's all we can do. I just wish there wasn't such a need."

"I bet your clients are glad they have you to talk to. Do you have any other job?" Tommy persisted.

This implication that Louanne had no income and was looking for a Sugar Mama made uncomfortable prickles rise up her neck. "I've worked in the library for eight years," she snapped, sounding colder than she intended. "Books are my life," she added. "I love helping people do research. You never know what you'll find when you start digging for information."

"I'm sure," laughed Tommy, stretching. She had an easy, contagious laugh which she sometimes used to hide her quick, contagious temper. She had heard the chill in Louanne's voice, and wondered if the book-lover thought the animal-lover was stupid. Tommy hated being patronized.

She reached for the front page of the local newspaper, which lay neglected on an adjoining table. "What do you think of this?" Tommy asked Louanne, referring to the headline about government cutbacks to libraries and educational institutions.

Louanne took the paper from Tommy's hand, letting her fingers linger. Tommy was slightly surprised, and looked thoughtfully at the other woman's dark, troubled eyes.

Louanne was looking at the front page. "Arggh," she sputtered. "The case of the South End Rapist. He's only being tried for the latest one, but we've heard about him for years. The cops are idiots."

"Have you met the victims?" asked Tommy. This was getting so interesting that she was only vaguely aware that her words might be politically incorrect.

"Not the one he's being tried for," sighed Louanne. She couldn't take her eyes off the article. "Who writes this stuff? Everything he did is described. He tied her up and forced her to—there was vaginal and anal."

"Male bastard," Tommy remarked calmly. "Why they like to do it without consent is beyond me." Louanne noticed that she had the bright blue eyes and freckled face of a healthy farm girl, but her energy was edgy and urban. Louanne decided not to think about consent.

"She's a teenage girl who met him in a chat room on the Internet," Louanne pointed out. "When will women and kids learn how dangerous that is?"

Tommy decided to play devil's advocate. "Do you really think that's more dangerous than finding a pen pal through a club that's been set up to bring people together, or even meeting someone at work or through a friend? Reaching out to a stranger always involves a risk because ya never know. And no one can promise you that someone else is perfectly safe." She paused. "Everyone wants something," she mused.

"Everyone," agreed Louanne. Tommy noticed a trace of bitterness in the set of her mouth. "But not everyone is an asshole."

"Doing it to someone who doesn't want it seems stupid to me," Tommy assured her companion. "I can't see what guys get out of that. But desire isn't a simple thing. Sometimes people don't know what they want until they see it, feel it, taste it."

The two women looked at each other for a heartbeat. Tommy reached for Louanne's hand, and it was not pulled away. Tommy heard a soft, answering sigh. "But don't some things, uh, hurt no matter what?" asked the librarian. She wanted to know.

"Some things," agreed Tommy. "But some kinds of pain are good, you know? And some—activities just need lots of good will and lube." She licked her lips. "And natural wetness. Encouragement. You gotta be willing and eager."

Louanne's eyes flashed, showing a mixture of feelings. "Eagerness isn't always appreciated," she countered. "Willing women get called some ugly names."

Tommy turned and squeezed Louanne's hand. "I have the greatest respect," she assured her, "for sluts."

The shared laughter of the two women resembled an impromptu duet. "Me too," agreed Louanne. "Would you like to show me your collection?"

"Of what?" prompted Tommy.

"Whatever you've got," responded Louanne. "Everyone has a collection of something."

Tommy snickered. "Sure, come to my place to see the sights." They stood up together, and Louanne was revealed to be half-a-head taller than Tommy. The shorter woman looked compact and fit in contrast with Louanne's willowy form and loose-jointed gait.

Tommy drove Louanne to an old brick apartment building that had a certain period charm, and pulled into the parking lot. She helped her date out of the car and herded her, with a warm hand on Louanne's lower back, up a short flight of concrete steps to a heavy wooden door with the name "Fairfield" on it.

In the tile-floored entranceway, Louanne faced a flight of wooden stairs which were graced with a curved black banister. Grasping it for support, she found it slick with layers of old shellac. Louanne was reminded of the 1940s detective novels that she had read as a teenager.

On the first landing, Louanne paused to catch her breath. Tommy circled her waist and pressed her crotch into Louanne's jeans-covered butt. "Need a rest?" Tommy chuckled.

"Just—for a minute," gasped her guest. Embarrassed by her weakness, Louanne moved forward as soon as she felt she could tackle the next flight.

Tommy's apartment was on the third floor, and Louanne was relieved when the number on the door came into view. She stood still, trying not to gasp for air. She didn't want to give the impression of being helpless or out of control.

"Why, babe?" Tommy asked. She smiled coolly. "Why did you climb up all these stairs with me?"

Louanne was taken off guard. "You asked me," she exhaled.

"So do you accept every invitation you get from people you hardly know?"

Louanne filled her lungs, clutching the railing. "Well, you don't seem dangerous." With alarm, she noted the common sense in Tommy's question. Louanne didn't like to consider herself a risk-taker.

"Because I'm a woman? Does that make me trustworthy?" Tommy barked with laughter. "Is that what you believe? Or maybe you think you're safe here with me because it was really your idea."

Tommy stayed behind Louanne, holding her by the waist so that her guest couldn't see her face. "How many times have you advised other women to avoid rushing off into the unknown?" she taunted. "Are you sure you could outrun me if you wanted to?"

This question sounded rhetorical, and Louanne didn't answer it. "Now you're here," Tommy reminded Louanne, her mouth close to her guest's ear. "You've worked so hard to get here that I bet you'd like to stay awhile. Welcome to my cave, honey." Tommy smoothly unlocked her door with one hand and pushed Louanne forward with the other.

Tommy closed the door behind her and ran a hand through Louanne's silken hair. "I like reckless women," Tommy purred. "They're usually bitches in heat."

Tommy calmly unbuttoned Louanne's cheerful checked shirt, exposing a lacy powder-blue bra cupping mounds of pink skin. Louanne sighed from the depths of her lungs—if possible, from her womb. "You want to play, don't you?" grinned Tommy.

"Yup," Louanne muttered. "It's been a long time." She couldn't look Tommy in the eyes.

"You must want a break from books and words," grinned the hostess as though reading her guest's mind. Tommy unzipped Louanne's jeans, and the taller woman pulled them down. "And we both know you can't think clearly when you want something, don't we?" Louanne was speechless, and it made her look younger than usual.

Tommy helped Louanne out of her underwear and threw it aside. Then she wrapped her arms around the naked woman and reached up to kiss her. The gentle pressure increased until Louanne's mouth opened and Tommy's tongue slipped inside. Slipping off her everyday common sense, Louanne moaned. A subtle tremor ran from her tingling scalp to her sweaty feet.

Louanne kicked off her shoes to bring herself closer to Tommy's height, but the difference still made both women feel awkward. Tommy thought of a solution. "Down," she growled playfully into Louanne's hair, pushing her forward with a hand on her back. Louanne slid gracefully to the floor, settling herself on all fours on the cool tiles of the hallway.

The hostess saw the tension that her guest was trying hard to control, and sensed her fear that she was taking an unreasonable risk, the kind that might lead to physical damage or to weeks, months, or years of scalding regret.

"I won't hurt you, honey," Tommy soothed her in the voice she used on frightened animals. "You need someone to take care of you and help you let go. I want to watch you, pretty thing. I won't push you too far. This time." Tommy grabbed a handful of Louanne's damp, messy hair and pulled it away from her face. She let it go and stroked Louanne's head, then her back and her sassy rump.

"Ohh," moaned Louanne. Her captor's touch and her suggestion that their relationship had an educational future were scary and exciting in equal parts. For once, Louanne really didn't know what to say.

Tommy was pleased to note that her captured stray was already losing her human vocabulary, but she wanted a clearer answer. "Okay?" she demanded.

"Okay," agreed the woman on the floor. *For now*, she thought.

"Good girl," gloated the animal-tamer. Her small, strong right hand slid down the crack between Louanne's smooth ass cheeks. Finding her cunt wetter than expected, Tommy pushed two fingers in as far as they could go, pressing one against a spongy cervix. Louanne inhaled sharply. "Bet you didn't think you'd get this much this soon," remarked the genial hostess, adding another finger and pushing rhythmically in and out. She could feel Louanne's startled cunt relax and then squeeze the trespassing digits.

Tommy changed her angle and her tempo. "I'm just getting started, baby," she smirked. "This is just to open you up. You can come any time you want." The words of the seductress had a dramatic effect on Louanne, whose breathing grew much louder. She came in quick, hard spasms, panting.

Both women breathed in unison. "So responsive," praised Tommy, sliding her free hand up to grasp one of Louanne's breasts. She gently withdrew her fingers from their warm home and slid them, one by one, into Louanne's mouth where they were sucked clean.

The woman on the floor wiggled with pleasure and shifted to ease the pressure on her hands and knees. "Oh, Tommy," she sighed. She rose up, and sat back on her heels.

The slap on her butt surprised her into sinking back down. "Stay," commanded Tommy. Her tone was good-natured, but it carried an expectation of obedience. "Stay down," added the pet fancier. "And no words, my bitch." She offered Louanne her hand again, and this time she felt a tentative tongue licking her palm.

Tommy was secretly impressed by her companion's willingness to try on a new role; as she knew from experience, it wasn't always this easy. Images of Louanne in costumes ranging from angel wings attached to straps that framed and supported bare breasts to bunny ears and a fluffy tail flashed through Tommy's mind. At the moment, however, her clit responded best to the challenge of bringing out the basic animal in the woman.

"You must be thirsty," remarked the new owner. "Are you?"

Louanne wiggled her rump and tried barking like the dog she knew best, an old terrier who still lived with her parents. "Stay," repeated Tommy, then she went to the kitchenette to fill a bowl with water.

Louanne prided herself on being a quick study, and she wanted her sensual hunger to be fully satisfied. She wanted to be on close terms with her own animal nature. Animal characters from children's books pranced and jumped and flew through her mind, and did shocking things before she could stop them. She imagined a naughty boy pig pulling down his new blue trousers and mounting a girl pig from behind while the wind blew her skirt up, grinning porcupines mating belly-to-belly, a sleek stallion pushing a huge red cock into a restless, whinnying mare, a mother mouse in an apron cuddling her fashionably-dressed (as of 1910) lady-mouse visitor, a thick-furred, bright-eyed collie lustfully chasing another bushy-tailed dog around a tree. In the real world, Louanne's pussy was so wet that she could feel the cool air of the apartment drying her pubic bush. She was certainly thirsty.

Tommy set the bowl of water on the floor in front of Louanne. By this time, the naked woman found it almost natural to crouch down and lap the cool water with her tongue and lips. "Ahh," murmured her owner approvingly, pulling her hair out of the way and tickling her neck. In some way, the casual familiarity of Tommy's touch felt more intimate than being fucked.

Louanne resisted the impulse to wipe her mouth, and raised her head to show her owner that she was finished drinking. "Good girl," approved Tommy. Louanne felt more refreshed by the praise than by the water. "You could wag your tail if you had one." Louanne shivered. She could guess what was coming.

"Hold still, Lulu." Tommy walked away. In a moment, she returned holding something like a wig on a stick. Watching it closely as Tommy approached her, Louanne saw that it had a bone handle carved in a series of knobs. A thick tail of black and chocolate-brown hair hung from one end.

The handle felt cool and slippery, apparently coated with lubrication of some kind. Louanne's anus was gently held open, and the handle was twisted against it until it slid in. Louanne gasped as the object pushed deeper and deeper into her in a rhythm like a pulse. "Hold it, girl," ordered her trainer, stroking Louanne's cunt lips to calm her. "Squeeze it."

Louanne squeezed. The foreign object in her ass felt uncomfortable, and she wondered if Tommy would pull it out if asked. Louanne didn't want to disappoint by showing herself squeamish, a chicken, a party pooper. She tried not to think about needing to poop.

"Nice, baby!" Tommy remarked, flicking the tail as it twitched with each squeeze of Louanne's anal muscles. The squeezing was nerve-racking, since it sent tremors into her cunt and threatened to send her clit into a frenzy. Louanne sensed that a good dog was not supposed to come while being fitted with a tail.

The tail-twitching lesson was so distracting that Louanne hardly noticed when Tommy left her for a moment. She returned with something else in her hands. "You need a collar," explained Tommy, showing it to her pet. The brown leather of the collar looked new, and a metal tag hung from it. Tommy adjusted the collar to Louanne's neck, giving her room to breathe but making sure that the slight pressure could not be ignored.

The proud owner attached a nylon leash to the loop that held the metal tag. Louanne was now ready to be taken for a walk.

The collared woman wondered what important information was engraved on the tag: an identification number? Record of vaccination for an actual pet? Apparently she was not supposed to know.

"I'll show you your new home, Lulu," Tommy told her. She tugged on the leash, and Louanne crawled after her as quickly and gracefully as she could; she was aware of how awkward she must look. Every movement jostled the hard plug in her ass, which was designed to make itself at home there.

Owner and pet entered a sunny room filled with comfortable, well-worn furniture from the 1950s, including a sofa and chair upholstered in a loud red-and-yellow flowered print. The crawling woman felt as if these large objects were inviting her to pee on them, and she wondered what the penalty for that would be.

"This is the living room," Tommy told her pet, "and you're not allowed in here on your own. This is where I entertain human company." Louanne felt as if Tommy could read her mind, and she felt heat rushing into her face.

The woman's sore knees welcomed the cool linoleum of the kitchen floor. "This is where you'll be fed, baby," her owner explained, "and house-trained."

The bathroom was next. "When you're dirty, you'll get washed in the tub," Tommy told Louanne. "Just like a person," she added. "I like to spoil my creatures, and I expect them to behave. No wiggling, no splashing. And no biting, ever." Louanne barked to show that she understood.

The bedroom came next. From Louanne's point of view, the four-poster bed looked incredibly high. An assortment of shoes and books lay scattered underneath. "If you're very, very good," promised her owner, "you get to sleep at the foot of the bed." Louanne was tempted to climb up immediately, but she held still instead, focusing on her breathing. Tommy casually wrapped the handle of the leash around a bed poster, then reached under her woman to cup her breasts, jiggle and stroke them.

Tommy rolled and squeezed Louanne's nipples until they each looked an inch long. The woman tried howling quietly, wondering if this reaction was acceptable. It was. A small clamp was attached to the pet's left nipple, and she yelped before she could get her reactions under control. Her owner smiled, and attached the other clamp. Louanne whimpered, and Tommy soothed her with long, slow strokes down her belly to her damp bush. An electric current seemed to connect the bone handle in her back entrance and the cruelly nagging clamps on her tits. "I know they hurt," her owner assured her. "It's only for a little while. You'll get used to them."

Crawling back to the kitchen seemed to take twice as long as all the rest of the tour. "Good girl," Tommy encouraged her. "Now you get a snack." She poured half a small bagful of nacho chips onto a plate, and set it on the floor. "There you go."

Louanne didn't see how she could eat the brittle, oddly-shaped chips without using her hands. The challenge appealed to her. She didn't feel hungry, but she wanted a distraction from the pressure on her nipples and in her butt. Most of all, she wanted to show off.

Tommy stood slightly behind her, watching. Louanne lowered her head and reached for a nacho chip with her mouth. Using her tongue and teeth, she was able to bite off a piece so that the rest fell back onto the plate. She chewed, swallowed and returned for more. The pile of yellow chips steadily grew smaller.

Finishing the last chip, Louanne felt full in every way. She realized that the inevitable was happening: her intestines were telling her that she had to take a shit. She whined and rubbed against Tommy's legs, hoping she would understand and show mercy.

"I bet you want to go outside," chuckled the owner. This was a possibility that hadn't occurred to the pet. Tommy grasped her tail and drew it out, twisting it on its way. Louanne was teased, relieved, and worried at the same time. She craved privacy as much as she needed air, and she wondered if she could control her bowels until she could be alone. She wished she had noticed whether there were any large bushes on the grounds outside the building.

Tommy spread a newspaper on the floor. She tapped it with her shoe. "Here, puppy," she grinned.

The woman gazed up, pleading with her eyes. How could she shit on the floor in full view of her new—what? Date? Girlfriend? Domme? Whatever Tommy was to her, Louanne was sure she would be disgusted to the core by the sight and smell of waste emerging from her new pet's protruding ass.

Louanne tried to crawl out of the room. "No, puppy," warned Tommy. She rolled up a section of newspaper and slapped her other hand with it as a warning. Louanne stopped, and shifted from one knee to the other. She looked at the newspaper on the floor, and looked away.

"Bad!" snapped Tommy. The rolled-up newspaper landed resoundingly across Louanne's lower cheeks. "Bad dog!" The newspaper landed again and again in a series of sharp slaps. The pet howled, but did not speak. "Here!" ordered Tommy, pointing to the square of newspaper on the floor.

Louanne was forced to consider the slippery nature of pride, and how much regret she might feel if she gave up now after coming this far. The saying "Pee or get off the pot" had never seemed so relevant.

Blushing hard, Louanne squatted, lowering her thighs as far as possible. She pushed, and felt the humiliating relief of the first turd emerging. It hit the newspaper with a soft thud, and was followed by another. Louanne let go, letting her human shame leave her body with everything else she didn't need. A stream of piss wet the newspaper and spread under Louanne's knees.

"Good girl," Tommy murmured into Louanne's ear, rubbing it. She sounded more impressed than before. Her pet realized that she couldn't use her hands or knees for anything other than holding herself up. They were wet with warm urine.

"Let's get you cleaned up, girl," crooned the pet-lover. Louanne was grateful when Tommy helped her to her feet and let the naked woman lean on her shoulder. Tommy half-carried Louanne into the bathroom.

Tommy turned on the taps, and steaming water gushed into the clean white bathtub. Three small red beads were tossed in, and bubbles quickly formed on the surface. Tommy waited until the water was halfway up the sides of the tub before turning it off. "In you go," she told her pet, patting her reddened butt.

The caress of warm water on Louanne's skin felt exquisite, even though it stung on her lower cheeks and increased the dull ache in her breasts. The woman positioned herself on all fours on the floor of the tub, finding the rubber strips that would prevent her from slipping.

Tommy filled a nylon puff with creamy soap, and spread it over Louanne's back, arms, and legs. She washed her thoroughly, and even shampooed her hair twice, rinsing it carefully under a stream of fresh water. The woman felt herself floating into another dimension.

Turning her head, Louanne was surprised to notice that Tommy had taken off all her own clothes, and she was adjusting a harness that held a flesh-colored dildo in the form of a penis, complete with veins. The word *patriarchal* flashed through the pet's mind, but she was unable to form a sentence around it. Another idea seemed to be forming somewhere on the edges of her consciousness; it seemed like a cloud formed from a vague desire, something that could assume a hard, firm, definite shape later on.

"You want to be bred, don't you, girl?" The question was rhetorical, since Tommy was climbing into the tub behind Louanne, who gave her a welcoming bark. A bizarre image of a rubber doll, fathered by Tommy's cock, popped into Louanne's mind, and she almost laughed aloud.

The device filled her to satisfaction, and she pushed back with enthusiasm. Louanne hadn't realized how desperately she wanted it until it was in, and then she knew how close she was to an orgasm from the first thrust. Tommy fucked her without restraint, and pulled the clamps off her nipples without warning. Louanne howled as she came, holding on to the sides of the tub.

The aftermath was tender. Tommy helped her woman out of the tub, wrapped her in a large, fluffy towel, removed the harness from her own loins, then devoted her full attention to drying every inch of Louanne's clean, glowing body.

"You're good, baby," the new owner told her proudly. "I want to enter you in a show." Louanne stared at her. "When you're ready," Tommy assured her. "You have what it takes to be a show dog. I bet some of the other owners will offer to buy you, but I'm not selling." Louanne seemed to withdraw into herself.

"You all right, baby?" the new owner asked with concern. "You can speak to me." Finding words again was hard; Louanne felt as if she had just been told to communicate in a second language. "Uh—yes, I'm all right," she answered, looking into Tommy's eyes. She was surprised at the depth of sympathy, affection, and anxiety she saw there. *So an owner could feel insecure. Of course.* "I'm fine," Louanne assured her. "I just didn't know there was a club for dogs and their owners."

Tommy was delighted. "You have no idea, honey!" she gushed. "You'll have a lot of fun. Really. And Lulu—" she seemed suddenly shy "—I'm so glad I met you."

The vague idea that had been tugging at Louanne's mind was taking shape. Tommy wanted the bitch in Louanne, and this was not necessarily an obedient pet. The woman, now restored to herself, realized that animals have strength and acute senses, they have teeth for hunting and claws for defense, they have their own ways. They can be intimidating. The humans who seek them out wouldn't really want them to be otherwise. Louanne smiled to herself, wondering why she had ever found it hard to see herself as tough and feminine at the same time.

Louanne rubbed herself against the shorter woman. "Oh yes," she assured her. "I'm sure we'll both get what we want." She vaguely remembered an animal character named Thomasina in a book from her childhood, and the memory tickled her. "You can trust me, honey." Louanne's smile was feral, and Tommy realized that she had finally found the right animal familiar.

Learning the Present Perfect
Andrea Miller

The woman who would substitute for me was already in the classroom waiting to observe my lesson. Hoping to be able to speak to her before the students arrived, I walked quickly down the hallway, my heels clicking on the linoleum. When I entered, the room was in twilight and she was silhouetted against the window. I snapped on the light and she whirled around. Surprise jammed my greetings in my throat. She had long, loose hair, a tight waist, and eyes that flicked from my face to my cleavage. She was a memory on the tip of my tongue, but until she smiled I couldn't quite place her. Then I hurtled back twenty years—to the first day of third grade.

Holly, the new girl, kept turning around in her desk to offer me sweaty pieces of chocolate and toothless grins. Her copper braid was a snake, a tail, a whip. And I thought she was prettier than any of the Mini Pops singers. That day we spent recess jumping rope together, beating a rhythm into the concrete right to pepper. Then a week later we were at my house, with Barbie clothes strewn everywhere.

Unlike many budding dykes I didn't cry when I found Barbie under the tree. I didn't hack her hair off and shove her into my toy box—to the very bottom, crushed beneath trucks and action figures. Instead I was the other kind of budding dyke; I wanted *two* Barbies. Holly and I were simple addition— one plus one equals two. Our Barbies could play together.

First we took their clothes off and snickered at their boobies. Then, deciding one of the dolls was a man, we laid them down, plastic on plastic, and ground their smiles together, making the sounds of pleasure for them. The sound of the letter *M*. The sound of lips smacking.

Autumn wore on and our Barbies rocked faster and faster until spent, then fell away like dead leaves and a new game was born. Of course, one of us pretended to be the man, a bad man who would touch the other in a very good way while she slept. I remember being the woman: lying motionless, my eyes closed as Holly circled my nipples, traced my slit. And I remember being the man: the softness of Holly's corduroys. The smell of her—of clean laundry and apple juice.

In the beginning we didn't remove any clothing and, instead of touching each other with our fingers, we used my rock collection. Small stones, smooth and rough, raked over fabric. But in time we discarded the rocks, our corduroys, and even the pretence of one of us being the man. And then it was just the two of us, trying not to get caught. I knew, almost instinctively, that we weren't allowed to play these games—we weren't allowed, yet I was unable to stop until one night in the spring.

Holly and I were having a sleepover—at my house, because my mother let me shut my door. We finished our licorice and soda, brushed our teeth, and, like good children, went to bed without asking permission to watch one more show. Then in the darkness Holly suggested we do something new, that we grind like the Barbies. Remembering that was the way the

Barbies had had sex, I hesitated. One of the Barbies had been playing the part of Ken, but Holly wasn't suggesting one of us pretend to be a man. I didn't want to have sex with a girl and hadn't, until that moment, realized it was possible. Nonetheless, Holly's idea was irresistible and so I reasoned that if we just stood up and left our panties on then it would be all right— that it wouldn't really be sex.

We hiked up our nightgowns, gripped each other's hips and began to move like two dogs I'd seen at a playground. Her crotch pressing against mine felt good—soft and hard and hot. Yet each thrust reminded me of the Barbies and I began to suspect that even the touching games we played were wrong— a wrong that went beyond Mom getting mad if we got caught.

"I don't want to do this anymore," I said, pulling my nightie down. "We're going to do it with boys soon." Holly whined and I wavered, still feeling a warm throb between my legs. Then, a heartbeat away from my giving in, she used the wrong word. "Can't we just *screw* one more time?" she said, sounding so dirty and grown-up that the blood rushed to my face and I answered with a firm *no*.

That summer I played sick the afternoon of Holly's birthday party and I didn't once invite her over for lunch. Then in the fall we were in different classes and I looked away when I passed her in the halls. Yet, secretly, shamefully, I thought of her on nights I couldn't sleep, and those nights became more frequent as fourth grade melted into fifth and sixth. Tiny hairs sprouted between my legs and it felt as if my swelling hips would split me open. I wanted Holly to stroke my new little fur and I wanted to see what changes had happened under her clothes. But Holly had long since stopped trying to catch my eye and she linked arms with other girls.

"Holly," I finally breathed as students started to file in. "You look different."

"So do you," she grinned. "You look good."

I colored and realized for the first time that all my students were sitting, watching, perhaps noticing that Holly and I were standing too close together. My students—eight in this class— were from across the globe and were here to learn English. "We should start," I said. "Sit wherever you like, Holly."

I hadn't planned the lesson well; I'd been thinking too much about my vacation, about cocktails rimmed with salt and the feel of white sand between my toes. Nonetheless, Holly appeared riveted—her gaze followed me everywhere as she rolled a pen in her mouth, biting and sucking it. She had perfect, glinting teeth and full lips. Nervous, I crossed and recrossed my legs, my thighs slippery with stockings and a surprising wetness.

"Have you ever eaten raw fish? Have you ever stayed up all night?" the students asked me, asked each other. And everything they asked took on another meaning, one thick with secrets. Finally, my hands shaking, I couldn't teach the present perfect anymore. I gave the students instructions for playing a game and I divided them into pairs.

At nine o'clock the class finished and the students trailed out. I picked up the teachers' book and sat down at the long table beside Holly, ready both to catch up and to explain what she should teach for the next week. Holly leaned forward and asked, "So what have you been doing with yourself?" Her expression was serious except for a trace of amusement in the corners of her eyes, and I took that as a sign; it was Holly, after all, who had taught me to recognize flirtation's pretty face. Until that moment I didn't know, however, that I'd ever learned to be so bold.

Instead of answering Holly, I leaned in hard and fast and she followed me—fell into me. Our mouths met with twenty years of urgency, and my tongue, rolling against hers, spoke a kind of apology, an explanation. *The boys I thought we should wait for didn't touch me like you did. I'm sorry I wasn't brave enough. I did desire you. I do desire you.*

Sliding off my chair, I knelt down in front of Holly and explored her thighs. Her fingers raked over my throat, nipples, and spine, and her cunt strained forward, filling the cup of my hand. And even through the layers of her clothes, I could feel a moist heat rising, urging me on. But when I reached for her belt buckle, she pulled back, glancing at the door.

"Don't worry," I said. "The school is closed. Nobody else is here."

Holly relaxed and let me undo her. She wriggled free of her pants and top and then slowly I rolled her sheer panties down her thighs, exposing the full and complicated folds of a grown woman. I ran a finger over her slick pink and made little teasing circles around her hole before plunging in. Her pussy gripped me and in my ear she whispered *more*. I drove a second finger in and pressed my thumb to her clit, rubbed it, rolled it. Felt that it was swollen. Hard like a pebble.

I moved in and out of Holly, rocking her into a rhythm. And when she started to pant, I buried my tongue in her center. She felt like a fish—slippery and strong—and she tasted like sea salt, like apples and onions. I lapped at her, her juices smearing my face, until suddenly she gripped my hair and shuddered, making quick tiny movements against my mouth, leaving my own pussy dripping.

Her head still thrown back, I pulled Holly off the chair and laid her down on the table. She watched me as I undressed— her eyes glazed, her legs parted. And then, naked, I climbed on top of her. Our bodies locked together, yet we slid against each other like seals. I could feel the roughness of her fur and the perfect pressure of her bones. I was moving faster, getting closer.

Opening my eyes, I looked straight ahead—out the window to a murky sky, a yellow moon and a city of windows facing ours. I realized then that we were on display, framed perfectly in the rectangle of our window. But I couldn't stop. Not until, grinding into Holly, my whole body shook and glistened.

Blowing Across America
Peggy Munson

The Panhandle Straddle

Talking isn't my favorite way to talk. I'd rather be a horse whis-
perer for cocks, cajoling them out of their downy slumber into
ice sculptures of air. I'm not speaking about cocks hiding in
nocturnal nests, but those that are as hard as signposts, posting
on bare backs through the happily saddled hours. Give me a
cock for each lonely plain, each motherless and fatherless maw.
I want to feel my jaw ripping wider for the traffic of soundless
talk. I want the distillation of sentences crammed back in my
throat. So fuck back my words and make them come out right,
as screams and primal sounds. I want to suck out the marrow of
this silicone shape, and make a body of this bone.

I hear the cowboys riding in, the sharp pinwheels of their
spurs rolling toward the pattern of my flesh. I'm crouched
doggie-style in a Day-Glo pink tent. One flap opens in front of
my gaping mouth. One flap fans a draft on my ass. "Best l'il
cocksucker in Texas," brags Daddy Spade. Rubber-dicked
cowboys shuffle a seven-card stud and stroke their bulges,
trying to win a turn. I watch the sidewinder curve of one

cowboy's hand as he fans out his cards like he's rubbing cum from a girl's mouth, then undoes his lone-star buckle to claim my cactus flower lips. "Let's see whut yew got, cowgirl," he says, standing just far enough away for me to strain for him with my mouth. An oligarchy of Daddies regulates my holes. Daddy Heart slides two stubby fingers in my pussy as the cowboy's hips twitch. Daddy Diamond rubs a dime of lube up my ass. Even if I'm not the best cocksucker in Texas, I am as hollow as a cheap wood flute. I give the guy a tiny hole rimmed with lipstick so that he'll push into my mouth. Boots strain forward, his hand yanks his dick, and he turns my mouth into a day at the bank.

Like cattle, the other cowboys move around me in a slow hunched dance, gathering the way sticks collect in a choked stream. I see the pressure building, dammed heat, the cowboys' sharp longhorns moving to stampede. It's the threat that makes me wet, the thought that I'll be crushed beneath this much iconic suede, flogged like hide until I'm soft enough to wear. My ostrich-skin boots hide their tips beneath me. Somewhere in my pussy is a lineage of old saloons, fringed vests and frilly petticoats, fertile ground where two rivers intersect after a buzzard stretch of dusty plain. I'm every cowboy's American dream—able to stand when I'm bruised: red-white-and-blue all over.

"Blackjack," says the second john in a cowboy hat. Daddy Club takes his wadded handkerchief out of my mouth—the one he stuffed in there as if I'd swallow my own tongue. Daddy Diamond mounts my ass, easing his cock in while the john takes his stance. "Such a good Wild West slut," says Daddy Spade, flicking his nail at my nipple and pushing my head onto the john's rod. This one's rougher. "Yew didn't know yew bargained for sumthin' this gamey in yer purdy mouth, didya missy?" he says. His cock scrapes the back of my throat. I can't breathe until Daddy Diamond rams his cock into my ass, pushing so hard the john's cock falls out of my mouth. Then they work me like a couple of lumberjacks with a bucksaw.

"Yeehaw! Got me a flush," screams another cowboy. He yanks at his belt and shoves the other john aside, barely giving me time to breathe before my mouth is stuffed with an even larger cock. Daddy Club has found my vacant pussy and he rubs the lip of his beer bottle against my dripping hole. He's singing, "Ninety-nine cock-wielding queers on the wall, ninety-nine cock-wielding queers," as another john steps up. The hard bottle goads its way inside of me, slipping in and out while I moan. The room clanks with rodeo buckles falling away. Their cocks rub my throat into rope burn.

These cowboys hold new railroad ties, silicone and rubber, cyberskin and glass, chasing fleeting parallels to the edges of law. They are nouveau outlaws, reinventing the gold rush, looking for a sweet glint wherever they can find a secret mine. They trace their rough hands on my crude map of nerves. They like to prospect and explore, especially when they've got a free and eager whore. I'm their favorite novelty since the invention of the mechanical bull.

They stuff my mouth all night. Outside of the saloon, the roads play a slow Pong match of tumbleweed. I hear the clatter of hooves, the creak of boots on the old wood floor, the snapping of belts, and then I suck the cowboys off. They have never seen a pair of lips this willing, or a girl who lives to suck Americana cock. They ram me as hard as planks, as simple as loading a gun. "Ain't she a pistol?" says the latest cowboy, stepping up to his claim. His rubber gun sprays its rubber bullets in my mouth.

The Cleveland Cleave

I am stuck on a repeating word that's like a gaping camera shutter. The word is *hole* and she has said it three times. The word *hole* is caught in the weir of my crazy muzzled mouth. She pours booze into the word. She says, "I'm going to fuck each (word) you have." The wretched ache of the word is so obvious. "I've got a boner from here to Columbus," she says. "And you'd better believe this state starts with O." The word is the noose she made to hang the piñata full of cheap candy she bought at a party goods store. The word is a lavatory in a vortex in a cheap motel. The word is resting on the other side of the Bible in the drawer, over the horizon where Revelations ends.

"Open your fucking hole," she says. She shoves the motel table out of the way and hangs the piñata by its noose from the dim chandelier. She opens up a plastic packet and pulls out a bootlace and wraps it around my wrists behind my back. "Kneel down and spread your hole," she says. I tilt my tipsy heels and then her hand pushes my shoulder down. She squats to position me, spreads my knees apart so that my skirt fans out around my knees and lifts my tits up so that my back arches. She raises my chin toward the light. She grabs the wooden paddle that is oblong like a cricket bat, and says, "Close your eyes." I hear an awful smack, but not on my ass. Once the candy beats me in the face I realize what she's doing. The pieces fall into my mouth, or bounce off my teeth, and they are not hard candy, but chocolate kisses, unwrapped.

She picks up strays and begins feeding them to me as I let the chocolate liquefy. The candy is so sweet, and when she shoves in her cock I start to gag and my eyes snap open. "No you don't," she says, roughing up my hair as she rams her cock into my throat. "Open your greedhole because I'm going to fuck every bit of hole you got." The bar in Cleveland where I met her was wall-to-wall carpet-munchers, but I felt her bulge against my ass when I slid through a pack of butches to get a beer. She lit one cigarette end to the next in the Chevy cab, but that was the only fragment of intimacy as the radio bent us slowly around a steel guitar. I thought we'd do it like a businessman and a mid-list whore, but I didn't think she'd fuck my mouth. I didn't think she'd do it like she didn't care if it was blood or spit running down my chin. My wrists were too tethered to fight, my provincial tongue learning French on the baguette. "Your lips are pretty around my cock," she said, as I started learning her groove, licking the tiny rut at the tip until her cock was shamed by my lipstick. Then she came so jerking hard and rough in my mouth that I almost fell backwards onto carpet as defeated as a pressed corsage. "Holy Toledo," she said, her cock slamming my sounds back to their harmonicas.

I didn't know women could come like that. I didn't know cum tasted like Pennsylvania chocolate, driven down a turnpike to the crosshairs of a rain-tamped field that ended in a door with a number full of beckoning hole. "Sweet mercy," she said, pulling her cock from the muted space. My pussy was dripping on the sandpaper carpet. When one hole closed, a new wind tunnel welcomed resistance. Her fingers grabbed at my cunt and fumbled for my clit. She looked at me fiercely as she shoved three fingers in. Her lips formed a beatific grin. "When there's a hole in the clouds it's always heaven," she said.

The Ivy League Incantation

Two people were trying to blow up something they really wanted, and I was one of them. The air was strangling bagpipes. The professor gambled with the buttons on my shirt. She wore pretentious glasses that made her seem serious and cagey. I couldn't believe how lucky I was to find a professor to fuck. She dropped *heuristic* and *epistemology* in pedestrian lines. When she led me back to her office and plowed me, her urban words were ground to stutter, and the masala that resulted was at once sweet and bitter. Broken of sentence structure, her skin became weak tea, eyes hidden in grass. When she stripped me to my threadbare cotton, we became the same quilted layers. She walked through East Texas fields, plucking the stars from their prickers. With flat palms, she crushed night mosquitoes into prayers, hoping for a woman as peaceful and unknowing as a deer.

It could have been great, but two people were trying to smoke a perfect thing to smithereens. Sometimes, her eyes would just disappear. She was thinking about Proust while I thought about her eyes. Her mind filibustered even when her hands were on my tits, until I pushed her head down. All academics need to suckle on something. "Does this make your queer theory cock hard, professor?" I asked her, but I was stroking the air, and her cock wasn't there. We were avarice and outline. Precipice and twine. My labial folds were palms on a throwing wheel. The thud of clay was her fist ramming into my cunt. I worked my pussy onto her. We had done it a hundred times, like a lecture. But our voices caught that time. Theory forgets how a body swallows a punch.

We were smoke-jumping through a terrible burn. We were fire and things that snuff. I had to blow on her to put her out. I soothed wounds she didn't even know. "I know you need it bad," she said to me one day. Her fingers went to pry their way inside. We leaned into a kiss, free-falling into paper space. She kissed my lips, my clit, everywhere. We barnstormed each red target. "Sweet. Sweet. Bittersweet," she said on alternate licks up the gild of my cunt, as she divided it like a book. "Do you want a girl job or a blow job?" she asked, as she sucked on my clit. She had to reinvent words like that. Going down on me was a "girl job," a trick birthday candle that flickered back after it was blown out.

We were afraid of our throats turning into flame, a long tunnel of trapped screams. Two people were learning the wick effect: how bodies can burn of their own rendered fat, until there is nothing left. We warmed our hands around our fear, talking about the news as if we were talking about ourselves, becoming less newsworthy in the process. On TV, we watched people burning in an awful fire, until our eyes were small white shells. We looked for personal warnings. The crematorium of misguided impulse. Bodies piled ten high, insects of people really, eyes shocked blank. These images burned our vision into a comfortable haze. New lust, the accelerant of skin, made us lose faith in a city of kindling. We only cared about means of egress.

Two people were trying to quell incendiary wants. Her hands skimmed the litigating daisies around my eyes: *Does she love me, love me not?* She shooed my errant hairs. She tickle-touched my forearm. There was something clawing in me when we kissed. Her lips could slay me, the way she pried my whole body open from one insertion point. I hated the weakness in my spine, the way I folded over like a limp napkin wanting to form a swan.

Two people were looking for a government, but only found ruin. All that existed was anarchy, a fiery red *A*. Two people were blowing up real hope with a graffiti game.

My fingers grabbed her belt buckle like a punk kid's collar, shaking her at the gut. I was fumbling for her theory cock. "Come on. Let's just find out," I said. "Let's see what we can be." Her hands weren't intellectual for a moment. They were brooding bits of rough-cut wood. "Then tell me that you need me," she said. "Blow your cover now." How long does it take to go from graduate school to ghost town? How long to disassemble crumbling grails? We were blowing it with doubt. We expected our demands to lead to outlaws and guns.

So we tried to outrun the burn. We took thirty paces, turned and aimed. Did her terse undoing make my chest begin to bleed or had my Technicolor dress begun to run? My brain ached with wondering. My heart kept beating for her like the automatic pilot that it was. She didn't know it, but I would have stayed with her to ash and dust. Instead, we panicked, and stampeded, and neither one got out first.

The Lakeshore Lick

The bully wind is beating someone up. It is training its punches on trees that make asthmatic whistles. She shoves me up against a chain-link fence. "I want your lips to bleed," she says, holding my collar. She thinks I need to suck on something. Pacify the baby and the baby won't scream. Pacify the baby and the opera will go on. The courtly midnight stragglers scuffle by in conversation past the scraggy silhouettes of slides and swing sets. She rubs my small hand up and down her cock beneath her Army pants, pulling me to the playground. I've spent the evening chattering like a manic boy and now she wants to stuff my mouth. "Be prepared, Boy Scout," she whispers.

The slide has terraces like an Aztec hillside. At the end, it looks like a conveyor belt in a factory. It looks like a place where people move their hands automatically, where the momentum stops but products keep pushing so the cans will move. She straddles the first hump of the slide, metal tagged all over by graffiti and hand smudges. Her legs are flung over the sides like she's a lazy Huck Finn in a canoe. "Generally, I spit on Boy Scouts," she says. "Usually I just cough a wad on them."

"I'm glad you didn't," I say. "I'm glad you were nice to me." Granted, *nice* is an overstatement. She grabbed me by one ear and led me to an alley. She made me trudge for blocks carrying her backpack. She harangued me on the way with rude remarks about the way I dressed, my country drawl, the way I moved. She alternately slapped my face until it burned and kissed me. She looked at me like I was barely palatable but she was barely picky. "Your mouth is shaped like a badge," she said, tracing her thumb on my lip. "Like a circle was sewn around it to keep it open. Stupid little vestibule."

We are from different sides of the Mason-Dixon Line. We are, like Civil War reenactments, a repetition of events. We are parts of each other. We are a severed one. It's as if we're fighting out of antebellum costumes, fighting for a future where divisions don't exist. But how naïve we are—to think that we can even fight the drives that make us fuck and suck and fall into dark corners. To think we can repair a country that's so different from itself.

She rubs her hand on her cock, teasing my need. She is shaped like what, like Italy? I'm too uncultured to know. She is shaped like a wolverine as it creeps, like a skinny kid who can nevertheless fight with a tire iron. Her long legs make their M over the sides of the slide. She has one button left to undo and her boxers are tufting out. I see the dick in there and I'm gulping air to get there. "When do I ever get a fucking good deed?" she starts. "When do I get to be a helpless old lady? I've got packages to be carried if you know what I mean."

"I know what you mean," I say, and give her a nodding glance. She looks at me with hostility. "I *do* know."

"Garrulous little wiener," she says. "Boy Scouts do not know when to shut the fuck up."

When I go silent, I hear the absence of the game of stickball that has ended blocks away, the stick that hands are wrapped around that might become a weapon. Wind is beating chain. The sound of cheap is making perky music in the yellowed lights. "I'm going to fuck your mouth so hard," she says suddenly. "I'm going to give you elocution lessons." Her hips are trying to squeeze her cock out of its cotton cage. Her eyes are careful tacks that spread out insect wings. "I'm not all that experienced at sucking dick," I say. I don't tell her I think about it all the time but haven't done it.

"You're a magician who can swallow fire, you understand?"

She takes her lighter from her pocket and she flips it open, thumbs a flame out of it. She holds the flame about an inch below my chin so that the tip of it could drill a hole into my jawbone. It goes from warm to hot. It goes from innocent to immolating. "Swallow," she tells me. I do. She moves the flame so that it echoes down my throat.

I can make crops grow, so I'm sure I can make cocks respond. I would like to tell her what I know of nature but we are in the city. There is nothing natural about the battle the grass fights to grow between the concrete cracks. In fact, it looks pathetic, olive drab because it's dry this time of year. She has got to haze me, or I'll be as lonely as that grass. I'll be a uniform of olive drab amidst a sea of red aggression. Her hands are poised like meaty spiders, thinking their own venom. Then there is her dick. It doesn't need to think. It's like bamboo. The universe is always saying, "There's a sky, and there's a beanstalk, Jack." The universe is just one cold unstopping taunt.

She pulls me down against the slide. I hit the metal with a *thunk*, my awkward limbs collapsing. I'm bent like a snake, my head and arms reaching over the curve to where she is. She yanks her dick out violently and shoves it in my mouth. "Take it all," she says, and pushes into my mouth. She's almost ripping out my hair to pull my head down on her cock. She is completely choking me. I'm trying not to lose my lunch. She pulls me off and I start coughing. "What are you—some kind of ballet dancer?" she asks. "You gag like a bulimic."

She doesn't know how tough I am, but I can't speak of it. I want to tell her how the boys at school once made me eat a cricket. The spine was crunchy and I didn't puke. A gang of rugby players wrestled me at recess and they forced the cricket down. I thought about its singing legs. How boys were just like crickets, making opera in their trousers shuffling back and forth. It made me horny thinking how the boys knew I was just a fag and not a girl, and probably beat off thinking of my frightened eyes. "I'll keep it down," I say. "I can. You'll see."

"You'd better fucking believe you will," she says. She slaps her cock against my cheeks. I slide my lips over the tip. I smell the black inside my nose, the city black. The light has turned into oil. Her knees are twitching but I hold them down. I want to make her feel my lazy fields. There is a world of singing legs—a night song made of friction. I force my mouth down on her shaft. I open up my throat. She's getting jazzed up now, and moans. She starts to rub the tiny bump above her dick, to shake and twitch. I want to hold her Zippo lighter to her mouth. I want her to believe she can extinguish everything.

But I am just a country boy without a trace of cool. My hands are ghostly pale. Girl hands that shape themselves to rings. My hands are small, effete. She grabs for one of them before she jerks and comes into the greening dark. She pushes into me like she is fighting concrete.

The Bloody Castro

She slips in out of nowhere. Against the white walls, in her uniform, she looks like an exotic plant that looks like an animal, something a topiary gardener would make. For months, I wanted to use the soldier as a verb, soldier on with her, make her soldier on with me. I watched her nimble hands uncover conflicts in an engine. I watched her shy and fumbling hands reach for her lighter. I thought about the way that she would touch me, as if she'd learned about adrenaline and how to use it.

The dark slips in like a cat. The stars collect like iron filings around the poles of the earth. The moon is a wet moon, the kind that lights up like ice under an eave. To my brain, it doesn't seem odd that the soldier is standing in my San Francisco apartment. "I know I shouldn't have come," she drawls, "But Mammaw made a red velvet cake." She holds up a plate with a sin-red cake on it. "Don't you think it's about time we ate the red velvet cake?"

The soldier is from the country of Louisiana. Hotter than a habañero bayou, where they eat things I wouldn't even spit into. Her favorite cake is whipped up with a whirling mixer into frenzied peaks of egg whites and then dyed the color of hell. I love the slow Southern motion, where a person can let cake melt on the tongue until it feels as sultry as velvet. It is like days that have dragged by, with such thoughtful hesitation, in the time before the soldier and I have grown close, that have made me stroke my own downy hairs and think of chintz and silk and velvet. I think of magnolia trees in their coming out gowns in my imagined South, where the world draws its vowels out as long as possible. As if moments of exclamation are all that matter.

I stroke my hand down the embarrassed heat of her face. I like the places where she is dented by dimples and accidents and deliberate destruction. She is as flawless as the most dilapidated motel I've ever fucked a reckless nowhere in. She makes me feel formative, like a country that will one day be safe. She speaks slowly, in that reptilian way of bayou people who are watching, counting everything. It is unnerving how she looks at me. As if she wants to love me on a rocking chair that never sleeps.

"You're like a kite," she finally says, looking at my body in a way that makes my pussy warm. "All sharp angles and delicate stretch of skin and a constant threat of impromptu flight."

She says this, and then our fingers start to let the sky uncoil.

As much as we're hot for each other, our touching takes some time. We want it to be perfect, virginal. Her narrow hands are just like mine—lost migratory birds. We have no homing skills. I contemplate Helen Keller and water—the moment when the water touched her hands and she knew it to be water. I think of water and of hands and revelation. It takes so long before she undresses me. I think how we live our lives blind and deaf with water running down and not knowing how to name it. It feels like silk, then anguish, then beauty, and finally water. I've longed for water to expand, to become beauty, and then grew scared and contained it. With her, I don't know if I should expand or contain. To be soothed might mean to be extinguished.

She slides her Army fatigues off. She wears her dick like she's a cub on awkward legs. It is wartime. The soldier has three days here before her deployment. People are running from their own hands. They are laying cinder blocks around their thoughts, censoring pacifist words. I hand her a bottle of massage oil and roll on my belly. She straddles me with her cock poking into my back. She talks to me about the art of war. Her hands slide down the gull wings of my shoulder blades, between the scaffold of my ribs, down to the dimple above my ass. She inhales sharply, then slides upward. "I read about the art of war," she says. "They make it sound like macho ballet, like boxing. The words they use are pride, discipline, courage, service. Those are good words, artful words."

"Yes, they are," I say.

"There's art," the soldier says. "And then there's war. I just realized I am fighting one to keep the other safe." The soldier's hands slide up the sides of my body, grown as dry as windblown buildings. She starts to kiss my neck, breathing hot down my spine.

The soldier hasn't filled out her swagger. I had forgotten, until I met her, what it meant to be that age. I forgot what it meant to fumble toward light, then remember to ask permission. There is nothing whimsical about twenty-five. Like a quarter, it sinks fast and hard. It falls on tails when you want heads. The soldier moves down the sheet over my legs, then lifts the fabric up and presses her thumbs into the balls of my feet. "And what is art?" I ask the soldier.

"Art is a battle of opposing forces that ends in beauty," says the soldier, sliding up to press her body against my back.

"Art is war?" I ask her, as I lift my ass against her cock.

"Yes," says the soldier. "And not the other way around."

I flip the soldier over and I start to bite her neck. I take my hand and languish on her cock. I'm dying to plant a flag, make it mine. I'm dying to feel it pushing in my pussy.

"I'd shed my blood for you, for *you*," the soldier says to me. I move my lips down, slide them over her cock. The soldier hasn't ever had a proper blow job. She can't tell Army dykes how much she loves her dick. At night, she jerks it, talking on the phone with me. We watched so many awful war movies, engorging an imagined space, but none of them has ever shown the way a tool of rage could just be coddled and remade. My fingers splay on her thighs, spreading her legs while my lips slide down the sides of her dick. My mouth can't get enough of it. I turn us both to blood alone, my reddened lips, her pulse and breath.

"You'd bleed for *me?*" I ask. I reach for her utility knife, the one we used to pop a cork. I pull a sharpened blade. My arm strikes her down like a bayonet. "You sure?" I ask. She gulps but nods. "Yes Ma'am," she says. She probably thinks I'm going to carve her up, but I only want to make a small point throb. I prick her finger, then prick mine. I lay our fingers on the piece of cake. The crimson of our blood soaks into the vermilion, making swirls of red. I blow on her finger to soothe the cut. I slide the fork into the place I bled and feed it to her mouth. I put the fork into the section where she bled and eat that piece. "Now," I say, and mount her with my pussy, easing down her cock. "Fuck me like you're reinventing velvet."

The Brothel
Isa Magdalena

"Are you all right, Vicky?" Sylvana asked as we stood inside a hallway at the bottom of a stair. She must have been referring to my state of confusion after our walk through the alleys of the red-light district on our way to the brothel where she worked. I'd never been in this area of the city, or to a brothel, for that matter, and was shocked by the crowds of men gawking and yelling at the women behind their windows.

"I want to come back here when we're not in a hurry," my lover, Martha, whispered in my ear. "I see more breast, more hip, more naked thigh than on most beaches I've been to!"

"Sure, honey," I responded, dazed.

Then, turning back to Sylvana, I lied. "Sure," I said, "I'm all right."

She gave Martha and me a warm hug, longer and warmer than necessary. When she let go of me she said, "I would give you a tour of the house, but all rooms are occupied." She turned around and before she began to climb the stairs, pointed to a heavy door on the left, saying casually, "Here is the domain of ropes, whips, and canes."

As I followed her, pretending I'd handled ropes, whips, and canes on a daily basis, I focused on the points of her black high heels, which aimed at me over the edge of every stair step. When I looked higher up, I saw her tight butt swaying to the left and to the right. It was dressed in close-fitting, deep, dark, red leather. Her waist was bare and her bra matched the pants. Silver snakes dangled wildly next to her long neck. And, though I didn't see it from the back, a frontal image of her was burned into my retina: dark red lipstick highlighted her large mouth, and makeup in shades of pink and gray made her blue eyes shine brighter, pierce deeper. The muscles of her arms were mighty and tattooed; her hair was very short, in an odd color of red. It occurred to me that this afternoon might become a little overwhelming, even if I was half in love with Sylvana. I didn't know which way to run faster, toward her or away from her. I knew Sylvana from the classes Martha and I were taking at Xtasia, a sex temple. We were taking the classes because I was nonorgasmic. In addition to the classes, we had decided to attend private sessions with Sylvana, who worked as a prostitute and was an apprentice *Hora* in Xtasia.

When we arrived on the first floor, Sylvana opened the door into what was evidently at one time a large kitchen, now old, that served as a lounge with funky couches and chairs. Every crack of this room smelled of feminine seduction. High heels, stockings, hand-mirrors, makeup, lingerie, leather, and all sorts of dresses were scattered around as if the wind had blown open all the closets and no one had ever bothered to put stuff back. It was a painful reminder of all the times in my life when I wanted to outfit myself in the traditional attire of the female species. I always failed. "Let's go to the next floor," Sylvana said, and I nodded in relief.

She led us up another flight of stairs and into a room which had no windows. It was decorated in black and dark purple paint and fabrics, except for the bed and the massage table, which were red with gold. A white candle, the only object on a small altar, stood out against a velvet curtain. The smell of incense filled the room. Next to the bed I saw a shelf that held a collection of sex toys. Most of all I noticed how silent this room was compared to the chaos of the streets below. I gladly accepted a glass of sparkling water from Sylvana and after a few minutes of polite conversation, she led me and Martha to the bed.

Sylvana kicked off her heels, sat down, and crossed her legs, saying nothing, then gestured to me to come sit on top of her in what they call "the position of Heaven and Earth" at Xtasia. I was to put my legs behind her back. This was easier said than done with my pants on. Her leather was evidently more flexible than my jeans. I managed the position, though not entirely balanced, and Martha settled behind me. Sylvana held me up firmly, closed her eyes, and at her suggestion we entered a brief period of silent meditation. Soon I was breathing more evenly and my heart had slowed. I was even able to calmly notice where I was: on her lap, her arms holding me up, my forehead touching her forehead. It was as if she had scanned me with some inner radar. I didn't mind. When I had become present with our bodies and our breathing, Sylvana said a prayer. She spoke thoughtfully and precisely, acknowledging and welcoming my blend of feelings: nervous and excited, turned-on and scared, hopeful and suspicious. I was about to embark on yet another adventure in search of my orgasm. I felt held, not just by Sylvana's arms and her lap, but also by her intention. Martha moved herself closer against my back. Her arms reached around me to Sylvana's bare waist.

Sylvana's breathing changed from deep and slow to deep and fast, then shallow and fast, and finally deep and slow. Martha and I breathed with her, as we had learned to do in the classes. I stopped when I felt somewhat dizzy, and so did Sylvana. But Sylvana's pelvis did not stop moving. It was rocking back and forth. She had started with a minimum of movement against me, slowly making her rocking stronger and bigger. Our foreheads were not touching any longer, instead our breasts met. Every time she rolled her pelvis down, she pressed against my breasts. Every time she rolled her pelvis up, she left my breasts empty. Every time she rolled her pelvis up, her pubic bone pressed into my crotch. Every time she rolled her pelvis down, she left my crotch waiting and wanting. When Sylvana's erotic energy got higher (which I had learned can happen just through breathing, squeezing the muscles of the pelvic floor and moving the pelvis), she slowed down, came almost to a halt but not quite. She leaned away from me, looked in my eyes while her fingers opened the buttons of my white shirt. She looked at me with those full red lips and I wanted to kiss her, but I didn't know what, exactly, the protocol was. I had never been to a whore. Let alone to a Hora. She brought her mouth very close to mine. I drew back because of Martha. I didn't know what the protocol was toward my lover, in this situation, either. Sylvana didn't come closer, but didn't stop teasing me, moving her tongue over her lips. She folded me out of my shirt with Martha's help, took off her own bra, took hold of my torso, and pressed and rubbed her breasts strongly against mine.

"We need to find and play with your arousal first to get you ready for penetration. You know that, right, Vicky?" Sylvana smiled. I nodded, as if I knew. "There are many ways to accomplish this. But this is how you turn me on today...," she said, while rubbing herself against me, pushing me away, pulling me back, pushing me away, pulling me against her. "Both of you together," she continued, "just think of all the possibilities...." She flung her head toward my neck, her teeth nipped at me. The shock gave me a rush. I grabbed her hard. Sylvana's arms easily reached Martha and pulled her against my back. It was a little clumsy but she managed also to remove Martha's shirt. I was pressed between the two of them like meat in a sandwich. The sounds of heavy breathing surrounded me like columns of smoke, and I thought I might faint or scream. Martha's familiar breasts, one smaller than the other, rolled against my back until Sylvana's hands came in between to fondle them. My lover puffed and pressed more strongly against me. Sylvana pushed her slowly back until she was leaning against the pillows. A second later I was leaning against Martha. Three seconds later my pants were opened at the fly. Then, while fingers searched around my waist and inside my jeans, they were slowly stripped off. Strong hands touched me so softly and with so much attention. They slid over my naked legs making a trail of goose bumps toward my belly. From there they slid in reverse, then back toward my belly again.

After a thorough investigation, Sylvana put oil on her hands and massaged my legs. Especially my thighs. Especially my inner thighs. And, after that, my belly and pubic area. She pressed, slid, explored. Though we were surrounded by a trancelike beat from the music she had started, I heard nothing but the sound of her hands over my legs, on the inside of my thighs and closer and closer to the cave in between. She slithered, she pressed, she kneaded, she grabbed. She picked up one leg, then the other, lifting them, spreading them wide, before placing them back on the bed. There I sat with legs wide in front of a Hora, leaning against my love, on a bed in a brothel. My vulva, heavy with heat, would have opened no matter how I might have tried to keep her private. My runner's legs softened under Sylvana's fingers. She put Martha's hands on my breasts to play with my nipples. I was being made ready. For what? To bake in the oven? To be taken? To be given? To be eaten? I was being made ready, but not entirely in the way I expected, if I expected anything at all. I assumed I was being prepared for penetration. That still scared me. I don't know why it scared me. Martha fucked me often at home, but that was different—we are lovers.

Half to my relief and half to my disappointment, Sylvana stopped massaging me and leaned against the stack of pillows on her end of the bed. She unsnapped one button after the other down the flap of her leather pants. First her curly hair appeared. Then, slowly, her ornamented jewel was revealed. We had seen it many times in class, yet, between the creases of soft leather it was stronger still, more provocative with the collection of golden and silver rings in her labia. She pulled her pants off, leaned back, relaxed, made a move with her fingers along her mouth to pick up some saliva. Then she brought her hand down, made a circle around her clit, and opened her labia until all the rings lay on the side with a red, swollen, and glistening path between them. In the middle of that path, between the deepest lips, a small dark hole appeared. Sylvana pressed down from inside. Her cunt opened up to show a little mouth. She squeezed and closed the mouth like a sea-flower opens and closes with the waving of the currents. She opened and closed, opened and closed, until a pearl of musky milky juice appeared. My eyes became big. I salivated. Her excitement penetrated me from distance.

"May I give you my arousal?" Sylvana said. "Just so you know that you don't have to do it all on your own. This is what we call *savayam,* masturbation, an erotic call to the core, only it is *dakir-savayam*—from me for you." Sylvana rose from the bed. She went on touching herself while placing one foot on the bed. Her eyes hypnotized me, utterly unashamed. With her fingers still on her cunt, she walked over to the shelf and picked up a V-shaped black dildo. Each of the twin phalluses was thick, medium-long, and (even I thought so) handsome. She rolled a condom over one side and smeared it with lube, with evident growing pleasure. She slowly slid her hand over it from top to bottom and bottom to top. And again. And again. And again, holding still at the top before sliding down. I thought she would devour the toy right then and there but instead she lay back down on the bed and let it rest between her legs. She went inside herself with two fingers, deliberately making sounds with the wet and swollen tissue. Her pelvis moved up and down, her torso lifted. Sylvana's movemenets on her own fingers were slow, deep, and wholly sexual. Her eyes were half closed, yet never leaving us. She pulled her fingers out, pinched her swollen clit, and pulled her lips. The rings made tiny sounds as they dangled against each other. It looked very beautiful. She looked very beautiful. It occurred to me that she looked so beautiful precisely because she was really enjoying herself.

I felt between my legs. I was dripping.

"I must seduce you," Sylvana said with a sultry voice, "not for my sake, but for life's sake."

"Uhhh...," Martha groaned behind me.

"What?" I said at the same time.

"Vicky, and you too, Martha, I must seduce you, so you can open up...," Sylvana sighed. "To find your full sexual power and pleasure, you need to open up, and to open up, I must seduce you...not for my sake, but for life's sake." Her voice trailed off. Both hands cupped her cunt. It was hard to believe that it wasn't for her sake. I mean, I trusted that it wasn't *just* for her own sake, but I didn't have the impression that she was having a terrible time. She picked up the dildo. Her legs were so wide and the cock was so big. She slipped it in as easy as a snake swallows its prey. My eyes sucked up the sight as her cunt sucked up the cock. She moved it in and out, gently, with no hurry at all. Her swollen red flesh parted and sucked, parted and sucked. It made me drool and sigh. My hips moved of their own volition. I told Martha to squeeze my nipples harder. Sylvana's chest was covered with perspiration and her movements became demanding and strong. She squatted, closed her eyes, and fucked the dildo hard and fast, holding on to one end of the twin phallus like a rider holds on to the pommel of a saddle. Her back and neck were arched backwards, her face distorted. She clenched her jaws, held still in midair, and fell back against the cushions, growling. She held her breath until a long sigh let all the air escape again. Then she opened her eyes, and the look in them seemed to move from being gone to being back to where we were. I went on touching my clit. Martha humped me from behind. Sylvana watched us as she moved her dildo quietly. Then she pulled it out, dried it with a towel, threw the towel and the dildo in a bucket on the floor, and reached down to wash her hands in a tub of water next to the bed. Her eyes never left us. When she dried her hands, I stopped touching myself. Sylvana leaned over and gave us a hug. She whispered in my ear: "Are you ready for me to massage you?" I nodded. Could I possibly become more ready?

"May I touch your clit?" Sylvana asked. I nodded again, leaning back against my lover. My clit was way past the stage of teasing, but Sylvana was busily trying to drive me insane. "I should say hello to her properly, shouldn't I?" she said. "Can't just come falling in the door, can I?" She caressed the edges of my clit with great gentleness. Then she stroked more force-fully—my clit, my lips, the space between my clit and my cave. I began to wonder if her teasing was intended to make me *beg* her to come inside of me. But that, I thought to myself, I would refuse to do. Begging was out of the question. Finally she took a latex glove, put it on her right hand, and asked if she could enter.

"Please…," was all I could say.

"Remember that I'm not trying to make orgasms, all right?" Sylvana said. "Instead I'm looking for gates, places in your body that hold resistance in order to protect you." I had heard about this before in class, but had forgotten. It was so hard to lie still. Normally I would have told Martha to fuck me hard a long time ago. So now I told Sylvana that was what I wanted. She refused. "That's your usual way," she said, "and it doesn't give you all you want. We're now trying something else." My body was screaming! "That's not easy, because your body is crying out for what it knows," Sylvana said, with an irritating compassion that ran square into my ever wilder impatience. She held two fingers inside without moving. "Vicky, relax," she ordered. "As terrible as it sounds, you must relax now...okay...breathe...yes...breathe into your belly. You have only two jobs, relax your cunt and breathe in and out of it...deep and easy.... See?" she asked with her eyes closed.

"See what?"

"Feel how you tense your muscles inside your cunt? You've got to let them go, baby, you got to relax them. You're not running a marathon right now, remember? They need to learn to let go."

I tried hard, but that was exactly the problem. I didn't know how not to try.

"Breathe into your cunt, baby...with every exhale let those muscles relax more...."

I couldn't do it. I felt how my muscles wanted to grab around Sylvana's fingers and I began to be very frustrated. "Let's do it in a different way," she suggested. "Squeeze your muscles as if you have to pee real bad and have to hold it...yes...hold it...hold it...until you can't hold it any longer...then let go...relax...." We did this about fifteen more times, and after each contraction and relaxation I could feel myself growing less tense inside.

Finally Sylvana seemed satisfied. "I want to tell your cunt that I won't do anything she doesn't want, all right? I want to learn to know her so she can know herself," she said. With the ungloved hand on my lower belly, and the gloved hand inside me, Sylvana's fingers made circles...pressed the ceiling of my cave...below...on all sides...shallow...deep...around my cervix...on and on. And I struggled to stay relaxed. As we had been told in class a hundred times, I felt much more sensation when I relaxed than when I was busy moving. In that moment I was immersed in the enjoyable feeling of fingers trying to loosen up knots in muscles. "This is your sacrum, this is your tail. Ligaments connect them to muscles we use for walking and running, all these tissues are connected." Sylvana explained in her scholarly anti-sexy voice which nevertheless cast a spell. She kept pressing gently as if she were massaging a tight muscle.

I didn't notice when her fingers had changed from massaging to fucking; it must have happened gradually. She slid back and forth through my slippery stuff without taking her fingers out. She roamed around, gliding in my wetness. I became the inside of an elastic, ever expanding, rubber ball. My body tingled all over. It made me rub my arms, shoulders, and chest. Sylvana didn't move hard or fast. "Nowhere to go..." I'd heard the phrase a thousand times in the classes. Sylvana reassured me that it was not easy to relax, to break patterns that had been ingrained in my body and mind as ruts of arousal. It helped that Martha and Sylvana were breathing and making sounds with me. Sylvana kept massaging, sliding, fucking, licking me inside with her fingers, never hard, always smooth; she swiped her fingers from left to right along my pubic bone; she came back to the ceiling and...hit a spot, which made me jump and scream!

"G-spot, baby...*zumah,* we call it...," she said and held her hand still. Her pressing on that spot had felt a bit too strong and I said so. But, immediately afterward I wanted to be taken that way, strong, again. I said that, too. "I won't...," was Sylvana's reply, her eyes glued to mine, "at least not yet. All that rough stimulation probably had the opposite effect of what you're looking for...."

"How so?" I asked, insulted.

"It can desensitize your tissue.... Put that on top of the assaulting messages we hear about sex..." Her concentration was in her hands, she pressed and released against my ceiling, steadily, firmly, but still in the same smooth way. "...And voila, a sensitive organ puts up walls...of course...."

I was well aware of the impact of the mind on the body, so I didn't need to argue with her. It just seemed that I was arguing with my own body.

Finally she will fuck me, I thought, when Sylvana consistently rubbed back and forth along the ceiling of my..."cunt," my "holy well." Sometimes I forgot to relax. As soon as I did Sylvana stopped moving. She said, "These are all little gates that try to distract you from feeling more...just give them time to relax again...and I'll see if they'll let me in...."

After what must have been at least forty-five minutes, during which time all three of us were busy being concentrated excavators of some sort, Sylvana groaned, "She's opening wider and wider, baby.... I'm going to add a third finger...if that's too much, let me know...and if I go too hard, let me know." It wasn't too much and it wasn't too hard. What she was doing just made it more difficult, again, to lie still. "You can move," she allowed generously, "just pay attention that you don't cramp up inside. And keep breathing, it will help you to relax."

Her fingers were pressing, caressing, and wiping several notches stronger now. I was breathing faster and deeper automatically. I pressed myself against Martha and my pelvis rocked up and down automatically. I wanted her to do me strong so badly! I thrust my pelvis toward Sylvana and she didn't stop me. In fact she encouraged me to move, breathe, and make sounds. She worked my *zumah* directly and methodically but also with restraint. Then the vibrator effect was there: her fingers pressed and released against my ceiling in rapid speed. I watched her strong shoulder as she thrust her arm and hand in and out of me. I closed my eyes. It felt as though her entire body was penetrating me. At the same time, Martha was holding me, moving with me, moving against me, breathing with me as if I was about to deliver a baby. Everything went faster and stronger. I couldn't keep track of everything going on inside and outside.

At last Sylvana did what I had wanted. She did me hard and fast. I grabbed her arm to encourage her to go even harder, but suddenly I could do no more. My insides tensed up. Sylvana kept going, even though I'm sure she saw the distress on my face. She still kept going. She pressed her fingers against my *zumah*. She pressed hard. I got mad. "Stttoooppp!" I screamed.

Immediately all action stopped. I burst into shattered crying.

Martha held and rocked me. Sylvana sat between my legs, her fingers still inside of me, her hand on my belly. "Cry, baby…crying is good…it brings our pain back to the underworld…," Sylvana said.

Her compassion made me hate her. I turned over to Martha and crawled into her arms.

Sylvana suggested that we lie together on the bed as long as we wanted while she went to a room next to ours. We could call her back to talk, if we wished, or we could wait to talk another time. "Just don't leave without saying good-bye, so we can have a formal closure," she said.

I didn't want to talk. I couldn't talk even if I wanted to. My feelings were tumbling like rocks in a mountain slide. I felt vulnerable and exposed beyond measure. I don't know what I would have done if Martha hadn't been there.

"I wouldn't have done what I did, if Martha wasn't with you," Sylvana explained later. "I wouldn't have gone that far. Your body doesn't know whether I'm friend or foe. It needs an ally more than anything else, someone who will stand up for her when she's been stepped on. That is Martha. But you were sure about what you thought you wanted. 'Fuck me hard!' you begged. Well, that's an old programmed rut that, in your case, lets your mind run over your body. Don't worry, one day you will want it again, once you've pasted your parts together. Then you'll be able to go as hard and as fast as you like."

Each time we came back for another session it became easier for me to relax and let myself "be done." It became easier to let go of wanting an orgasm. I learned to stay with the sensation in the moment and not grasp for something I didn't even know. My body and I began to trust Sylvana as an ally and Martha became more and more actively involved.

In the middle of our fifth visit I was laying still on top of Martha, my flat belly perfectly fitting on her round one. Sylvana sat behind us, between our wide-open legs. I heard a new glove snap over her hand. I was so turned-on, yet I also felt an unexpected sensation, the sensation of "nowhere to go." Martha rocked me up and down. I heard a second glove snap onto Sylvana's hand. One hand played with my bottom and teased my bottom-hole. The other hand played with Martha's clit and the entrance of her cave. From Martha's increased breathing and loud moaning, I could tell Sylvana must have gone inside her with a few fingers. Sylvana slid her other hand inside my cunt, massaging me with precision. I pushed against her without tensing up and I pressed against my lover, my clit on her pubic bone. Martha was hot and moving, but wasn't in a hurry either. Something deep inside my belly began to slowly split me open. My body moved, yet I wasn't the one moving it. I flew in the air, yet I was riding the earth on my lover's body. I felt fused to her. Whatever aroused me from inside fucked her, penetrated her, insisted I flood myself inside her warm, greedy, panting flesh. When Sylvana pressed my G-spot it didn't feel sharp the way it had at other times. I grabbed Martha so tight she gasped for breath and stuck her nails in my back. Sylvana's fingers took me again, and this time my riding, diving, flying, and pounding poured me out into a scream so long and so loud that I didn't notice I screamed until it stopped. I sank on top of Martha. I cried. My body waved like a serpent waves out of its old and too-tight skin. I cried. I laughed. I looked at my love and my midwife in wonder, pulled them closer against me, and slid silently into a timeless, worry-free space.

One
E. Robinson

The rain pelted the window as if willing Lazarus to rise from
the dead. It was the same miracle that I had desired too, to be
raised from the dead. It was just how I felt, three weeks into a
five-week business trip. Pent up and frustrated like a panther
caged and not drugged, watching her prey escape. I wanted
my drug.

I was in London, in December, shooting a commercial for a
stateside snack company, with lots of special effects. It had
been a long haul. It had rained the whole time of my stay. So
there were weather delays and lots of standing around under
falling water. It was Sunday around eleven o'clock in the morning. I was staring out the window, watching the rain and the
tourists, skimming the U.S. papers and longing to be home.
I had decided to go to the dining room that particular morning,
bored of my own private room, as luscious as a suite can be.
I was distractedly sifting through the English version of an
American breakfast. They just don't quite get the potato thing.

The small, blue, formal dining room was full but beginning
to empty when I noticed a handsome couple seated over by

the wall. Well, actually I noticed her. She was beautiful, in the way that I like it, wild, understated and simple, very little makeup. For a moment I wished she was mine, then I noticed her husband, or at least the man she was with. Like the good predator that we all can be, he looked up when he felt me eyeing his woman. He was handsome. Both had dark hair that fell loosely around their faces. They could have been siblings. He had a strong jaw and round brown eyes that invited you to play. I was caught. I had just been imagining her pulled down to the edge of my bed with me on my knees before her, face buried in what I imagined to be a lush brown mound. My tongue first flicking in and out and then lapping it up. He surprised me, and smiled back. A confident man at that! I liked this couple and silently wished them well. I forced my gaze back down to my paper.

Halfway through an article on the presidential scandal at home I felt a presence and looked up. It was the man. "Excuse me," he said, "I couldn't help but notice you're enjoying Rachel?" His accent was faintly German, his manner discreet.

It was my turn to be confused. "Excuse me?" I mimicked.

"The woman I had breakfast with, Rachel. She was pleased that you became aware." Well, all right, I thought to myself, I have become aware and it pleases the lady. I was wet already.

"Please sit down," I said, and motioned for him to have a seat. He smiled that easy playful smile again while I scanned his hands for a ring. He didn't have one. "And so you thought you'd come over and…," I encouraged.

"Well," he said, almost at a loss for words, "We are from Austria, we have been here many days, it is raining, you see?" We both looked out the window. The goddamned rain was getting to everyone. I nodded. We were silent. It was okay. I turned my gaze back toward the Austrian and noticed that he had gently placed a hand on his lap, which was visible as he sat back from the table. I couldn't help it; I blushed and averted my eyes. "You don't like me?" he asked, a little surprised. I looked in his eyes, which showed neither malice nor perversion, just a kind, easy fun. He didn't move his hand.

"No, it's not that," I said. "I was just expecting a quieter day."

"I should leave you alone?"

"No stay, continue, I'm fine." He smiled and gave himself a little squeeze. So sure were his motions I couldn't be sure I wasn't imagining them altogether.

"She likes you. She also appreciates a beautiful woman." His first flattery; I didn't like it nearly as well as the unspoken, but I nodded, accepting. A semi-successful actress in a previous life, I had spent time in front of the camera, but I didn't trust it. I must have grimaced. "But you are beautiful, as you know? Should I not have said?"

Nice, attentive, I thought to myself. "But what about your wife?" I asked. "You don't mind my interest?"

"Wife? Rachel, no." he chuckled softly at his own joke. "She is beautiful and I should be so lucky, but no, I'm afraid my boyfriend would not approve at all, he is very jealous." This time there could be no mistake, he rolled the shaft of his semi-hard penis, which I could now see clearly through his snug black pants, against his thigh. He smiled.

"Boyfriend?" I wanted to get this straight.

"Yes, I enjoy women but not nearly as much as men."

"I see."

"Do I disappoint you?" he asked, leaning farther back in his chair and stroking himself. I shook my head. "Rachel travels with us from time to time. She is good company but she is easily bored. She needs more than men for company." He removed his hand. He was fully hard now, and I noticed for the first time the fullness of his lips. He followed my eye and slid his tongue along his bottom lip. We stared at each other a moment longer, as it rained steadily on. "Would you like to join us for a drink?"

I searched the window for an answer. He stood, as if it were finished. I hesitated a moment. He offered his hand. I took it. My female hand felt small in his warm, large, masculine one. It had been a long time since I had held a man. I rose. He released it, waited for me to pass and we left the dining room, which had suddenly become claustrophobic.

At the lobby, he touched my elbow and motioned to the glass doors that led to the terrace. "We are in the bungalow," he said. I hadn't even known the hotel had a bungalow. We walked to the door and I squinted through the rain. "There is an awning," he said, and pointed to the far left. Funny, I had never noticed this discreet emerald awning before, leading directly out to a small cottage. The cottage was the same color as the hotel, white with green trim, and it had a small wooden side porch, facing a tiny English garden.

We stepped out into the rain. He sheltered me from the wind. The path curved a little so you couldn't see the front door. About fifteen feet away he touched me on the elbow again. I stopped. He stepped in. Standing, he was about three inches taller than I am. He smelled clean and musky. "I would like to kiss you," he said, and then he leaned in and did just that, tentative at first, but direct. Surprisingly, the feeling shot through me. His lips were supple and firm. He pulled me closer. I felt his erection swelling. He ground into me. I had one hand behind his neck, the other stroking his long cock. I felt unbelievably forward and aroused. We pulled apart, a string of saliva between us. He laughed, swiped it with his hand, and crinkled his eyes and said simply, "Good." I smiled at my shoe. "My boyfriend, Stefan, he is jealous but simple, don't be afraid, he will treat you well."

"And Rachel?" I asked.

"She is a woman, no? Whatever she likes," he answered. "I am Josef." With that he stepped away as if the deal were done, and led me to the door.

He pulled open the screen and I noticed there were potted geraniums scattered about and four metal deck chairs leaned up against the house, away from the rain. A miniature painted glass seascape hung in the center pane of the door. He pushed it open. "Stefan, Rachel, we have a guest," he announced.

From out of nowhere a handsome, muscular blond appeared, smiling and scowling at the same time. He had brown eyes as well, which for some reason pleased me. I don't know, perhaps it gave him depth. He was shirtless, the top button of his faded jeans unbuttoned to reveal a light-brown trail of hair; he held a white rag in his hand. Josef took a step toward him, pinched his nipple, and let his fingers trail down toward his cock as they kissed. Stefan grew hard at his lover's touch and now it was my turn to be jealous. I wrinkled my eyes and smiled. I had never been witness to such a direct display between men. Again I surprised myself by liking it. Josef eased himself around to Stefan's side, so I could get a better look. I smiled and forced myself to take in the room.

The place was done in the same dark, gentle tones as my suite, royal blue, burgundy, and gold. It looked like the three of them had been there awhile as there were funky nude statues placed here and there, candles, and a large print of Dali's *Time* leaning on the wall. I could see now that the place Stefan had emerged from was a small kitchenette. Josef and Stefan were still kissing. Josef was kneading his nipples, Stefan yielding. I moved closer and ran my fingers down Stefan's rippled stomach, tracing the trail of hair to where his now fully erect penis lay smashed against his jeans. I heard a match light and looked up; there on the couch was Rachel, lighting a cigarette and watching impassively. She looked even more beautiful than before, having changed into a night-blue dress with a low neckline and silver chain. I traced the outline of Stefan's cock to its head and then walked toward the couch.

"Hello." I said, "I'm Beth." She nodded and offered her hand. I took and gently kissed it, awkward but somehow fitting. She smiled.

"Rachel," she said. "Please sit down." She patted the couch next to her. I sat. She offered me a cigarette. I shook my head. "You don't mind if I smoke, then?" Her accent was ever so faint. I shook my head. I must have wrinkled my nose because she smiled again and put the cigarette out. She uncrossed then recrossed her legs, turning toward me and leaning back on the couch. She could easily drop her arm and touch me. I admired her slender figure and soft perfume. I moved closer and leaned back. "It is raining still, no?" she asked.

"I don't see how the English can stand it," I said. "It makes me feel like a caged animal." My nerves were all jangly.

"And what animal would that be?" she asked calmly.

"A panther," I said without hesitation. She dropped her arm and touched me. I couldn't help it; I was aroused and anxious, and I flinched.

"You like to be petted," she said, "and you like to chase." She stroked my arm. I bristled, I didn't like to be pegged so easily, and honestly I had never thought of it before. I started to pull away. She held my gaze and gently squeezed my arm. I breathed deeply. She smiled and peered further into my eyes. "Which is it that you like more?" she asked. I took another breath.

"That depends on who I'm with," I said.

"With me?" she asked, letting her gaze fall to my breasts while stroking my fingers. I had to remind myself to be calm.

"This," I said softly. "I like this." She smiled.

"Good." I scooted in closer and took in her beauty. I watched her eyes, dark brown and almond-shaped; her mouth, a faint touch of dark lipstick and a smile. I wanted to know this woman who was making me feel so uneasy and so good.

"Yes," she said.

"And I'd like this," I said as I leaned in to kiss her. I tried to match Josef's balance of purposefulness and gentleness, with one hand on the couch, the other instinctively reaching for her waist. She opened her mouth and I fell forward, delivering small kisses at first, with the tip of my tongue. She tasted like blackberry wine and smelled of good soap. She leaned into me. We must have kissed for quite a while, dancing, chasing, and exploring each other, because when we stopped, candles were lit and both men were shirtless and pouring wine. I decided I wasn't going to care about what any of it meant anymore; I would just go with it.

I picked up my glass and handed her the other. Josef and Stefan held their glasses aloft. We toasted each other silently and I moved myself closer to Rachel to kiss her again, and was pulled into her once more. Her lips were soft and full, her desire plain and uninhibited. Running my hand up her spine I felt her energy build and follow me. I slid my hand around to one of her breasts, taking a nipple between my fingers and squeezing. She let out a soft moan. The sound of her voice, female and willing, drove me on. I squeezed again, harder this time. She went erect in my fingers. She pulled me on top of her, sliding her leg between mine and roughly against my jeans; I almost came in the process. She laughed at my eager-ness. "So like a young boy, no?"

I sat back, legs straddling her belly, and pulled off my belt, not wanting to grind the silver buckle into her skin through the dress. Sitting up, she took the belt from my hands. I kissed her face, the top of her head, her mouth—that delicious supple mouth. I love kissing; for me it is one of the most sen-sual aspects of making love. I can tell right away if it's going to happen just from the kiss. Stefan, whom I had forgotten all about, slid in behind me on the couch, stroking himself, full erection exposed. I took another sip of wine, and before

I could swallow Rachel reached up and grabbed my hair. Fistful of dreadlocks, and she was pleased. She smiled and pulled me in. "I am thirsty, too." She drank the wine from my mouth while I began opening the buttons on her dress. Stefan pressed himself into me as the last button gave way and her dress fell open. I leaned over her, tracing the outline of her clit through the lace of her plum-colored underwear. She leaned back onto the couch and stroked my hair. I undid the front hook of her bra and ran my tongue around the edge of her nipple, licking, sucking. Stefan slid his hands under my shirt and unhooked my bra, squeezing tight; electricity shot through, pushing me back into his dick. He laughed and unbuttoned my pants. I knew I wasn't going to last long and wondered what had become of Josef, whose lover didn't seem to be so jealous now.

Out of the corner of my eye I saw motion and there was Josef, naked and muscular as he approached the couch, full erection in hand, pulling his balls. He came up behind Stefan, who turned and took him in his mouth, taking him fully and swallowing while constantly stroking his own hard cock.

I stared down at Rachel's beautiful slender body and tugged at her panties. She lifted her hips and slid out of them. There was nothing I could do but follow. I raised my arms and Stefan pulled off my shirt. My pants were now loose at my knees. I arched forward for her to touch me, to take my wetness into her hands. I wanted to taste myself on her. She started lightly as her fingers explored me, sliding in and out, smearing wetness onto my ass and thighs. Spreading my wetness onto her lips and breasts. Her fingers found their goal and plunged hard inside me, my body convulsing and rising. I pulled away, leaning back to lick my own juices off her breasts and then down her belly. My hands teased her clit and squeezed her nipples until my tongue found her whole and swollen. Ass in the air, I dove into her wet pussy, teasing with the tip of my tongue. I flicked and sucked, using my fingers to stroke my way through her beauty and into her soul. She moaned, her fingers once again entangled in my long, thick dreadlocks.

She was ready; I could feel her. I pulled her whole clitoris into my mouth and she was writhing. Then Stefan was suddenly awake at my ass. I felt first cold and then wetness and then he was inside me. This was a shock. I hadn't had anal sex in years. I started to pull away. Rachel forced my head down into her sex—her lovely musky rich sex—and I didn't care. I wanted this now. I wanted to smear it across my face and breathe her in. I plowed my fingers into her. Stefan matched my rhythm and I could no longer think. The pain of his dick forcing its way into me wrestled with the pleasure of each stroke. I screamed into her pussy. He fucked me slow and hard. Rachel bucked beneath me, calling my attention back to her clit. She arched and I plunged my fingers even further, harder. I didn't care if it hurt. She squeezed my tits and I exploded into hyperspace. She arched her back again and we were both inconsolable. Stefan thrust hard and shot into me. Josef, somehow behind him, yanked Stefan's head back, planting a kiss; sweat rolled down his chest as he screamed his release.

I floated. Breathing and floating back down to earth, I found myself on top of her, her arms around my waist. She kissed my forehead, my lips, and smile. I could smell myself on her and it pleased me. She lifted my face to hers.

"To the bedroom, then?"

Does She Look Like a Boy?
Tara-Michelle Ziniuk

When I ran through the door at work I was glad I had done my hair and makeup on the way. For the past while, my boss had been pestering me to be "as ready as possible as early as possible." She and I both knew that I didn't look quite like this when I wasn't at work, but I'm not sure she understood my untended body hair or my refusing her invitations to tanning salons. I'm a femmey girl, no doubt, but not the type to get all glammed up without occasion to. The other girls at work were the straight girl equivalent to high-femme all the time, manicured and face-masked; they also did not understand.

I kissed Darlena on both cheeks then bolted to the walk-in closet, which had been home to much slut-gear as well as my personal dressing room for nearly two years. I breathed in the scent of other people's perfumes and overcompensating chemical detergents, all stale and mixed together. Not a minute after I closed the door and stripped down to begin a frantic search for my PVC bra and corset set, Darlena walked in behind me.

"The four o'clock guy called back," she began *(oh please don't tell me he cancelled and I rushed here for nothing)*, "and he wanted to know if you looked like a boy."

I laughed. "Did he look at our ad?" I asked.

"Apparently not. I directed him to the website but his Internet service was down. I wasn't sure how to respond so I just joked back with him and said, 'Well no, sir. Did you want her to?' And he said yes."

She was reading me for a reaction. This was not an environment that had fostered any sort of gender-bending positive play in the past, save a few male clients who liked to wear pantyhose. My first instinct was that it was a crank call and I was wasting my time, *grrr*.

"So, you think he'll be a no-show?"

"I don't know, he sounded pretty sincere, and you're here now. Do you have a hat?"

I spent the next fifteen minutes scrambling to get out of my makeup and find masculine clothes amongst the leather and stilettos. I settled on a white dress shirt from an unclaimed bag of uniforms and schoolgirl attire, and found a white tank top to go under it. One of the other women at work had left behind a pair of dark-blue jeans with a wide black belt still in them. I pulled them on and they fit snug against my ass and thighs. I found a black cock in a box of sex toys and rinsed it in the sink before resting it against my already constricted cunt, and allowed myself to feel its stillness, rubbing my middle finger along the shaft. I positioned it so that it would be noticeable but not tacky, and zipped up the now very fitting pants.

When I came out of the washroom Darlena was waiting for me with the only hat she could find, a black cap with some anonymous Celtic symbol on it. It would do. I looked myself over in the full-length mirror. I certainly didn't look macho, I looked faggoty. I hoped that was the idea. The hall clock read five-to-four, the hour I anticipated the caller's arrival.

It was a good scene to have been called in for, more interesting than the bulk of them. I knew only that it was to be a dildo-training session and that this particular client had not seen any of the other girls before. I hoped he wouldn't have any huge unavoidable flaws, specifically that he didn't stink and wasn't eighty years old and waiting for his next heart attack. Though these possibilities occurred to me, I somehow was not as panicked as I had often found myself before. I was quite intrigued by this character who wanted curvy lipstick-lipped me in drag. Why hadn't he booked a call with a male Dom? I imagined complicated answers to this question until there was a knock at the door. I poured some water for myself into a crystal wine glass and went into the room to meet my new submissive.

He was definitely more masculine-looking than I had been able to pull off, an interesting element for the scene. He looked young and wide-eyed. He appeared willing and nervous, but not fearful. "Very nice to meet you. You will call me Master," I said, in what I liked to call my best warm/cool voice. I had impressed myself already by remembering that today I would be "Master" as opposed to "Mistress." I extended a hand and he shook it firmly before kissing it. I hadn't been sure of what to expect, but this pleased me. He was blushing as I motioned for him to have a seat. "We'll just have a little chat and then get things started." He nodded. I was unable to read his anxiety. "We use the code words *yellow* and *red* here, yellow for caution, red to stop the scene. You are familiar with these?" Another nod. "Have you done this before?" I asked genuinely.

"Similar things, but not exactly." He certainly was not talkative.

"But you do have experience with BDSM and you feel confident that you know your limitations?"

"Yes, Master." I could tell by his immediate submission to me that he did. He kept his eyes lowered, but I could see his wanting in them. There was no reason to take up more of our time together. I settled into character easily.

"I am your Master. You will do as I say, when I say to. You will be polite and courteous, and appreciative that I have taken up my valuable time to train you." As I stood he dropped to his knees in front of me.

"Yes, Sir. Thank you in advance for spending your time on me." He offered me a thick black collar with metal rings, and I thanked him by securing it tightly around his neck. He bowed his head and touched his nose to the polished tip of one of the too-large black army boots I was wearing. I rustled his hair before pulling his face up by it.

"Very good. Now why did you come here today?" No answer. "I asked you why you came here today."

"I came here to please you, Master."

"Now go back to what you were doing." He curled by my feet, tracing his nose along the seams of the boots. Then he did the same with his entire face, resting his cheek against my ankle. He slowly licked the stitching around the soles. Before he was quite done with the second one, I interrupted. "Back up on your knees." He was taller than me, and upright on his knees reached higher than my waist. I pushed him back so that he was sitting on the backs of his heels. His eye level was just below my swollen crotch. He seemed to look straight through the tops of my thighs. "You see something you like?" My voice was softer this time.

"Yes, Master. I do."

Again he lowered his head. I felt the rush of excitement that I was intending for him electrifying my own body. We made eye contact, and though his body looked tough, the steady eyes that met mine looked like they had been hurt. They were focused now on something else. I nodded simply, testing to see if he did as well. A small well-hidden smile appeared as he faced my body. He ran his face along the zipper of my jeans, like he had done with my boots. He was slow and careful already so I didn't have to direct him. He pressed his face harder and harder into me. I could feel myself getting wet as much as I tried not to, as he started kneading my cock with his face. His lips ran over it through the denim, as he looked up for my approval. He looked brave and small. I gave him another nod and he gently started kneading with his teeth. I tried my hardest not to release the gasp in my chest that so desperately wanted to be let out.

I decided to regain control of the situation and, unzipping the jeans, took the dick out inches in front of his face. I ran my fingers over his mouth and he sucked and lapped at them with his soft tongue. I thrust myself into his mouth. He gave me the sweetest, fiercest blow job I had known, putting everything into it. He let his mouth handle the cock expertly, paying attention to its curves and shape and not leaving out anything. He was in tune to my hips' rhythm and worked with and against it. I allowed myself to breathe heavily to let him know he was doing well, but I restrained myself from making any other sounds. I didn't want to stop him, but I wanted to make sure I took over the scene before I came. I backed out of his soft wet mouth. This time when I looked at him he looked less bashful and more confident, like he had regained some of his pride giving head like that. "Did you like that?" I barked. He did not flinch. He licked his lips and gave me a look I had come to know well through various female lovers. "Did *you?*" they asked silently.

"Yes, very much. Thank you." He blushed, smiling obviously this time. "Master."

I wanted to see if he was hard but was unable to tell because of the way he sat. I moved along quickly, because he had paid good money for the hour, but also because I was incredibly turned-on and didn't want to ruin the moment. "You want more?"

"Yes. Please, Master."

"Are you going to behave yourself if I give you more? You are already very lucky to have been allowed to suck your Master's big cock like that. You know that, don't you?"

"Yes, Master. Thank you." He played along, knowing full well what he was entitled to during the session.

"Okay then, you must promise to be on your very best behavior. Bring me a condom, boy." I wanted to continue as much as he did and was pleased that he returned quickly with the basket of condoms and a bottle of lube. I pretended to eye the bottle he had handed me quizzically. "Oh, you were expecting me to go easy on you, were you?" I toyed with him, for both of us. He lowered his head in response, looking like a child about to break out in giggles. I imagined him being a strong butch lover of mine as I snapped on a glove and prepared to ready his waiting ass. I had him face the whipping post on the other side of the room and undress from the waist down. Off came the work pants and a pair of gray-specked boxer briefs. I noticed he kept his body pressed tight against the post. "Are you nervous?"

"No, Master." I didn't push it, as it was ideal positioning for my own fantasy. I instructed him to step back and make sure he kept his forehead touching the post. He complied with my demands easily, and I threw in a threat about the disciplinary actions I would be forced to take if he squirmed out of position.

I entered him at first cautiously, with one finger, then two. I realized very soon that he had more experience than he had let on. I ran my other hand through what I assumed to be sweat on his inner thigh. He was moving his body accordingly, so I knew he wanted to be fucked. I thought about what he had said when he came in about not having done "exactly" this before, and wondered what specifically he had meant by that. Was he a fag experimenting with women? A "straight man" who frequented cruise parks, having anonymous lovers nightly? Maybe he had played out similar scenes with a woman lover before, who had since left him or become ill. I speculated for a moment too long and then snapped back to reality. Or as close to reality as I chose to make it: he was my handsome boy-dyke slave, a fine butch bottom, helplessly awaiting my hot femme dick to enter and take him over.

Caught up in my own imagination, but not so much that I wasn't paying attention, I spread the soft asscheeks before me and circled the tip of the silicone dick between them. I had, at some point in this fluster of daydream, work and sweat, remembered to put on the condom. One last time I pushed my lubed fingers in and out firmly, and then pushed myself into him. He let out something between a squeal and a sigh, sounding like a young boy. I liked the power I felt hearing his surprisingly high-pitched sounds and continued to press myself into him and pull back. As this motion quickened and we fell into each other's rhythm, I began to grind my dripping cunt against her ass, playing with her insides. I pretended that the increasing sweat pouring down his legs was sweet girl cum and held the inside of her thigh against the palm of my hand.

I noticed that as he got more turned-on and as the fucking became rougher, he pulled away from me more, and pushed his weight against the post. I brought my arm around to the front of her neck. It was soft and tight. I ran my knuckles against his jaw, finding that his teeth were clenched. I ran my hand along his jawline, also soft and unusually free of stubble. His face was trembling with what seemed like fear.

Leaving one hand on his face, I slowly moved the other hand around to the front of his thigh. It was sticky wet and also trembled to my touch. I tried to stay strong and stern, but was both confused and excited. As I inched my hand upward he jerked away from me. I pulled her close to my body. The hand I had rested on her face came down and pressed against her collarbone. I felt the tiny recognizable ripples of a tensor-bandaged chest.

She heaved the heavy sigh of someone exposing a skeleton. I moved my hand between her legs, revealing for certain the truth to my fantasy and this boy's well-hidden identity. I sighed a sigh of relief, of pleasure, of the unknown future. I sat down on the floor, leaning my back against the wooden post. I pulled her down and continued to hold her against me. My hand ran through her sweaty hair. We had not yet made eye contact. When she finally looked at me her eyes were intense and concerned. "Are you mad?" they asked. I flashed her the same sexually charged and wanting smile she had given me after sucking me off.

"Are you?" my eyes asked back.

About the Authors

LISA ARCHER is the pen name and alter ego of a San Francisco–based writer. Her stories have appeared in *Best Bisexual Women's Erotica, Best Women's Erotica 2002* and *2004, The Erotica Reader, Awakening the Virgin 2,* and *Pills, Thrills, Chills, and Heartache: Adventures in the First Person.*

SARAH BARDEEN is a freelance writer and editor, music critic, and poet living in the San Francisco Bay Area. Her reviews have appeared on National Public Radio's, "All Things Considered" and in various print and electronic media. Some of her best friends are lesbians.

BETTY BLUE is a neurotic sex-kitten in San Francisco who is fighting a losing battle against the urge to stab people with forks (cuz you know it's all fun until somebody loses an eye). Her fiction has appeared in *Best Women's Erotica 2003, Best Lesbian Love Stories, Best Lesbian Erotica 2002* and *2003, Best Bisexual Erotica,* and *Tough Girls.*

Under her real name, CHEYENNE BLUE writes rural travel guides, and often blends outdoor themes into her erotica. Her writing has appeared in *Best Women's Erotica 2002* and *2003*, *Best Lesbian Erotica 2003*, *Mammoth Book of Best New Erotica 2002*, and several websites. Visit her website at www.cheyenneblue.com.

RACHEL KRAMER BUSSEL (www.rachelkramerbussel.com) writes about books, sex, smut, and music. She is the reviser of *The Lesbian Sex Book*, coauthor of *The Erotic Writer's Market Guide*, and coeditor of the lesbian erotica anthology *Up All Night*. Her writing has been published in *Bust, Curve, Diva, Girlfriends, On Our Backs, Playgirl, Rockrgrl, The San Francisco Chronicle*, and in over twenty anthologies including *Best Lesbian Erotica 2001*, *Best Women's Erotica 2003*, and *Best American Erotica 2004*.

KATE E. CONLAN is a young New Zealander traveling the world collecting stories and people. She yearns for a purse puppy but makes do with sporadic emails from friends and family for long-distance love. She is unhealthily addicted to her computer and loves the sound of rain on her tent. Her favorite thing in the whole wide world is a Cox's orange apple in March, handpicked and shined bright on the edge of her shirt.

TINA CRISTINA MARIA D'ELIA is a power femme mixed-race Latina lesbian feminist, activist, performance poet, actor, and playwright. She was a Boston Amazon Poetry Slam winner and OutWrite Festival Slam finalist; her work has been published in *Sojourner, The New Our Bodies Ourselves,* and *Fragments*. She has appeared in the films *Hard Love and How to Fuck in High Heels, One, A Haunting, Sexual Healing, Exploring Butch/Femme Desire, Simone's 24,* and *Shut Up Josephine!* She is currently at work on a film based on her one-woman show.

MARÍA HELENA DOLAN says, "You can know a lot of things about me, but the basics are: I love women, and I fuckin' hate George Bush and all he and his pals stand for. I say put tax dollars into community gardens, not long-range bombings. Do I have to say more? You betcha. Just let me unleash my collection of Southern-accented erotica and my Lesbian Vampire Mother novel on an unsuspecting world. Any takers?"

BETHANY HARVEY is a writer, editor, and artisan from the backwoods of West Virginia and, more recently, the backwoods of northern Florida. Her goal in life is to make a living writing fiction so she doesn't need a real job. Most of her fiction is about being young and queer in the New South, but, unfortunately, she did not write "Breathing Water" from personal experience.

DEBRA HYDE's lesbian smut has appeared in *Best of the Best Meat Erotica, Body Check: Erotic Lesbian Sports Stories, Ripe Fruit: Erotica for Well Seasoned Lovers, www.suspectthoughts.com,* and *Prometheus Magazine.* She is a regular contributor to both www.scarletletters.com and www.yesportal.com, maintains the pansexual weblog called "Pursed Lips," and writes erotica for everyone. Debra flags right and wishes she looked less femme.

ABBE IRELAND's stories have appeared in *The Ghost of Carmen Miranda, Skin Deep, Best Lesbian Love Stories 2003, Burned Into Memory,* and *Underneath It All.* Abbe currently hangs out in the Arizona desert with a herd of neutered tomcats—an odd life dynamic for writing lesbian stories, but it seems to work.

ISA MAGDALENA is a teacher and lifelong student of the erotic, using the language of hands and body in her experiential classes and coaching. She developed and taught workshops for XOX and the Body Electric School in the '90s. Her forthcoming book *Take Off Your Clothes, Beloved* shares her vision of a transgressing paradigm of sex and gender that embraces both sacred and profane. Her Sex Coach website is www.xtasia.info.

MIRIAM R. SACHS MARTÍN is hotter than flamin' hot Cheetos, and wetter than the Lexington Reservoir. She loves to muck around in the place where poetry becomes intimacy and the word becomes song. She's a five-foot one-half-inch Cuban Jewish dyke who loves East San Jose, where she lives, teaches English as a second language, produces the spoken word event "Fierce Words Tender," and in every way worships things both feral and feline *(purrrowrr!)*.

SKIAN MCGUIRE is a working-class Quaker leatherdyke who lives in the wilds of western Massachusetts with her dog pack, a collection of motorcycles, and her partner of twenty-one years. Her work has appeared in *Best Bisexual Erotica 2, Best Lesbian Erotica 1999, 2001, 2002,* and *2003, HLFQ,* and the webzines *www.scarletletters.com, www.nestovipers.org, www.storymistress.com,* and *www.suspectthoughts.com.* She has also appeared in *On Our Backs,* and will soon be in *Bad Attitude.* Her chapbook, *LoveSexGod&Everything,* won the 2003 Cambridge Poetry Award for best poetry publication. A collection of her erotic fiction, *Remote Control and Other Weegee Stories,* will be released shortly by Top Dog Press.

ANDREA MILLER has a degree in English literature and a degree in journalism. She is currently teaching English as a second language in her Canadian hometown, but she has also taught in Korea and Japan. If her employers happen to read this, she wants them to know that she has never fucked anyone on a table at work.

PEGGY MUNSON has been in seven editions of *Best Lesbian Erotica*, as well as in the collections *On Our Backs: The Best Erotic Fiction*, *Tough Girls*, *Genderqueer*, *Hers 3*, and *Best Bisexual Erotica 2*. She has also published work in *The Best American Poetry 2003*, *Blithe House Quarterly*, *Literature and Medicine*, the *San Francisco Bay Guardian*, and elsewhere. Check out her latest projects at: www.peggymunson.com.

KRISTEN E. PORTER is an acupuncturist, teacher, director of a nonprofit, and the founder of Dyke Night Productions, which hosts a weekly lesbian dance party in Boston. She has been published previously in *Skin Deep* and *Faster Pussycats*. She has never been to Missouri, but longs to one day leave the city for a rural existence of raising babies on a farm with her beloved.

ELSPETH POTTER's credits include *Best Lesbian Erotica 2001, 2002,* and *2003, Best Women's Erotica 2002, Amoret,* and *Tough Girls: Down and Dirty Dyke Erotica*. She's written stories involving fisting at a hot spring, a threesome in a zero gravity chamber, and a cell phone set on vibrate. "Wire" is a sequel to "Camera," which appeared in *Best Lesbian Erotica 2002*.

JEAN ROBERTA writes erotica, reviews, articles, and opinion pieces for various publications, mostly colorful and obscure. She teaches first-year English courses at a Canadian prairie university. During the past twenty years, she has been proud to watch the queer community in her town progress from silence and shame to its present visibility. Her stories have appeared in *Best Lesbian Erotica 2000* and *2001*, *Wicked Words 8*, and in numerous other anthologies.

E. ROBINSON lives, works and makes her home in the City of Big Shoulders, the Windy City, Holy Cow!...Chicago. She earns her keep as an ad producer. This is her first published erotica.

SPARKY's work has appeared on *www.dykediva.com*, *www.technodyke.com*, *www.darkplay.net* and *www.playbutch.com*. She can be reached at sparky@geeklife.com.

JERA STAR writes erotica, handcrafts wooden spanking paddles, and dreams of running away to the circus. Her writing has appeared in various Canadian magazines and lesbian erotica anthologies.

RAKELLE VALENCIA is a confirmed bug-eyed pervert of the "trysexual" nature (try anything). New to writing, she looks forward to joining the ranks of the *best* erotica writers and is awaiting the contracted publication of her novel, *Mail Order Bride*, a lesbian-themed Western, under the pen name of R. C. Kayelle.

KYLE WALKER's work has appeared in the anthologies *Best Lesbian Erotica 2003* ("Luck of the Irish") and *A Woman's Touch* ("Why They Are Called Bad Girls"), and on the Internet ("Sticks and Balls" at hottlead.com). "Paisley Comes Back" is from a novel-in-progress, *What People Want*. Kyle recently appeared in Ed Valentine's *Women Behind the Bush* at En Avant Playwrights.

JEWEL BLACKFEATHER WELTER is a snarling little lynx of a creature who lives in an Illinois town with a Greek name amidst fields of grain and honey. Currently, she conducts interviews with well-known people for *Numb Magazine*, where she has earned death threats for her interview with Noam Chomsky, was sent loads of chopsticks for her interview with Yoko Ono, and wrote an elegy for Gwendolyn Brooks. Sometimes she cries when it rains, other times she howls. Both are good things.

JENI WRIGHT is currently living in New York City, where she misses the lush landscapes of Connecticut. A seven-year resident of Washington D.C., she developed her writing vice by performing poetry at Mothertongue events and keeping lots of journals, many of which were written on her rooftop. Currently she reviews books for *www.africana.com* and *www.coloredgirls.com*, while attending the public interest program at Queens College. She can be reached at savorydc@hotmail.com.

KRISTINA WRIGHT is an old-fashioned girl with a hedonistic heart and she happily admits to being a contradiction in terms. Her work has appeared in the anthologies *Bedroom Eyes: Tales of Lesbians in the Boudoir, Best Lesbian Erotica 2002, Ripe Fruit, Sweet Life,* and *Best Women's Erotica 2000,* as well as e-zines including *www.cleansheets.com* and *www.scarletletters.com.* She lives in Virginia with her very supportive husband and a menagerie of pets. Contact her at KristinaCW@aol.com.

FIONA ZEDDE is a transplanted Jamaican lesbian currently living and loving in Atlanta, Georgia. She spends half her days in the city's fabulous feminist bookstore, Charis Books and More, and the other half chained to her computer working on her first novel and an endless collection of smutty stories. Yeah, she went to college for that.

TARA-MICHELLE ZINIUK is a Toronto/Montreal writer, performer, activist, warrior, and princess. She is half of the spokenword-cello-sex-noise+politix project "Black Licorice Theory" and writes the column "Lydia Lane Is Not My Name" for *Trade: Queer Things* magazine. Her work appears in various places and publications and is upcoming in the erotica anthology *Burned Into Memory.* Tara-Michelle received a Toronto Arts Council New and Emerging Writers Grant, and is currently working on a collection of poetry.

About the Editors

MICHELLE TEA is the author of *The Passionate Mistakes and Intricate Corruption of One Girl in America, Valencia,* which won a Lambda Literary Award for Best Lesbian Fiction, and *The Chelsea Whistle.* She was the recipient of an award from the Rona Jaffe Foundation, as well as a *San Francisco Bay Guardian* Goldie Award for Literature. Michelle is cofounder of the Sister Spit all-girl open mic and national tours, and continues to bring performers around the country on cabaret-style tours. She writes for the *San Francisco Bay Guardian, www.thestranger.com, www.nerve.com, On Our Backs,* and *Girlfriends* magazine. She is the editor of two anthologies, *Pills, Thrills, Chills, and Heartache* (coedited by Clint Catalyst) and *Without a Net,* an anthology of writings by women and trannies who grew up poor and working-class. A collection of her poetry will be published by Manic D Press in 2004.

TRISTAN TAORMINO is the award-winning author of three books: *True Lust: Adventures in Sex, Porn, and Perversion, Down and Dirty Sex Secrets,* and *The Ultimate Guide to Anal Sex for Women.* She is director, producer, and star of two videos based on her book, *Tristan Taormino's Ultimate Guide to Anal Sex for Women 1* & *2,* which are distributed by Evil Angel Video. She is a columnist for *The Village Voice* and *Taboo Magazine.* She has been featured in over three hundred publications including *The New York Times, Redbook, Glamour, Cosmopolitan, Playboy, Penthouse, Entertainment Weekly, Vibe,* and *Men's Health.* She has appeared on CNN, "Ricki Lake," NBC's "The Other Half," MTV, HBO's "Real Sex," "The Howard Stern Show," The Discovery Channel, Oxygen, and "Loveline." She teaches sexuality workshops around the country, and her official website is www.puckerup.com.